MW01243371

EMERGENT LIGHT

THE REWIRED SERIES
BOOK 3

ALEXANDER MUKTE

Three to Five Publishing, LLC.
2107 N. Decatur Rd., Ste 438
Decatur, GA 30033
www.threetofivepublishing.com
This publisher is not responsible for websites (or their content)
that are not owned by the publisher.

Names: Mukte, Alexander.
Title: Emergent Light / Alexander Mukte.
Series: The Rewired Series.
Identifiers:
Library of Congress Control Number: 2022919389
ISBN 978-1-952030-08-6 (paperback)
ISBN 978-1-952030-09-3 (ebook)
Subjects: BISAC: FICTION / Visionary & Metaphysical. |
FICTION / Magical Realism. | FICTION / Own Voices.

EMERGENT LIGHT

1

AWAKENED WITH PURPOSE

THE WHITE FLASH OF LIGHT WAS SO BRIGHT IT AWAKENED MALIK, compelling him to open his eyes. The crashing thunder that followed seemed to echo through the house. Malik turned his head to watch the rain out the window. Beyond the beads of rain trickling down the pane, he saw another succession of lightning bolt flashes, all quickly followed by thunder so close that each roar shook his home. Nursing a baby had caused his wife, Magaly, to become a light sleeper. Malik turned to see if she was awake, but her side of the bed was empty and still made. *Did she fall asleep in the nursery again?* Malik wondered, pulling himself out of bed and heading upstairs to relieve her.

Malik moved through the dark, barely feeling his own steps as he made his way up the stairs and down the hallway. Almost too quickly, he found himself in a bedroom that was both incredibly familiar and strange. The room had the same feeling of warmth, love, and familiarity as that of their son Aries, but something was different. Another flash of lightning illuminated the room enough for Malik to see he was not in his son's nursery. Instead, he was back in his childhood home, the one from before his parents' divorce.

Malik stood in what used to be his dad's upstairs office. It, however, was not how he remembered it. There was now a dresser next to the door, a bed along the opposite wall, and a rocking chair facing the window. The chair looked just like the one his grandmother had gifted them for the birth of their elder son, Noah.

"How did this get here?" Malik said softly.

The chair glided back and forth, as if someone were rocking in it. Malik reached out and spun the chair around, expecting to find Noah there, as he often did at home. The hair on Malik's arms raised when he realized no one was there.

Oddly, Malik did not feel scared; he felt more aware. His attention was pulled to the window overlooking the backyard. He glanced down at the old tree stump he used to play on when he was a boy. Several people were standing nearby in the glow of the full moon, untouched by the rain. Scenes he could scarcely identify passed before his eyes, yet he knew they were significant. In a moment, it was over; the faces and places washed away like watercolor paint swirling down a drain. His mom, his grandma, and Magaly were the only faces that remained.

Then farther back in the trees, he saw the familiar fair skin, dark hair, and thin frame of an old friend. "Callie," he whispered. To his surprise, she met his gaze.

Malik backed away from the window. "This has to be a dream."

"It is, and it isn't." Callie's voice came from behind him, startling him.

Malik wanted to turn and look at her, but he hesitated, recalling her request the last time he saw her alive. Callie wanted him to remember her from the before times, not the end times.

"No need to look away," he heard Callie say.

Malik turned to see his friend as she was when they were teenagers. She was healthy; her smile was vibrant. That same smile had been a ray of hope in some dark times. Even a beautiful life has its dark times. The house trembled as he felt the weight of those heavy feelings pulling on him.

"You can release those feelings." Callie gave him a nod of assurance. "Believe it or not, this is a wonderful dream."

"What do you mean?"

"Don't worry, you'll see."

"I'll see what?"

Callie took a few steps closer. "Do you remember the last thing I told you?"

Malik's mind pulled him back to the hospital room, where he sat holding his oldest friend's hand. He felt another wave of sadness until Callie's voice brought him back.

"No," Callie said, "not that. Remember what I said."

"That you know why all of this is happening, why everything is happening?"

"That's right," she said with a smile. "Everything happens for a reason. You'll get to see more of that reason soon."

"Am I dying?" Malik asked.

Callie's eyebrows shot up in surprise, and she quickly replied, "No, no!" She then seemed to consider the idea, shrugged her shoulders, and said, "Well, the old you maybe."

"What do you mean, the old me?"

She shook her head. "Never mind that. Listen," her voice was steady and focused, "what you and Magaly are doing for those boys is amazing. You've found it."

"Found what?"

Callie smiled and mouthed something that Malik could not hear.

"What?" He leaned closer. Callie's mouth was moving as though she were saying something, but Malik couldn't hear anything. The only sound was a loud, high-pitched whine. It sounded like a swarm of mosquitoes. He glanced up and around, feeling as if they were upon him, but he saw nothing. His first instinct was to swat, but his arms wouldn't cooperate.

"I can't hear you," Malik tried to shout, but he couldn't even hear his own voice.

He looked out the window for the source of the noise and caught sight again of his mom and grandma holding hands. A sense of calm came over him, and his muscles relaxed. The sound had reached a peak and was now softening to a dull buzz. Malik closed his eyes and inhaled deeply. Once he fully exhaled, the quiet returned. He opened his eyes and saw Callie still standing there, assessing him.

"What?" Malik asked, but she didn't answer. Before Malik could repeat himself, he heard a loud voice coming from the walls of the house. "Wake up!"

Malik jerked awake, his eyes darting around the room. He was back in his bedroom with the full moon's rays beaming through the window. Magaly was peacefully sleeping next to him, her head turned toward the baby monitor on her nightstand, her curls cascading across her satin pillow cover.

And then he heard it: "Daaadaaa."

2

A BAD DREAM

NOAH HAD BEGUN HAVING MORE VIVID DREAMS OVER THE PAST FEW months, and unfortunately, they had been disturbing his sleep. Malik sat up and hopped out of bed, his eyes now open wide, his adrenaline pumping. He knew he needed to soothe Noah before the boy's calls woke the baby. *Please, don't wake the baby,* Malik silently begged. Malik glanced at the clock on his way to the stairs: 3:58 a.m. *Of course,* Malik thought, tiptoeing up the stairs in a feeble attempt to minimize the sound of the creaky wooden floorboards in the old home that once belonged to his grandfather.

As soon as Malik reached Noah's bedside, his son whispered, "I had a bad dream."

Malik kneeled and placed his hand on Noah's forehead. "I know. Do you want to talk about it?"

"No," Noah said. "But can you stay in here with me?"

"Of course," Malik replied. How could he say no? Malik shifted around all of Noah's stuffed animals, or "babies" as his son liked to call them, to make a small sliver of clear space.

"Can you also turn on my elephant light?" Noah asked.

"No problem," Malik said as he searched for the plush night

light. He discovered it near the foot of the bed. "How did you get down here?" Malik scolded the toy, trying to make his son smile. Malik turned it on, clicking until he got to Noah's favorite color. Green stars and crescent moons glowed along the walls and ceiling. Malik placed the elephant next to Noah's pillow. "How's that?"

"Perfect," Noah said. "Are you still going to stay with me?"

Malik settled in as best he could next to his son. "I'll stay here until you fall asleep." Content with that, Noah closed his eyes and hugged his stuffed tiger. As Noah's breathing slowed, Malik listened for any rustling in the nursery next door. The baby seemed sound asleep too.

Malik peered over at Noah. He saw the scar that went from the corner of Noah's left eye toward his temple. Malik replayed in his mind the doctor's words: *"A half an inch to the side and he could have lost that eye."*

He would never forget that day. Malik had stepped out of a meeting in London after noticing multiple missed calls from Magaly. He remembered the panic in his wife's voice when she told him there had been an accident at Noah's daycare. Noah was the only child injured, and they were on their way to the emergency room.

Malik tried to shake the image from his mind and just be thankful it wasn't worse. *I can't believe I was halfway around the world*, Malik thought.

Malik inhaled deeply, grateful to be more present for his family. Noah fidgeted and rolled over, causing Malik to hold his breath. Malik tried to get a peek at his son's face without disturbing him. Satisfied that Noah was sound asleep, Malik exhaled and relaxed again. He considered going back to his own bed, but decided not to risk waking Noah. Now that his house was in a peaceful state, it was time for Malik to close his eyes. He needed answers, and while these nights weren't conducive to the profound thought that often came with deep sleep, he could still let his subconscious do some work.

How do we reach one billion?

Malik imagined what it must have been like the day the daycare groundskeeper burst into Noah's classroom in a confused state. Malik volunteered with the man frequently, painting and doing repairs, and knew him to be exceptionally kind and responsible. The man was so handy that Malik occasionally sought his help with repairs around the house. Anyone could see that the groundskeeper, a veteran, cherished his job and all the kids at the daycare. *That poor man*, Malik thought, slowly shaking his head.

How do we reach one billion? And will that be enough?

MALIK SHIFTED in the toddler-sized bed, felt a knot in his neck, and realized sweat had collected on his chest. He cracked open an eye to see the sunlight streaming into Noah's room. Malik rolled his eyes as he reminisced about getting those curtains four years ago. "Those definitely are not blackout curtains," he muttered. He looked over to see Noah was no longer next to him. Malik stood up and stretched his stiff back before starting downstairs. When he got to the living room, he saw Noah curled up on the couch with a picture book.

"Morning, buddy," Malik greeted his son, who looked up and grinned before returning to the colorful illustrations.

Malik walked to the kitchen and turned on the coffeemaker.

"Daddy," Noah said.

"Yeah," Malik replied.

"Did you have a bad dream last night too?"

"I don't—" Malik couldn't remember his dream. Well, not all of it. He knew it was intense, but he believed that it all ended well. "No, I didn't. I think I had a wonderful dream."

Noah scratched his leg. "I dreamed I got bitten by a bug and I was itchy."

Malik didn't remember all the details of his dream, but he knew there was something to do with mosquitoes. He lifted his son's pajama pant leg to see if there were any bug bites. "Do we need to put any cream on it?"

"No, I'm okay," Noah said, his eyes focused on his book. "Daddy."

"Yes?"

"Can you make chocolate chip pancakes?"

"Sure," Malik said, as he poured a cup of coffee.

"Dad?"

"Yes?"

"Can we visit GG and Nana today?"

"Not today," Malik replied.

"Why?" Noah asked.

Malik knew this question was coming. "Why" always came after any answer other than "yes." "Because it takes time to get out there. Plus, GG's been needing to rest more lately, and we will need to tell her ahead of time to ask if it's okay if we come to visit."

"We should call them today."

"That we can do."

"Daddy?"

Malik sat down on the couch. "Yes?"

Noah scooted across the couch until he was sitting right next to Malik. "When's my birthday?"

"Next week," Malik said. He could hardly believe Noah was about to turn four.

"When we talk to GG and Nana, we should ask them if we can spend my birthday with them."

"Is that what you want to do?"

Noah nodded.

Malik rubbed the tight curls on the top of Noah's head. "All right, my boy, then that's what we'll do."

As Malik started to stand up, Noah asked, "Can you wait, Daddy?"

"Sure," Malik said and settled back down next to his son. He listened as Noah flipped the pages and told Malik the new things he noticed in the images.

"See, Dad, this page is dark because the lights are out in the room. Look, the owl is the only one with its eyes open. And then on this page, it goes back to white because someone turned on the light. Look at the owl. Now it's the only creature with its eyes shut. That's because it's the only nocturnal animal there." Noah looked up at Malik with those bright, intelligent eyes.

"Ah, I see. I think you're right." Malik marveled at how thoughtful the illustrations could be in a good children's book. He enjoyed seeing his son discover unique details with each reading, and was often blown away by how observant the child was. After a while, Malik pulled out a puzzle for Noah and moved toward the kitchen.

As he was making pancakes, he heard Noah carrying on a conversation. "See, silly," Noah said with a giggle. "We can't go see GG and Nana today." *What did he just say?* Malik wondered, creeping closer to the couch, out of view. He peered over Noah's shoulder to see his son's tan rocking horse, which he called his "sweetheart." Noah liked to carry it with him wherever he could, chatting with it as though it came to life when no adults were watching. "We have to fly all the way there. We'll go next week." Then, in a louder voice, Noah said, "Dad?"

"Yeah?" Malik said, backing away from the couch.

"How much is a week?"

"It's seven days. Do you remember, like *The Very Hungry Caterpillar*?"

"Oh, that's right," Noah said. He turned back to his

sweetheart, and Malik heard their conversation continue. "Daddy said maybe we would be there for my birthday."

IT WAS STILL EARLY, and Magaly and the baby were still asleep. No doubt they were making up for the nighttime feedings. Aries still woke up every few hours to nurse, so Magaly had to grab any window of sleep she could. With the pancakes now done, Malik walked outside and sat on the back deck. The vibrant reds of the male cardinals gliding across the backyard were a striking contrast to the green canopy of the oak tree that had just bloomed. Malik settled into his seat and inhaled as deeply as he could, feeling his chest puff up. He let out an audible exhale, pushing out until his lungs were empty. Malik took a few more deep, cleansing breaths, taking in the subtle sweet smell of spring.

Now, with his mind clear, he was back to the question at hand. *How do we protect a billion more people from solar flares?* Malik closed his eyes, pondering this. *Is one billion even the correct number? How?* Malik envisioned the countless hospitalized people suffering from overexposure to solar flares. As his chest tightened, he thought, *Fear.* He breathed again and recited to himself, *I am present. I am capable.* "I don't know how," Malik whispered, "but I will figure this out."

Malik heard the creaking of the deck door and turned to see Noah standing there, now wearing his giant panda T-shirt and cargo shorts.

"Can we go to the zoo today?"

"I'm not sure. We need to see what time your mom and brother wake up."

"My sweetheart says that today is the perfect day to go to the zoo."

Malik stood up to check the time. They preferred to get there right as it opened, to stay ahead of the crowds. "I don't know,

Noah. We need to let your mom get some sleep, and by the time she and your brother wake up, it may be a little later than we like to go."

"Don't worry." Noah looked back inside the house. "Aries is awake."

"Really?" Malik walked inside and heard the second-story floorboards creak.

"Good morning," a voice rang out from the top of the stairs. Magaly walked down slowly with the baby in her arms. She saw Noah's outfit, smiled at Malik, and said, "I guess today is a zoo day."

3

A TRIP TO THE ZOO

MALIK TURNED LEFT INTO THE SPARSELY POPULATED PARKING LOT outside of Zoo Atlanta. It was a sunny and cool day. There was still a little moisture on the grass, showing the blazing Georgia heat hadn't won the temperature battle just yet.

"We're here!" squealed Noah. Malik glanced in the rearview mirror and watched the boy clinch his fist. "I'm so excited."

"Me too!" Magaly chimed in. "I hope the orangutans are out today!" Malik loved the joy she had in these moments, how it radiated off her.

Malik pulled the car into a shady parking spot. "Remind me, Noah. What's your favorite animal to see?"

"Um… the tiger and the clouded leopard. They're part of my cat family."

Malik looked over at Magaly, sitting in the passenger seat. She shook her head and smiled. "Who's cooler—your cat family or us?" Malik asked, tilting his head back at Noah with an eyebrow raised.

"Not everything is a competition, Dad."

Malik laughed as he pressed the button to turn off the engine.

He made eye contact with Magaly, who had just finished rubbing in sunblock. She was so cute, with her bouncy ponytail and baseball cap.

"You and your sunscreen," Malik teased her.

"It's good for our skin, no matter what shade we're blessed to be," she chided him.

"Fair enough, my love," he replied. "You get cat man, and I'll get the baby?"

"Oh, stop," Magaly replied with a grin.

Malik got out of the car and retrieved the stroller from the trunk. He opened the rear door and was greeted by a big gummy smile from their almost six-month-old. "Hey, little one! You ready for the zoo?" he cooed to Aries as he moved the car seat to the stroller.

With Malik pushing the stroller and Magaly holding Noah's hand, the family walked across the parking lot toward the entrance to the zoo. Malik pulled his phone out of his pocket to pay for parking when it lit up and vibrated with an alert. "Oh, no."

"What?" Magaly asked.

He quickly opened the Singularity Group Solar Flare Alert app to see the details. "There's a solar flare that's going to hit in five minutes." Malik assessed their options for shelter, and in unison, he and Magaly said, "We should get back in the car."

"But why?" Noah whined.

Magaly's voice was calm. "We are not going home. We just have to wait in the car for a little while."

"But what about those people?" Noah pointed at a couple of zoo volunteers across the lot in their brown khakis and navy-blue shirts.

Malik passed the stroller to Magaly and picked up Noah. "I'm sure they will find a safe place for cover as well. Now let's go."

Once at the car, Magaly parked the stroller, popped the car seat back in, and hopped into the driver's seat. Malik went straight to the front passenger seat and opened the door.

"Aren't you going to put me in my chair?" Noah asked.

"Not for now," Malik said, climbing in with his son on his lap and closing the door. Malik's phone lit up again. *One minute left,* he thought, as he stared at the mostly vacant parking lot. His eyes followed the two zoo volunteers who were still out there. He willed them to hurry.

"I don't think they're finding a safe place, Dad," Noah commented.

The windshield grew darker until it was completely opaque, which shifted Malik's focus to the technology shielding his family from the solar flare. Malik felt a surge of pride in the protective glass his team at the Singularity Group had made.

"You made this, right, Dad?" Noah asked, pointing to the glass.

Are we entangled? Malik wondered, not for the first time. "Well, some really, really smart people I worked with used their brains and their imaginations to figure out a way to make this special type of glass that protects us from the sun's hot rays."

"You mean solar flares?" Noah asked.

"Yes, exactly," Malik said. Just then, the windshield lost its opacity, turning back to a clear, visible glass.

"Why is it not dark anymore?" Noah asked.

Magaly jumped in. "When the glass turns dark, that means solar flares with harmful energy are touching it. When the harmful stuff goes away, then the glass clears up, which means it's safe for us to be outside."

"What about them?" Noah pointed at the pair of zoo volunteers who had tried to hide underneath an overhang.

"I don't know, baby. But they look like they are okay," Magaly replied.

"Yes, they do, don't they?" Malik said and intuitively looked at the dashboard clock to note the time, which read 9:02 a.m.. Malik set a timer on his phone for eighteen minutes and twenty-five seconds.

"What are you doing?" Magaly asked.

"I'm testing a theory," Malik said, eyes still on his phone.

"What's a theory?" Noah said.

Magaly answered, "It's a belief or an idea of something that will happen."

"What's your theory, Dad?"

Malik looked up to find both Noah and Magaly studying him. "A scientist who has been doing a lot of research came up with an idea that some people feel sick from the solar flares after about eighteen minutes. Anyway, let's get this zoo visit started."

As Malik and Magaly fell into step outside the car, she asked in a low voice, "Who was this? Anatole?"

"Yep," Malik said.

"Has anyone heard anything?"

"Nothing yet."

4

THE LION EXHIBIT

MALIK NAVIGATED THE STROLLER THROUGH THE ROPE MAZE THAT LED zoogoers down the brick walkway toward the entry booths. They waited at the end of the roped-off section for the next available attendant to wave them forward. Malik's eyes moved from kiosk to kiosk, noticing each person was still getting set up in their booths. Malik scanned the surrounding area. "That's strange," he said.

"What?" Magaly asked.

"We're the only ones in line."

"I saw some other people getting back into their cars before the solar flare hit," she responded. "Plus, we made it here right at opening time today."

"Ah, that's probably it," Malik said. "Whatever the reason, I'll take it. We'll get to take our time going through today. Plus, the atomizers are the most effective with lighter crowds."

"Who is Adam?" Noah asked.

"Who?" Magaly and Malik said simultaneously.

"You said Adam's eye," Noah responded. "Was it hurt like mine?"

"Oh, no," Malik said. "We said atomizers. You've heard us talk about them before, right?"

"I think so. They're at the zoo?" Noah asked.

Malik kneeled to Noah's height and pointed to the roof of the covered zoo entrance. "Do you see those large black machines that are fastened up there?"

Noah followed Malik's finger. "The ones that spray water?"

"That's right." Malik nodded. "My granddad, GG's husband, invented those machines. They call them atomizers."

"Why?"

"Why do they call them atomizers?"

"No, why did GG's husband invent them?"

"You know the virus we talk about sometimes?" Malik asked.

"Yeah," Noah said.

"Well, back then, it was new, and there was a great deal the doctors needed to learn. They made medicines to treat it and make it less severe, but the virus kept changing all the time. GG used to have to wear a mask anytime she left her house. Then smart doctors and scientists learned that the virus did much more than make you sick. They discovered it could live in your body, even after you stopped sneezing and coughing, and over time, it could damage your lungs, heart, and even your brain. So, my granddad, Zach, invented those machines as an additional treatment. They spray a natural medicine that doesn't let the virus stay in our bodies and hurt our organs, prevents new strains from developing and spreading, and helps us stay healthy."

"Did he pass on?" Noah asked.

"He did—"

An attendant waved them over, interrupting the conversation. Malik felt the refreshing, gentle mist of lemon-scented air as he walked up to do the facial recognition. He hit "Approve" once the attendance confirmation popped up on his phone. Then he pulled up their membership key and held his phone out toward Noah, anticipating what came next.

"Ooh, I want to do it," Noah's voice rang as he lunged forward and grabbed Malik's phone. Malik exchanged smiles with the attendant while Noah held the phone as high as he could reach.

The attendant touched the glass with her finger. "Thank you," she said and gave Noah an enormous smile. "You're all set. Enjoy your day!"

Malik held himself back from pointing out the advanced two-way Singularity Group vision glass to his family before walking away. One side appeared to be a see-through window, while the other side could have an array of screens to suit the user. Malik wondered what she was watching on her side of the glass.

"Thank you!" Noah shouted as he sprinted toward the flamingo habitat right by the entrance. He leaned up against the railing and stretched onto his tiptoes to get a better view of the birds. "Whoa!" Noah turned back just enough to confirm that Malik and Magaly were paying attention. "Did you know flamingos get their color from what they eat?"

"I think you may have mentioned that before," Magaly replied. "It's a pretty pink, isn't it?"

"Yes!" Noah said.

Malik let Aries hold his finger as he talked to him. "There's so much for you to see, buddy. I'll try to get you out in a bit." Aries seemed content for now, observing something beyond Malik's head.

"Okay, Noah," Magaly said. "Do you want to go straight to see the tiger and clouded leopard, or do you want to go left to…"

Noah interrupted Magaly with an enthusiastic, "Let's go see if Grumbles is out today!" Malik watched as the little boy jumped down from the railing and darted off and to the left.

"Wanna see a rhinoceros?" Magaly asked Aries, walking alongside Malik as they trailed Noah to the next location. They all stopped to see Grumbles having some breakfast, then started on toward the elephants. The woman volunteer who had been outside during the solar flare walked by. Malik smiled at her as she walked past, and she seemed to try to smile back, but something was off about it. Her smile looked more like a grimace. Malik paused and glanced over his shoulder in time to see her stumble and stagger as she continued down the path. He checked the timer on his phone. Six minutes left. Malik got an uncomfortable feeling in his gut and thought through his choices. *If I do this, and I'm wrong, it could be bad. They might ask us to leave… If I'm right, I could save a life, or maybe even two.*

Noah was already up the hill by the elephants. Malik called out, "Wait there, Noah." He then handed the stroller over to Magaly, who looked at him questioningly.

"What's up?" she asked.

Malik hesitated, then said, "I'll be right back."

"Is everything okay?"

"It will be. If Anatole is right, then I should probably go get some help."

Her look of concern deepened. "He hasn't been wrong yet, has he?"

Malik hurried back to the ticket attendant that helped check them in, but she was busy. He saw the next attendant was free and stepped up to address him. "Excuse me?"

"Yes?"

"I think that one of your volunteers is sick," Malik said. "Can you call 911?"

"What happened?"

"She walked past me near the rhino habitat," Malik pointed over his shoulder, "and went toward the eagle and the tiger habitats. She looked like she was in pain, and I saw her stagger. I'm worried she might collapse."

"Oh, no!" the attendant said sympathetically, searching over Malik's shoulder for any sign of an emergency.

Malik continued. "I think she's the same person I saw caught outside during the solar flare this morning."

Malik heard someone in the distance call, "We need some help over here!"

The attendant heard it too, his sense of alarm now heightened. "I'll call it in right now!"

Malik heard the attendant relaying the message to someone on the other end of the phone. Meanwhile, a couple of zoo employees went running in the woman's direction. Malik decided the situation was being handled, and he hastened to catch up with his family.

As Malik got within view of the elephant habitat, he heard Noah shout, "Dad, where were you?"

Malik began his reply, "I had to—," but he was cut off.

"We're going to see the lions!" Noah said, too excited to wait for Malik's response, and then raced up the hill toward the lion habitat.

Malik merged with Magaly. "Were you able to get help?"

"I told some people at the front. They're calling it in." As soon as the words left his lips, he heard the sirens in the distance. "I just hope she's okay." Malik shook his head, wishing there was more he could do. He felt Magaly's soft hand rub the back of his arm.

"You did the right thing," she said.

"Come on, you guys!" Noah called to them.

Malik tried to shake it off and bring his attention back to his son, who was enthralled with the lions. This habitat had two viewing areas: An outside viewing area, which was farther up the hill, let visitors view the lions from afar. The covered viewing area they were approaching offered visitors a closer view. It was positioned at the bottom of the lion habitat and looked like the entrance to a cave. There was a thick glass barrier between the spectators and the regal creatures they were there to see. Sometimes, when they got to the zoo early enough, the lions were lying right there against the glass. This looked to be one of those mornings. Malik saw two of the giant males lying together, still asleep. And then there was the third, standing right in front of the glass, eye to eye with Noah.

Noah gave a low, playful, "Roooaaarrr."

He could swear that the lion's head alone was Noah's height. The lion shifted his gaze to Malik, which was enough to make the breath catch in Malik's throat. The lion's eyes were enormous and focused. His thick mane created a vibrant halo with its hues of gold and black. "I don't know why I'm always surprised at how massive they are," he said to Magaly. "One day, I want to go on a safari."

"Oooh, me too. That would be incredible," Magaly agreed.

"Can you imagine seeing these guys in action?"

Just then, the two brothers jumped to their feet, and all three lions focused on something that was out of view. A second later, they ran off toward the far end of their habitat, and a chilling scream pierced the air.

"What's happening?" Noah asked. Magaly had the stroller and was pulling Noah to her as well.

"Wait here," Malik said and dashed to where he could see the outdoor viewing area. A couple of zoo workers ran by. The foghorn sound of the timer came from Malik's phone, and he felt the knots tighten in his stomach. It was 9:20. There was no more time left; the eighteen minutes expired. *The other volunteer...* Malik didn't need to see what happened. He knew.

Malik felt a small hand grip his. He looked down to see Noah holding his hand. "Daddy, I think something bad happened."

"I think so too."

"I think we should go home."

"That's a great idea."

.   .   .

As they walked across the parking lot, Malik watched his son, head down and shoulders slumped. The little boy stared at his shoes, placing one foot in front of the other. "Hey, buddy, you know what?"

"What, Dad?" Noah said, without looking up.

"Do you want to go see Nana sooner?"

Noah gasped and looked up from his shoes to search Malik's face. "Yes."

"Why don't we go tomorrow?"

"Really?" Noah squeezed both fists tight.

"Sure, why not?" Malik said. He silently looked to Magaly for agreement and was met with a smile.

"But don't we have to fly?"

"I'll book the flight as soon as we get home."

Noah turned to Magaly. "Mom, is he serious?"

Magaly nodded her head. "He is, baby. You've got some packing to do later!"

5

WELCOME TO NEW YORK CITY

ONCE MALIK HAD CARRIED THE BABY, STILL STRAPPED INTO HIS CAR seat, into the house, Magaly asked, "Can you put Aries down for his nap? He shouldn't need to eat."

"Sure," Malik said.

"Look at that!" Noah pointed at the car seat. "There must be aphids on Aries."

Malik saw the telltale bright orange and black dots of ladybugs on the car seat above Aries's head.

"Why do you think aphids are on the baby?" Magaly asked.

"Because everyone knows ladybugs eat aphids." Noah's tone was all confidence.

"Oh? And what are aphids?" Malik asked.

"They're the tiny bugs in my nature game," Noah said. "They always try to eat the plants in my garden."

"Ah, got it," Malik said, unbuckling Aries and hoisting the baby up so his chin was on Malik's left shoulder.

Noah collected the ladybugs and rushed to release them outside before he began running laps around the living room. "Can we watch a family movie?"

"Not right now," Magaly said. "I'm going to make lunch, and then I think you should have some quiet time."

"But I'm not hungry or tired."

"We didn't say that you needed to nap," Magaly continued. "You can work on a puzzle or play quietly with your toys."

"Can I do one of my dinosaur sticker puzzles?" Noah's face brightened.

"Of course," Magaly said, and then paused. "Babe, are you hungry?"

Malik turned, knowing that was directed at him. "Not really. Breakfast was pretty filling."

"Neither am I," she said. She walked over to her desk and searched through a stack of books. Aries was restless in Malik's arms, so he turned the baby around to face outward. They both watched as Magaly continued to search the house for something.

"What are you looking for?" Malik finally asked.

"I can't find my sketchbook," Magaly said.

When Magaly stepped away from the hospital, she had searched for an outlet that would engage her mind and allow her to learn something new. She sketched whenever she had a moment. She had been working on eyes, noses, and ears, trying to work her way up to portraits. Magaly would even thumb through her old medical school books and sketch the complex muscles of the arms and legs. She was quite talented.

"I know where it is," Noah said. "I'll go get it!" Noah darted out of the room and Aries did his best to watch where his brother was going. Malik turned the baby back around, trying to give him a better line of sight to Noah. After a moment, Aries's head became heavy on Malik's shoulder.

"Alright," Malik whispered. "I'm going to go try to lay him down."

"Good luck," Magaly whispered back. They both knew that

getting Aries to sleep in his crib could take anywhere between fifteen minutes to an hour. That's if they could get the baby to lie down at all.

MALIK SETTLED into the rocking chair in the nursery and waited as the baby fidgeted with the folds on Malik's shirt. The morning's events at the zoo played back in Malik's mind, and he tried to push out the feelings of unease. Malik closed his eyes, breathed deeply, and rocked in the chair until the baby seemed asleep. Malik gently laid Aries in his crib and held his breath as he backed away. The baby made a small fussing noise, and Malik froze. When no crying followed, Malik sat back down in the chair, thinking, *I'll just stay nearby for a little while and make sure he's settled.*

A BRIGHT LIGHT caused Malik to shift his shoulder, expecting to nestle into the soft microfiber of the glider. Instead, he felt his cheek scrape against a rough surface and the knotted muscles in his neck ache. Malik quickly realized he was no longer reclining in the nursery chair and was not even safely at home with his family. Malik urgently pushed himself up to sitting to gauge where he was. The foghorn alarm from his phone sounded again. This time, it was much louder and reverberated off the surrounding buildings.

Malik tried to focus on the cause of the sound, but he became distracted once he recognized where he was. The first thing he identified was the bronze statue of a young girl standing in front of the iconic Wall Street bull in New York City. *I'm in the Financial District,* Malik thought, as pressure filled his chest and his heart raced. *How did I get here?* He hurriedly stood up, hoping to avoid being trampled by the throngs of busy inhabitants and photo-hungry tourists he expected to see here. Now on his feet, Malik felt the pinprick of goosebumps crawl up his arms. He turned in a complete circle, and all he saw around him were rows and rows of people lying still on the ground.

Malik held his breath in an attempt to become completely silent, and he strained to hear a voice, a laugh, a footstep, any sign of life. He locked his eyes on one person, a woman lying on her side, wearing a red dress that clung to her ribs. His inner dialogue was loud in his mind. *Please move, please move.* Her ribcage lifted, just barely. *Oh, thank God,* Malik thought, relieved that she was breathing and hoping that meant the same was true for all the others.

Malik couldn't move without stepping over people. Next, Malik saw a man wearing a charcoal suit, white shirt, and a royal-blue tie whose head lay upon his designer backpack as if it were a pillow. Malik watched the man's chest expand and retract. *Are they all asleep?* Malik wondered as he looked around at the bodies, all perfectly placed, as if each had picked a spot to nap.

Malik reflected on the last time he picked his son up early from daycare, which was during nap time. Each child had a small blue, yellow, or red mat and a little piece of floor to themselves to rest. *Not the time. Stay on track.*

Malik turned his attention back to his surroundings. He leaned down and gently nudged the shoulder of the man lying on his backpack, but the man did not awaken. After a few more unsuccessful attempts at waking people, Malik saw the street sign for Wall Street and headed that way.

Malik pulled his phone out of his jacket pocket and unlocked it to find the red triangle with an exclamation mark in the center, which signaled a solar flare. A coronal mass ejection flashed in the distance with enough intensity that Malik lifted his hand to shield his eyes. Once his eyes recovered, he closed the alert, and then a calendar reminder popped up for a meeting at 40 Wall Street. *I don't know what's going on, but I need to get inside as soon as possible.* Malik made his way toward the meeting destination as fast as he could without stepping on anyone.

A block or two down the street, Malik halted midstep when a small motion caught his eye. A person lying on the steps of the Stock Market Exchange had moved. Malik looked up and down the street to find a handful of other people awakening. *Oh, thank you,* was all Malik could think. He thought about walking toward the people, but he first had to identify a clear path through the still dormant figures around him. Once he identified a route, Malik glanced back up to see that the others who had been awake had disappeared.

Now in front of the gold-plated building entrance and glass doors, Malik stepped up to the security screen for facial recognition. When Malik heard the lock on the door open, his stomach tightened with anticipation of what was inside. Malik slowly tugged the heavy door open and took in as much as possible before walking over the threshold. There was no movement anywhere, just a continuation of the sprawl of well-dressed bodies on the pink marble floor. He took a few steps into the building, his own reflection the only movement in the polished gold panels that lined the wall.

Is this a dream? He stood still in the entryway, again listening for any sound. Nothing. Not even the AC or the atomizers were humming. *This can't be.* Malik saw the guards cuddled behind the check-in desk. Something made him walk past their bodies and take the elevator to the twenty-seventh floor. Malik had often traveled to New York before he took his leave from the Singularity Group and had attended many a meeting in this very spot.

When the elevator arrived at the twenty-seventh floor, Malik hesitated to step out. He placed his hand on the door to keep it open and waited. Usually, Malik could hear the phones ringing as soon as he stepped off the elevator. The team would be on the phones as early as six in the morning, fielding calls from their Asian team members. Yet, on this day, Malik didn't hear a single ring or greeting. There was simply… silence. Malik jumped at a sudden loud buzzing of the elevator, warning him the door had been held open for too long. Malik stepped out and let the door slowly close behind him.

Now Malik had a clear view of the office. Everyone was sound asleep at their desks. *This has to be a dream,* Malik assured himself emphatically as he rubbed the area between his eyebrows. He shut his eyes as hard as he could, feeling his eyelids tremble, and whispered, "Wake up, Malik! C'mon, wake up!"

A bolt of lightning caused Malik to open his eyes in time to see the sky turning gray through the large office windows, which looked out on a helicopter landing pad. Another lightning bolt crashed down right in the middle of the H, quickly followed by thunder that made the entire floor quake. Malik instinctively backed away from the windows and surveyed the room for somewhere safe to stand. "Please wake up, please wake up," he whispered to himself as he saw more bright flashes of light out of the corner of his eyes. There was a brief pause before thunder roared so loud it could've been playing through a loudspeaker inside the building.

Malik stood there, his eyes shut, as he felt the building first shake, then sway. He took a deep breath and a slight jolt shot from his feet to his stomach, making it vibrate. It was a feeling that he'd only experienced a few times when he was out in California during a mild earthquake. The feeling in his stomach settled, and Malik felt goosebumps again. He squeezed his eyes tightly until a blinding white light forced him to turn away.

. . .

MALIK JERKED awake and realized he had fallen asleep in the nursery. Rain was falling, making a pleasant pitter patter on the roof. Suddenly, a flash of lightning was so bright and a clap of thunder so loud it was hard to separate from his dream. Malik was sure it would wake the baby, but to his surprise, Aries was sprawled out in his crib in a deep, peaceful sleep.

6

THE CREW IS BACK TOGETHER

JESSICA SAT IN THE CHAIR ON HER PATIO, APPRECIATING THE CHILLY early morning air and hugging the soft blanket around her shoulders. Pink, orange, and red light had just broken through the dark of the night sky. Jessica watched the few remaining stars go into hiding while the sun peeked over the distant hills. She heard some movement behind her and turned to see the tall, lean figure of her son-in-law bend over the fireplace. Jessica never minded the cool mountain air. In fact, she preferred it. Ever since her daughter, Nia, and her husband, Jonas, had moved in, they insisted on making sure a warm fire was always burning to keep Jessica healthy. She had told them it wasn't necessary, but they didn't listen. Their intentions were good, so Jessica let them fuss over her a little. Jessica chuckled softly, and thought, *If only they knew.*

Ever since she had traveled to the Point, her body had never felt better. She was never too hot or too cold. She was always just right. *I can't even remember the last time I was sick,* a realization she hadn't shared with anyone other than her late husband. She inhaled sharply as a memory flashed into her mind of being barely conscious at the Point. *It has been such a long time. How long has it been?* She tried to remember the last time she had visited her friends there. As the sun continued to rise, so did a feeling of excitement in Jessica's chest.

The dream home that Jessica and her late husband had built was on top of a hillside outside of Newberg, Oregon. Jessica had chosen the property, which backed up against an old-growth forest, while Zach had made most decisions on the design of the home. Jessica loved watching the rabbits and deer come out every morning. This location was also perfect because it allowed Jessica to be stealthy when traveling, drawing no suspicion. Ever since her work had been completed, she hadn't felt compelled to travel back to the Point, though it had been on her mind as of late. Today, however, was the perfect day to make the trip.

The early light enabled Jessica to see the fog spreading across the grass. That familiar mist reminded her of her old companions and all the adventures they had been on. Jessica closed her eyes and filled her lungs. As she exhaled, a low fluttering sound made Jessica crack one eyelid to see the green and blue plume of a hummingbird, the rapid beat of its wings allowing it to hover just inches away from her face. Now with both eyes open, Jessica watched the small bird zip to the trail entrance that led to the woods before it paused again mid-flight. *I'm on my way,* she silently told it. *Although I haven't been sick,* Jessica gripped the arms of the chair and pushed herself up to stand, *age takes its toll.*

She looked down at her wrist and caressed the bezel around the skeleton watch's face with her thumb and index finger. She smiled as she saw the gears turning away under the transparent face. Jessica turned her head and studied the inside of the house for a minute to ensure no one was there to see what was about to happen next. After she was sure there were no witnesses, Jessica turned her attention back to her watch. The gears had stopped moving, and the sub-dial now showed the number eight. Jessica inhaled until her lungs were full, then she pressed her index finger on the sub-dial.

The white cloud moved fast, and as Jessica exhaled, her body became weightless. This feeling of floating in the air was always accompanied by a tickling sensation inside her stomach. She smiled, thinking about all the times she had experienced this feeling while traveling with Ori and the team in her role as the Scribe, and how the sensation of traveling never got old. It made her feel like a kid again, her dad pushing her on a swing, and her calling back to him, *"Higher! Higher!"* That was the first time she experienced and learned to love that fluttering feeling in her gut.

Once Jessica stopped floating, the clouds dispersed quickly, and she had a peaceful bird's-eye view of the planet. Suspended, she watched as countless lightning bolts—in quick succession— struck various locations of the planet. Then the fog whisked her along. *I love this.* The wind on her face was warm and comfortable, one of the few signs of how fast she was traveling. Another clue was the array of vibrant colors that streaked around her. Now and then, the greens and violets would radiate more brightly and extend, giving Jessica a feeling of love and comfort. She inhaled deeply once more and prepared to disembark.

The landing was always smooth. Before she knew it, she was striding through the forest; her legs knew what to do. She loved being here. Her soul, mind, and body loved being here.

"Hey, Jessica."

She turned to see Tony arriving as well, wearing a navy-blue shirt and brown khakis.

"Where are you coming from?" Jessica asked.

Tony pulled the glasses off his face. "The zoo."

"Which zoo?" Jessica asked as Tony quickly walked past. He didn't answer. *Something must be up,* she concluded, extending her gait to keep up.

Tony glanced over his shoulder at her. "I see you got the meeting invitation."

She nodded. "I even got a reminder, in the form of a hummingbird. What's going on?"

Tony laughed. "I'm glad to see that you are still in flow."

"Did you expect anything else?" Jessica smirked before her smile fell away. "What happened?"

"Someone jumped into the lion habitat at the Atlanta zoo."

"Are they okay?"

Tony shook his head.

Jessica covered her mouth with her hands. "Oh, my."

"That's not all."

Jessica braced herself, awaiting what Tony would share next.

"Malik was there."

"Please tell me that the babies weren't with him."

Tony's shoulders stiffened in reply.

"I have to check on them," Jessica told him, considering whether to turn around.

"I think this meeting is important for you, and for them. We'll share more in the team meeting at the house. It might help."

JESSICA FOLLOWED Tony out of the woods and through the orchards that bordered part of the estate where Ori, Evelyn, and the rest of the crew typically resided. As they passed by trees full of ripe apples and pears, Jessica focused on keeping stride with Tony until they reached the large stone manor. "I think they're waiting on the porch," Tony said, leading the way around the large mansion to a covered porch supported by stately columns. Jordan was lounging across a broad armchair, with her legs hanging over one armrest and her back and head arched over the other. Vau, who was lying on a couch, swung his legs around and jumped up as soon as he saw Jessica.

"Jessica!" Vau boomed and spread his tattooed arms wide for a hug. He wrapped Jessica up so tightly she could barely move as he lifted her into the air. "I'm sorry we had to pull you away from your family. We know how precious your time with them is."

Jessica lightly patted Vau's shoulders before he returned her to the ground. "Don't worry about it. I'm here whenever you need me; you know that."

"I wish it were under happier circumstances," Jordan said, lazily pulling herself up from the chair. She walked slowly around Jessica, inspecting her. Jordan gave a single nod of satisfaction. "You look good."

Jessica narrowed her eyes, suspicious of the compliment. "Thank you?"

"For an old lady," Jordan said, and they both let out a laugh and hugged.

"You missed me. Admit it," Jessica said.

Jordan rolled her eyes. "You wish."

"So, are you gonna tell me what this is all about?" Jessica asked. The faces of her three friends immediately lost their mirth.

After a lengthy pause, Vau started, "Did you hear about…"

Tony cut him off. "I already told her."

"About the zoo?" Vau asked.

"Yep," Tony confirmed.

"That's just the beginning," Jordan said.

"Give her a minute, guys. Let her settle in," Evelyn said as she joined them outside. Evelyn was different. Her light gray pantsuit and white blouse were uncharacteristic for the Evelyn Jessica knew. It made Jessica feel like she should be back in the Str8 Truth Media office, pitching stories to M. Evelyn's curly hair was now a darker chestnut brown and flowed down her back. Like everyone else here, Evelyn seemed timeless, but unlike most of the others, she often changed her hair.

"It's been a while." Evelyn smiled, leaning in to give Jessica a hug. "Don't mind this getup." Evelyn brushed at her outfit. "I've just come back from being in the field. You, on the other hand, look great."

"Oh, you're just saying that," Jessica said. "My knees aren't what they used to be. And the gray has fully forced out all the black in my hair."

"No, I mean it. And thank you for coming on such short notice. I wish we could let you enjoy the rest of your time in peace."

"I'm happy to help however I can. Plus, I haven't seen you guys in…" Jessica paused. "I don't even remember how long it's been since I was last here."

"That's the beauty of living in the present, right? Time becomes a very relative thing."

Professor Raziel and Ori then approached the porch from somewhere on the grounds.

"Why, Jessica, what a lovely sight," the Professor said.

Ori smiled at her. "Don't be too critical of those knees of yours. You made it here in quick time."

"He's right," Evelyn said. "Anyway, I know you must be curious about this meeting. We'll explain everything soon."

"I'm ready when you guys are," Jessica assured her.

"Perfect." Evelyn turned to Jordan. "Let's catch up first. What's the report?"

"It's just like you said." Jordan looked at Ori. "Incidents are popping up more frequently, and people don't seem to be connecting the dots. It's getting bad."

Professor Raziel said, "Nothing is good or bad; it just is."

Ori rubbed his chin and stared off into space. "Well, the good news is we saw this coming. It's not ideal, but we knew this could be a result."

Jordan turned to Evelyn. "How was your trip to Washington, DC?"

Evelyn pursed her lips. "Budget issues and a lack of data and understanding around solar sickness are making them think the solar flare infrastructure is no longer needed. There is a lot of debate about it though, so we still have time, but not much. We need Anatole."

Jessica's ears perked up when she heard the uncommon name.

"And how did the other DC aim turn out?" Ori asked.

"As well as expected," Evelyn said with a shrug, "considering I couldn't make direct contact. But enough events have been set in motion to lead her in a new direction. How about you? What did you find out?"

"I've confirmed that my impact on their consciousness becomes mostly ineffective when there's too much brain fog. Once a mind reaches this point, their decision-making ability and control weaken to where…" Ori paused as he appeared to search for the right words.

Vau came to his aid. "Yeah, we understand."

Evelyn gave an audible exhale before she turned to Tony. "Did I leave any trace?"

"No," Tony said. "You're clear." He turned to Ori. "Your trip to the park was good too."

"Good," Ori said.

"How did he seem? Were you able to identify any alternatives?" Evelyn asked.

Ori appeared thoughtful. "He's… I think this is still the path forward."

"Are you sure this is the direction we have to go?" Jordan asked.

Ori remained silent for a moment, his hand on his chin, staring at the floor. He then shook his head from side to side and looked Jordan in the eye. "I, unfortunately, don't see another way."

The tension in the room was palpable. Ori then broke his eye contact with Jordan and slowly turned to Jessica. She asked, "Is there something I can do to help?"

Everyone seemed to have taken that as a cue, and they settled in around her. She took a seat on the couch between Tony and Vau.

"Where should I begin?" Evelyn spoke to herself.

"The virus," Ori said.

"Right, right." Evelyn focused on Jessica. "Thanks to you and Malik, we were able to right the course regarding the virus in a frontline existence. You and Zach got your time back, and a solution was introduced much earlier, which dramatically reduced the impact of the virus, putting humanity in a better position to prepare for the reset."

Jessica nodded, as her mind flashed back to seeing Zach in the assisted living home. She shivered, and for the millionth time, felt grateful they had rewritten that story.

"The impact of that mission went even further," Evelyn continued. "That treatment led humans to further explore how to tap into the tree and fungal network and created a newfound widespread appreciation for the healing powers of nature. This significantly slowed deforestation, which was previously at a critical point. And this all also helped stop the backslide into the third growth phase."

"The more people in the fourth growth phase of owning one's time," Ori elaborated, "the more people who will inevitably move to growth phase five."

Vau leaned toward her and whispered, "The ability to master multiple things and consciously manifest."

"Thanks," Jessica mouthed in reply.

"Which brings us to the reset," said Evelyn.

"The solar flares," Jordan explained. "Well, in tandem with Earth's magnetic field. Overexposure to solar flares is preventing enough people from having the mental capacity to reach the fifth phase."

Evelyn continued the explanation. "Every several hundred thousand years, Earth's magnetic field gets weaker, allowing more cosmic rays to penetrate the atmosphere, including harmful solar flares, otherwise known as coronal mass ejections. The more intense particles the sun ejects have become increasingly detrimental."

"Given the slowing in deforestation, the tree canopies will protect the earth, but they can't protect humanity as well," Jordan added.

Ori spoke up again. "Too much direct exposure to these more potent solar flares causes brain fog, as Jordan alluded to. It is also causing emotional instability, along with erratic and dangerous behavior."

"The solar flares tinker with you on an atomic level," Jordan said.

"That's why you guys mentioned Anatole earlier?" Jessica looked at Evelyn for confirmation. "The scientist, Anatole Patterson, whose research was focused on this? He was on his way to a solution, right?"

Evelyn frowned. "A solution that needs to be finished."

Jessica felt a fresh wave of sympathy as a memory of attending the funeral of Anatole's partner flashed into her mind. "His focus is elsewhere, and understandably so. It will be very difficult to get his mind back on this work. He blames himself for what happened."

"We understand," Ori said. The area was quiet until a light breeze blew, followed by the tinkle of a wind chime.

"Jessica," Evelyn said, "we believe Malik is the key."

7

MALIK IS THE KEY

"Malik?" Jessica searched each face from Evelyn to Ori to Jordan, who turned away, avoiding eye contact. "Okay. Why are you telling me this?"

"We would like your permission and help in recruiting him," Ori replied. "We want your support and blessing to bring Malik to the Point for training."

Evelyn spoke again. "Since Malik was so helpful with the virus, we believe he is the perfect candidate."

"But that's a reality he no longer lives in," Jessica protested.

"True," said Ori, "but he's the same person with the same heart and mind."

"And beyond that, he is still connected to your family's work with respect to the virus, and Malik understands it all intimately," added Evelyn.

"How are the two related?" Jessica asked.

Evelyn nodded toward Jordan with an expression that said, *"Do you want to take this?"*

Jordan cleared her throat. "They aren't exactly, but the virus served as a preview of what was to come. It was trying to hack your bodies, looking for areas of vulnerability. That's why so many saw such an array of effects. It would attack the lungs of some people, the heart of others, the brain in others. Those were considered the severest of cases. But the most lingering, difficult-to-diagnose issues were found to be the long-term effects of the virus that had been lying dormant and hiding," Jordan rubbed her stomach, "in the gut."

"We don't believe the virus was trying to kill you, but to colonize your body," Tony said simply.

"Like bacteria?" Jessica asked.

"Yes!" Jordan stood up and extended both hands in Jessica's direction. "You, your bodies. You guys are the host of the oldest life-force on the planet."

Tony chimed in again. "Your bodies were created to be a cozy place for your microbiota, bacteria, to live."

"When Nia was a baby, the doctor talked about the colonization of a baby's stomach." Jessica remembered trying to soothe her daughter, wishing there was more she could do to ease her little tummy. "And now her husband talks sometimes about feeding our microbiota when he cooks for us."

"Jonas is on the right track," Professor Raziel spoke up for the first time. "More people need to understand why that's important, one's microbiome. Your ability to coexist with trillions of microbes is really the reason humanity has survived this long. As long as humans keep being made, these microscopic life-forms have a home. You are the perfect host for them. And your ability to create and quickly adapt to your environment means that your species has the greatest chance of longevity."

"The bacteria, they were the beginning of life. There was nothing here before them. Now, they are connected with everything your body does and feels," Vau said.

Professor Raziel continued, "For the unconscious, the microbiome has more control over your cravings and your actions.

A healthy human body depends on bacteria diversity, which provides checks and balances."

"Without those checks and balances, the body can become very ill," Vau added.

"Or worse," Jordan said, "completely take control."

"While the body serves as the host to the microbiota, the brain and its advanced ability to create—that is uniquely human." Professor Raziel inhaled deeply. "Creativity sets you apart from the rest. Without that, you will no longer be the optimal host, and the reset is upon us."

"The solar flares," Vau jumped in, "accelerate the growth of certain microscopic life-forms, particularly the bacteria. Millions of years ago, this injection of energy was needed to create a planet habitable for evolved life to form, but now it is a threat to humanity."

"How so?" Jessica asked.

"When exposed to these coronal mass ejections, if you have a healthy microbiome, everything should multiply in a balanced way," said Tony. "However, if your gut bacteria is less than stellar and is unbalanced, then aggressive bacteria will overpopulate and force out other bacteria, causing people to make unbalanced decisions."

"You don't need a perfectly healthy diet; you just need enough of the beneficial bacteria to offset the harmful ones. That's always been the case. But now, with the solar flares, everything is multiplying so quickly that people don't have time to make the corrections," said Vau.

"It's like the worst pop quiz ever," Jordan said.

"And then what happens when harmful bacteria takes over?" Jessica asked, though she had a bad feeling she already knew the answer.

"Take the zookeeper who leaped into the lions' habitat for example," Tony said. "There is a particular parasite that can only thrive inside the intestines of a feline. It's called Toxoplasma gondii."

"Okay," Jessica said.

Tony continued. "Well, that parasite is focused on surviving, that's it. That poor person probably contracted the parasite by accident, while cleaning the cat litter or by eating uncooked meat. Perhaps there wasn't a balanced gut to keep the bacteria in check. Add in the solar flares, and that particular parasite multiplied in the small intestines to a point where it impacted the decision-making of the brain."

Jessica must have looked skeptical because Jordan spoke up again. "It's been observed in some animals, like rats, where this parasite will find its way to the brain and alter how the rodent views the threat of a feline. The parasite is known for altering the brain's activity as it relates to fear."

Jessica rubbed her temples. "This is quite a lot to process."

"We know," said Evelyn apologetically.

"See," Jordan exclaimed. "And that is a parasite that most experts know about."

"Anatole's solution," Evelyn said, "once complete, will help save billions of lives. We need Malik's help. We'll be seeking alignment to recruit him at the Council meeting today."

Jessica was silent as she digested this.

She finally spoke, still feeling uneasy. "I don't know if Malik would or even could finish Anatole's work."

"Malik's genius is the only one actively trying to solve this problem," Evelyn said. "And we believe Malik could help us get through to Anatole."

"But... I don't know," Jessica said. "He would spend a lot of time locked away, obsessing over formulas and calculations." Jessica shook her head. "I don't want that for him."

"We understand how you feel," Evelyn said. "We don't either, for him or his family. You just have to trust us."

A wave of panic caused her to stand up from the couch. "The last time I was at the Point, I lost almost fifty years of my time…"

"Your situation was different," Ori said. "Time passes differently for different people. When you came to the Point, your conscious mind was affected, and you had lost your memory. That's why you lost so much time while here. But for a person who consciously lives in the present, then time at the Point will pass as fast or as slow as they choose."

Evelyn spoke again. "Right now, Malik and Magaly are living a very present lifestyle. Now is a great time for them to be recruited."

Jessica paced as she considered this. They were her friends. She knew she could trust their level of intention and thoughtfulness. She rehearsed the conversation in her head, thinking about what she would say to her grandson.

"Don't worry, the words will come when it is time," Ori said. "Malik showed great promise when we needed him. He has a strong connection with his intuition, and he wants to make the world a better place. He will make a great fit."

Evelyn gave her a warm smile. "If the Council agrees he can be recruited, then he will become an asset for Gabriel and Aja. This will allow him and his family to lead a life more beautiful than one could ever hope for."

"You'll want to give him this," said Ori, handing her a folded piece of paper.

Jessica unfolded the paper and saw it was a Newberg address. "What is this?"

"That's the address for Lotus," Ori said. "She's a human being, just like you. Lotus lives by the old way, following the signs, going on the journey. She will give Malik some guidance and some much-needed words of wisdom to help him stay rooted."

"It's time for us to be on our way," Professor Raziel said. "The others will arrive soon."

8

THE COUNCIL MEETING

THE GROUP STARTED ON THEIR WAY TO THE COMMAND CENTER, LED BY Professor Raziel, Ori, and Evelyn, who was now wearing a long, blue-and-green, sleeveless linen dress that flowed to the ground, hiding her feet.

Jessica trailed behind with the others and noticed Jordan was deep in thought. "Jordan, you okay?" Jessica asked.

"You should think about whether you want Malik and his family to be a part of this," Jordan said, still staring ahead.

"Why wouldn't I?"

"Don't worry about her," Vau said. "Jordan is just projecting her fears and her experiences onto Malik."

"What experiences?" Jessica asked as the path narrowed and forced them to walk single file.

Tony led, followed by Jordan, Jessica, and then Vau, who gently tugged the back of Jessica's shirt to slow her down a little. In a low voice, he told her, "Jordan's parents had incredible manifestation powers."

"Malik likes to help everybody," Jordan said over her shoulder. "He's just wired that way."

"I thought that was part of what made him an ideal recruit," Jessica replied.

"Yes, there's nothing wrong with that. It's important that he's kind," Vau said. "But giving help when someone doesn't explicitly ask for it can cause unintended interference. And some problems won't be meant for him to solve. They may be opportunities for others to achieve a deeper level of existence. With the gifts he'll have, he'll need to focus on his priorities. He'll learn these things though."

"Plus, it could make him vulnerable," Jordan said. "But it's more than that."

"So, what's your concern?" Jessica asked Jordan, genuinely curious.

Jordan stopped and turned to face Jessica. "Assuming there's alignment today and we move forward, with your experience and your help, I fully expect him to become exceptional. And with us honing his abilities as well, he could tap into a level of manifestation powers that haven't been accessed in a very long time. Essentially, the waiting time between Malik's ideas and their fruition will be all but removed."

"He will be fine," Vau assured her. "We'll be training him to be disciplined."

Jordan lifted her chin higher into the air. "I know that, but it's the boys I'm thinking about."

"What is it you fear for the boys?" Jessica asked, wanting to understand.

"Many parents try to imagine a life for their children—a job, a path, a partner—forgetting that their children are and will be creators of their own worlds. I've seen parents do more harm than good when they try to identify what they think is the best life for their offspring. And if, or when, Malik has this power, there will be little room for error," Jordan explained.

"He and Magaly will need to be open to the gifts their children receive and where the nurturing of those gifts takes them," Vau said.

"The children will also come to understand the power of manifestation at an impressionable age," Jordan said. "Malik must stay present for them so the same energy that gives him power can also help his children bear power responsibly. Malik and Magaly must protect the boys and their gifts for as long as they can until the children discover who they are."

Vau locked eyes with Jessica. "We would not do this if we thought that those kids or even Magaly and Malik would be in any danger."

"Let's get a move on, guys!" Tony's voice called from ahead, putting an end to the conversation.

JESSICA FOLLOWED Tony and Jordan into the command center, where she saw Gabriel and Carlos taking their seats around a large black table so polished Jessica could see their reflections. Carlos donned a well-tailored three-piece suit. Gabriel, on the other hand, was dressed with more flare. She would expect no less. He was wearing a fitted shirt that had a silver sheen to it, and he was showing a bit too much chest.

Jessica observed Aja enter and approach Ori, Evelyn, and Professor Raziel. They seemed to discuss something while glancing at Jessica. Aja nodded her agreement with whatever was discussed, then she made her way over to Jessica.

Aja looked divine in an emerald-green dress that trailed behind her as she walked, becoming transparent along the edges and camouflaging with the sleek black marble floor that seemed alive itself, with its pulsing pink, purple, and white veins. In her calm, regal voice, Aja greeted Jessica with a warmth that made her feel special. "Jessica, I hoped you would be in attendance for this."

The bangles on her wrists clicked, and her ebony skin glowed as Aja opened her arms for a hug.

Jessica leaned into the embrace and smelled a delicate aroma of lavender. An image of her parents floated into her mind from when Jessica was a little girl. After a moment, Jessica realized she was still holding onto Aja, rocking from side to side. *There's always something about her that feels like home.*

Jessica didn't want to let go, but she pulled herself away, breaking the spell. "It's great to see you. It's been too long."

Aja smiled and held Jessica at arm's length. "You look wonderful, dear."

"Thank you," Jessica said.

Aja continued. "Your willingness to risk your time and your life the way you did will never be forgotten. We are forever grateful to you."

Evelyn walked up to get Aja's attention. "We should probably get started."

Jessica heard part of their conversation as they walked away.

"How was your trip?" Aja asked.

Evelyn replied, "We will see."

"Be careful," Aja warned, looking toward Gabriel, then back at Evelyn. "You don't want to step on anyone's toes."

"I know, I know," Evelyn said. "But it was necessary."

Jessica stored the fragments of conversation in her mind.

Ori paused briefly as he walked by her. "Let's touch base afterward?"

Jessica nodded and then went to take a seat in the viewing area next to Vau and Tony, who now had a stack of tall, violet-colored books on his lap. The cover of the top book glowed where Tony's hand rested.

· · ·

AJA KICKED OFF THE MEETING, addressing the now full table. "Thank you all for joining us today. I know we have been meeting more often now that the major event is upon the frontline existence at seven point eight three hertz. Last we met, we established Earth was back in a sustainable position across all existences. There have been improvements across deforestation, desertification, and pollution, all of which is allowing the forests to heal themselves. We, however, are still assessing the state of humanity and had asked both Evelyn's team and Gabriel to gather more information. In addition to that update, Evelyn has indicated that she will seek our alignment today on something that her team deems imperative to humanity through the reset. Evelyn, shall we start with the update?"

"Yes, thank you, Aja." Evelyn took the floor. "As you all know, in the age of Pisces, humanity needs to move together. Thanks in large part to Jessica and Zach," Evelyn nodded to Jessica and several of the Council members turned to acknowledge her, "we now believe this is achievable. The early containment of the virus has prevented the rising discord previously seen. On top of that, the completion and launch of Aldermin7500 has ensured that people are exposed to the same credible, objective data. There are fewer micro-realities and a broader shared truth."

"I'm seeing this as well," Gabriel confirmed.

"Wonderful," said Aja. "That bodes well."

"Another positive sign," continued Evelyn, "is the level of awareness and rate of ascension. Following the virus, we actually saw significant increases in self-reflection, particularly regarding how people were spending their time. A larger percentage of people began pursuing passions they had always dreamed about but feared doing."

"However," Gabriel weighed in, "the coronal mass ejections are jeopardizing this."

"That's right," Evelyn said. "Overexposure to these harmful

solar flares is creating a debilitating brain fog. It's responsible for erratic behavior that can only lead to fear and chaos. What's worse is that it affects one's ability to think creatively, solve complex problems, and multitask."

Professor Raziel spoke up for the first time. "For humanity to continue to push forward, around twenty percent need to retain their creative faculties. Twenty percent could pull the rest forward and effectively rebuild a lasting civilization, helped by the reestablished written documentation of important historical knowledge completed by our Scribe." He gave Jessica an appreciative nod.

"How long would it take for the forests to be healthy enough to protect humanity as well?" another Council member asked.

"Too long," Aja answered.

"One scientist, Anatole Patterson, has come close to discovering a solution for the harmful impacts of the solar flares," Evelyn said. "But he abandoned the work after a personal tragedy."

"I've confirmed as well that no one else is close to solving the issue," Gabriel said. "Unfortunately, most people do not even know that the solar flares cause the brain fog and erratic behavior."

"We've been assessing whether there's a way to move Anatole forward again," Ori said. "He has become very isolated though. Casual interactions in his everyday life will not only be scarce, but they wouldn't be meaningful enough given his current emotional and mental state. His dreams would have to be the way, and even that will require something special. He suffers from insomnia, and his subconscious is on guard. We'd have to use someone he recognizes and trusts."

"Jessica's family knows Anatole, as they provided support for his research. She has done enough for us, though, and we agreed she would spend the rest of her time with her family," Evelyn said. "Here is where we get to the special request."

"We believe Malik is who we need," said Ori. "This clearly would involve more than a standard recruitment. He would need to be extensively trained, and his awareness would need to be enhanced to a point where he could enter dreams. He'll need to become a Universal Citizen."

Evelyn jumped back in. "He doesn't know it, of course, but he's already proven himself to us. His heart is pure, and his curiosity knows no bounds. And his genius is the only one that not only understands what's happening, but is actively searching for a solution."

"Could he get to a cure?" asked Carlos. "If he's searching for a solution, could you let that play out?"

"He won't be able to get all the way there without Anatole," Ori replied. "And we won't be able to bring them back together in their reality initially. We've considered all the options."

"This training, how far would it go?" asked Gabriel.

"It would have to include the mastery of himself and his world," Ori said.

"Are you talking frictionless manifestation?" asked Gabriel.

"We believe he's likely to achieve that, yes," said Ori.

The room fell quiet. Aja leaned back in her chair while Gabriel shifted in his.

It was ultimately Silas who broke the silence. "Do you think he'll want that kind of power?"

"He won't," Ori said. "But in time, he will accept it."

"Ori, Evelyn, are—are you two sure about this?" Carlos exchanged glances with them, a wary expression on his face. "It could easily get out of control."

"He's our best option," Evelyn said decisively.

"Can we grant that level of power again?" Gabriel asked, and everyone at the table turned to Professor Raziel.

Professor Raziel considered the question, running his hand over his beard, which Jessica noticed looked more salt and less pepper. "It has been long enough. No one would consider it humanly possible." He turned to Aja. "As long as you are comfortable with it."

Aja had been taking everything in with her usual calm, attentive demeanor. She gave Jessica a kind smile and said, "Malik comes from excellent lineage." She then turned to Evelyn. "He's shown an ability to pursue, with great belief, that which is not seen. We know he can walk alone to receive gifts that can be used for the greater good." Her brow knitted as she continued. "My only concern is for his children."

"They too are of excellent lineage," Evelyn said. "Malik's partner, Magaly, is full of grace and kindness."

"Another worthy recruit," Ori agreed. "Their children, and their children's children, for generations, will be raised in the present, fully aware of being aware, and knowing the power of words and imagination."

Aja's smile returned. "Then I have no objections."

Gabriel was silent for several moments. When he finally spoke, he said, "I'd like to propose one condition."

"Which is?" Evelyn asked.

"Malik can only manifest solutions when he is specifically asked. And," Gabriel raised his index finger, "he must live an isolated lifestyle that will make it challenging for those with destructive intentions to seek him out."

Evelyn, Ori, and Professor Raziel exchanged looks before Ori spoke. "That can be done."

9

A FAMILY TRIP

THE DRIVE FROM THE AIRPORT TO HIS GRANDMOTHER'S HOUSE WAS easy enough. It had been over four years since Malik had been there, but he used to spend every summer running around in the woods behind the property, picking leaves off trees and stuffing them into his pockets, pretending to be a successful businessperson like his granddad. Malik felt a twinge of sadness, thinking about the spark that went missing after his granddad had passed away. Malik regretted that he hadn't visited often once he took over at the Singularity Group. The last time they came was for his granddad's funeral, when they found out that Magaly was pregnant with Noah.

Noah's going to love this place, Malik told himself with a sense of certainty that this would be good for everyone. He slowed the car by the call box in front of the tall black metal gate. A mixture of large trees and shrubs blocked both sides of the gate, making it all but impossible to see what was on the other side of the property line. Malik rolled down the window to cool, fresh air, a welcome change from the thick, humid air from home.

"Wow, look at all of those trees," Noah said. "I bet we are

going to see a lot of creatures. I saw a cow back there." Malik turned to see Noah twisted around in the car seat, pointing behind him toward the neighboring farms. Noah faced forward again and said, "This looks way different from Nana's house."

"You know this is Nana's new house too, ever since she and Opa moved in with GG," Magaly said.

"What happened to the other house? I liked the road runners!" Noah moved his arms back and forth as if he were running really fast in his seat. "And the jackrabbits. And the…" Noah's voice grew loud with excitement as he stretched his arms wide. "The… the… Harris's hawk. Dad, did you know they are the only hawks that hunt in packs?"

Malik smiled as he regarded his son. "I didn't know that."

"Nana and Opa go back there sometimes," Magaly said. "Those are definitely some cool desert animals."

"But," Malik interjected, "you're right that there are going to be a lot of creatures to see here." He reached out his arm to press the four-digit code his mom had given him but paused once he heard the low humming of the motor on the gate and saw it slowly open. "They must see us." Malik drove the car forward on the gravel road. Once through the gate, the house emerged atop a lush green hill against a backdrop of dense tree canopies.

"This place looks great. I'd almost forgotten how wonderful it is out here," Magaly said. "Are they still thinking about turning this into a bed-and-breakfast?"

"I don't know," Malik said. "My mom changes her mind every day. Plus, you know GG. She's all about privacy."

"Do I get to eat my breakfast in my bed?" Noah asked.

"Oh," Magaly said. "That's not what I meant. I was talking about a type of hotel."

"GG's house is a hotel?" Noah asked.

"No, buddy," Malik said. "It was an idea Nana mentioned, but this house is not a hotel."

Malik stared at the house, settled so perfectly into the hillside. It was bigger than he remembered, three stories of stone and wood beams with large floor-to-ceiling windows facing the gate. *That's probably how they knew we were here.*

Malik drove up the paved driveway that ended in a gravel parking lot behind the home. On the other side of the parking area, there was a new extension. It appeared to be a barn or some other large storage construct connected to a glass room with yoga mats and exercise equipment. Surrounding the back of the property and extending up the mountainside were walking trails that vanished into the thick woods.

"I'm totally going to take advantage of that yoga studio," Magaly said.

"It looks pretty amazing," he agreed.

"Why did Nana and Opa move in with GG?" Noah asked.

"They didn't want GG living out here all by herself."

"Because her husband passed on?" Noah asked.

"Your great-grandfather," Malik said. "Yes, that's right. And she's getting older."

Malik turned off the car and opened the door to the sound of his mother's voice. "Welcome, welcome!" She had stepped out of the house and was walking toward them, arms extended. Malik got out of the car to give her a hug, with Magaly following suit.

"It's great to see you, Nia," Magaly said before she turned to the house. "This place looks incredible!"

"Thank you, but you'll need to make sure you tell Jonas that. He's been doing most of the upkeep. He'll be back soon. Jonas has fallen in love with the walking trails and farming. He spends almost all day outside," Malik's mom said before she peered around them into the car. "Now, where are those babies?"

"Nana!" Malik heard Noah shout. Nia opened the door and helped him unbuckle from the car seat.

"How was the flight?" Nia asked.

"It was great," Malik answered, then realized she had probably intended that for Noah.

Noah extended his arms wide. "We had an entire plane to ourselves."

Nia's eyes slid over to Malik. "You chartered a private jet?"

"It was last minute."

Nia turned her attention back to Noah, squeezing him and kissing his cheeks. "I have some cookies waiting for you inside."

"Yay!" Noah squealed and dashed toward the house.

"Wait," Malik called after him, and Noah slid slightly in the gravel before he came to a complete stop. "Grab your backpack." Nia laughed as they both watched Noah sprint back to the car, grab his backpack from the back seat, slip it onto his shoulders, and then run to the house again and disappear inside.

"I'll go make sure he doesn't eat all the cookies at once," said Magaly, holding her bag on her shoulder and following behind Noah.

"I'll grab the baby," Malik replied, and walked around the car with his mom in tow. He opened the door, and she smiled into the back seat.

"That baby is getting so big."

"I know," Malik said. "He's already wearing twelve-month clothing."

"Get him all the way out," she demanded. "I want to hold my grandbaby."

Malik laughed, unbuckled Aries, and handed him to Nia.

She held him close in front of her so she could look into his face and rubbed noses with the baby. "'Cause we know I don't get to see you that often."

"Mom..." Malik started.

"But that's changing now, isn't it?"

"Mom..."

"Let's get you inside out of this cold weather," Nia said as she took the baby inside. "Speaking of spending time with people, have you heard from your father?"

"I got a message from him a few months ago. Things seem to be going well. His shuttle is scheduled to make contact with the station by the end of the year."

"Good. I'm glad to hear that his adventure is going well."

Malik grabbed the baby's diaper bag and his own backpack and couldn't help but ask, "Really?"

Nia arched her eyebrows at him. "Of course. This was your father's dream. Are you surprised?"

"Well," Malik searched for the words, "you guys just really haven't maintained much of a relationship since the divorce."

"Your father was hardwired to put work before everything. That's just how he was. I used to get angry that he couldn't seem to break away to spend more time with you, but you turned out well, so..." Nia shrugged, "what's there to be upset about anymore?"

"Aww, thanks, Mom," Malik said with a grin.

"I'm so happy you took some time off work to spend with your family." Nia nodded to the baby in her arms. "Especially at their ages. It's a really special time you can't get back."

"I couldn't agree more," Malik replied.

By the time they walked into the house, Noah was sitting in front of a computer at a kid-sized wooden school desk with a matching chair that Malik's mom had found at an antique store.

"Hard at work already?" Malik asked.

"I have an idea for a movie," Noah said, then took a bite of his cookie.

Malik glanced at the computer screen and saw a long string of ones and zeros. He patted his son's shoulder and said, "You'll have to tell me about it later."

Magaly had taken a seat on the floor next to a colorful mat and smiled up at Nia and the baby. "Look what Nana got for you, little one." Malik's mom lay Aries on the mat on the floor and sat down across from Magaly. They took turns playing with his feet and flashing different toys in front of him. Aries cooed and squeaked and kicked his legs.

Malik grabbed a chocolate chip cookie from the kitchen counter and took one large bite before asking his mom, "So Jonas and Grandma are getting along well?"

"Oh yeah, they adore each other. She even let him spend time in your granddad's study," Nia replied, and then looked up at him. "Though he was a little nervous being in there."

"Nervous? Why?" Malik asked.

"He knows how close you and my dad were. He worried it was an intrusion."

"If Grandma is comfortable with it, then so am I." Malik shrugged. "Besides, Jonas is great."

"I know," Nia replied. "And I think he has found settling into retirement a bit more difficult than I did."

"Are you guys considering the whole bed-and-breakfast thing?" Magaly asked.

"No, we nixed that idea," Nia said.

"How come?" asked Magaly.

"Mom didn't want just anyone coming out here and staying with us. Plus, she was adamant that we have plenty of space for you and the kids to live here."

"Live here?" Magaly asked, sounding as surprised as Malik felt.

"Mom, we're just here for—"

Nia put her hands in the air and shook her head. "I know. I told her that too. So look out, she may try to sell you on moving out here."

"Got it," Malik said. "How do *you* like being out here, by the way?"

"It's actually pretty great. Your grandfather did a great job adding in-floor heating and plenty of fireplaces. I just stay in front of one of them most of the time."

"It's even more spectacular than I remembered," Malik said.

"Especially on a warm, sunny day!" Nia continued. "I mean it. And Jonas has all kinds of ideas. He's talked about making wine, jarring honey, getting chickens." Nia let out another laugh. "The possibilities are endless for that man. Jonas should be collecting some things for dinner as we speak."

Malik paused. "Collecting dinner? What do you mean?"

"He's all into foraging now. He'll probably want to tell you about it," Nia prepared him.

"What does he forage?" Magaly asked.

"Mushrooms mostly. He is even part of a group of amateur... What is it called?" Nia snapped her fingers. "Oh yes, mycologists."

"Does your mom eat them too?" Magaly asked with a smirk.

"She likes them! I am just as surprised as you are, but they seem to have bonded over them. And..." Nia gently bobbed her head from shoulder to shoulder, "they aren't that bad."

"Go, Jonas!" Magaly said.

"He honestly does a great job cooking with them. He and his buddies swap recipes. You'll see."

"Well, I'm glad that you all are getting along," Malik said. After his dad left, he wasn't sure how the family would evolve. Then Jonas—who had spent most of his adult life working in Germany—came into the picture. Malik's mom kept her new crush a secret for a long time, so Malik assumed there was a reason, and that reason being what his grandma would think. "Where is GG?"

"She's probably out on her back patio."

Aries fussed on the mat, and Magaly picked him up. "I think it might be nap time," she said.

"I can read to Noah," offered Nia. She got up off the floor and ruffled Noah's hair. "I have some books I think you'll like."

"If you guys are good, I'm gonna go check in with GG," said Malik.

"I wanna see her too!" cried Noah.

"Nap first," Magaly told him. "Then you'll get some good quality time with everyone." Then to Malik, she said, "You go ahead."

As everyone else made their way toward the bedrooms, Malik went toward the sliding glass door at the back of the house. There, he found his grandma sitting in a chair, staring out at the rolling hills.

10

DEEPLY ROOTED DREAMS

MALIK STEPPED OUTSIDE, AND HIS EYES IMMEDIATELY LOCKED ONTO movement in the distance. It was a large raptor, swooping low along the side of the mountain. He first recalled the red-tailed hawks he was so used to seeing in his neighborhood in Atlanta, but it was much too small and missing the signature red tail.

"Do you see the Merlin Falcon?" Malik's grandmother whispered without looking up. Her coily white hair came down to her shoulders, and while her wrinkled hands showed her age, the brown skin on her face was smoother and had a pleasant glow.

"I do," Malik whispered back as a second falcon swooped in, the two dancing and soaring in the gust of winds.

"You used to love watching the 'giant hawks' in our backyard," she said, doing her best impersonation of a young Malik. "This is a good sign." His grandmother finished writing something in her journal. "I figured you would come soon."

"I know I should come more often... I just..."

She looked up at Malik over the frames of her glasses, and he noticed her brown eyes were now looking cloudy in the middle.

"Baby, I know you have a lot going on. You do not have to explain."

"I know, but Mom—"

His grandma cut him off. "She gives you a hard time, but she understands. You've got to do what you've got to do. We just appreciate what time you can give."

Malik smiled. A sense of ease came over him. The moment was fleeting though, as flashes of his dream came back. "Grandma, I had this wild dream that this virus turned the world upside down. People were doing awful things, kidnapping people to find a cure. You had dementia or something…"

"I know, Malik."

"That's the thing," Malik said, as he felt his shoulders relax. A feeling of relief allowed him to take a deep, cleansing breath. "Somehow, I figured you would." Malik sat down in the chair next to his grandmother, and they continued to gaze at the falcons. "I've been having all sorts of dreams. They're becoming more vivid and feel strangely real. The part that makes me uneasy is that Noah has been saying things lately that make me think he's having these dreams too."

His grandmother seemed surprised for the first time, swiftly turning her head in his direction.

Malik could read her anticipation, so he continued. "In my last dream a couple of days ago, there was something to do with our old house and mosquitoes; it's all so foggy now. The next morning, Noah was telling me about his dreams, and he mentioned mosquitoes. My friend Callie—I don't know if you remember her—but she has been in them too." This was the first time Malik had spoken about his dreams aloud to anyone other than Magaly. Slightly embarrassed, he backpedaled. "I know it sounds crazy but—"

His grandma's face grew stern. "Don't call your dreams crazy."

But she said nothing else. She studied him for a moment and then went back to the view.

"Anyway, I'm hoping a change of scenery will help."

"How's business going?" she asked, startling Malik with the change in topic.

"All is well there. I'm trying to truly take the time away, and everything is in good hands, so I don't check in much."

"I think it's great that you're spending this time with your family."

"Yeah, and it feels right. Though my mind is having trouble leaving one thing alone," Malik confessed.

"Really? What's the one thing?"

"I—I don't know if I'm ready to talk about it. There's something I think I can figure out. I mean, I think I have to figure it out."

His grandmother nodded. "Then you will. You've just got to keep the faith."

"I know, you're right." Malik was a little ashamed that his faith did waiver. *I see a bigger purpose, but what if I can't get there? What if this is a foolish gamble?* Malik shook the negative ideas out of his head.

"You know your grandfather would be so proud of you," she said.

"You think?" Malik asked, hoping she was right.

"Oh yeah. All he ever wanted was for you to be happy and do what you felt you were meant to do." She patted his knee. "It's not easy to walk away from a job like that."

"No, it isn't," Malik agreed. "And the time I have already gotten to spend with the boys has been beautiful." Malik stared at the ground before admitting something else. "I feel kind of bad."

"Why's that?"

"I don't remember as much of this time with Noah. I wish I did."

"Oh, but it's okay," his grandma comforted him. "You're spending time with him now, and that's special too. And just know, any decision made for your family is always the right one."

The two of them sat on the patio in silence for several minutes as the falcons soared higher in the sky, coming in and out of view.

"Do you mind if I poke around Granddad's office while the kids are napping?" Malik asked.

"Not at all," his grandma said. "Once you are done, get some rest and we will chat more later. Alright, baby?"

"Alright," Malik said, and he took his leave while his grandmother stared off into the distance with a slight smile on her face.

11

THE SCIENTIST AND THE SOLUTION

MALIK WAS SLOW TO WALK INTO HIS GRANDFATHER'S OFFICE, WHICH he found overwhelming. It was one of the few rooms in the house that was two stories. The office was in a corner of the house, allowing for two walls of floor-to-ceiling windows. The third wall, to his right, was almost entirely a built-in bookcase. There was a large live oak desk made from the two-hundred-year-old white oak tree that had been in the front yard of his grandparents' house in Atlanta. He recalled how upset they had been when the arborist told them the tree was sick and there was nothing left to do. When they finally had it felled, they took great care to recycle as much as possible on the property, using the wood chips to protect the ground and roots of the other trees. And they also had custom pieces of furniture made, each beautiful and one-of-a-kind, like this desk.

As Malik sat down, he rubbed his hands along the polished desktop, tracing the grain. The desk faced the door, because his grandfather insisted on never having his back to any door. His grandfather never explained why, but Malik used to get a kick out of watching his dad and grandfather at a restaurant, as they danced around who would sit in which seat.

On the fourth wall alongside the door, there was a massive stone fireplace. Sitting on the mantel was a row of souvenirs that his grandfather had collected throughout his travels. Above that hung a large map of the world that was new to Malik, but looked quite old in age. The map had the brownish-yellow tint common to the antique documents and books his grandfather loved collecting. Malik then looked to the side and scanned the bookcase as he leaned back in the chair. That's when he noticed the ladder, which was used to reach the higher shelves of the bookcase, was connected to a rail that went well above the rows of books he could see.

Malik climbed the ladder to find shelving set further back into the wall, filled with small hardcover books, almost the size of a journal, each with a plain green spine. Malik pulled one out and noted that the cream-colored cover had no words either. *What is this?* He opened the journal to find rows and rows of zeros and ones. *What in the world?* Malik replaced that book and checked another. *Hmm, the same.* At the very end by the wall, Malik spotted a small section of books with black spines that had a leather shoulder bag resting on top. *I've seen that bag before,* he thought as he picked it up to explore the contents. Malik's grandfather had used this bag whenever they went on family vacations. Despite his grandmother's insistence they be present, his grandfather would sneak work in with this casual bag.

Malik climbed back down the ladder, sat at the desk, and opened the bag for further investigation. Inside were several large envelopes stuffed with documents. He opened the first to find correspondence between his grandfather and Anatole Patterson. Malik flipped through and then grabbed another document at random. This one was different. It was titled, "Draft Abstract:

Coronal Mass Ejections and Their Impact on the Human Microbiome." As Malik read the small font, underlined words drew his eyes: "lead," "neurotoxin," "chlorofluorocarbons," "stratosphere," "1923." Malik spied his grandfather's scribbled notes at the bottom of the page. "Stratosphere damage + reduced tree canopy permits more harmful solar flares through. Triggers harmful reaction in the body on micro-level. Anatole's serum balances and protects against." The notes seemed to end in mid-thought. He sifted through more documents when he noticed one of the cream-colored hardcover journals among the papers.

MALIK RUBBED his eyes to get relief from the burning sensation. He'd been sneaking into the office every chance he had when the kids were sleeping or otherwise being entertained by his mom and Jonas. *I must have missed something,* he decided as he studied the thick report, which now had pink, yellow, blue, and green-colored page markers sticking out in every direction. The sunlight streaming in the floor-to-ceiling windows was fading. Malik stood up and turned on the light before leaving the room to grab a snack in the kitchen. When he returned, he was surprised to see his grandma sitting in the chair behind the desk, thumbing through the colored tabs.

"How's it going?" she asked.

"Pfffttt…" Malik sighed audibly. "It's going. I have to be missing something. There has to be something I've overlooked."

"Maybe," his grandma said. "Or maybe you should take a different approach."

"Like what?"

"You can ask for help, you know. You don't need to solve everything yourself."

"Help from whom?" Malik scoffed. He immediately regretted

the outburst. "I'm sorry. I'm just tired." He moved a stack of documents from the chair opposite his grandmother and flopped down, slouching low.

"So, tell me." His grandma's voice was calm. "What are you doing in here?"

Malik motioned to the stacks of papers spread across the desk. "That's all the correspondence between Granddad and Anatole Patterson from back before. I've been trying to wrap my head around it all. If I do, then maybe I could pick up where he left off and finish his work. I was hoping to find some new pieces of information here that would help."

"No luck?"

"Not really. These outline several of Anatole's experiments, but they mostly show how to identify different triggers or causes for solar sickness. I knew he had theories about how to approach a serum that could act as a solution, and that he never finished the work. I was really hoping to get a better handle on what he discovered along the way so that I could, in the best case, get a jump start on finding a solution. In the worst case, I could avoid making the same mistakes. But right now, it just seems like there are countless possibilities," Malik said. He pulled himself up out of the chair and walked over toward the windows. "You know, I haven't seen him since the funeral."

"Anatole?" his grandmother asked.

"Yeah." Malik gazed out the window and noticed the waning moon over the tree line.

"Neither have I."

"Did you know him well?" Malik asked, glancing her way. "I mean, I know you and Granddad privately funded his research together."

His grandmother nodded and said, "Your grandfather worked more closely with him, but Anatole and I were friendly as well.

We all met together when your grandfather and I were considering supporting his research. He was incredibly impressive, and we knew he was onto something important. Your grandfather became his primary contact."

"That was around the time that Granddad transitioned the Singularity Group leadership over to me, right?" he asked.

"Yes, I believe so. He had more time on his hands and wanted to fund other passion projects. This was one of them. Though he had a sort of agreement with Anatole to be hands off."

"Was that hard for him?" Malik asked, making his way back to the chair across from her.

"Yes and no," his grandma said. "Your grandfather didn't like to bother motivated people while they were working. Plus, this research was Anatole's life's work. He wanted to figure it out more than anyone, so we knew we didn't need to hound him." His grandma smiled as she glanced off, caught up in a memory. "What we didn't realize was how often Anatole would be on the move. We wouldn't hear from him for months, then out of nowhere, he would send your grandfather a message from some new location with news of a breakthrough. Moving around seemed to help the ideas flow."

Malik observed her tap the draft abstract document with the underlined words before she said, "There was probably another reason too. Once Anatole confirmed there was a connection between solar flare reactions and industrial pollutants, he became paranoid. I'm not saying it was unfounded, as he had upset some powerful people, lost funding and support, and was receiving a great deal of pressure. Others like him stopped their research because of similar situations. So he bounced around and would just mail us envelopes of his latest results, annotated with updates and changes. Each return address was from a new location."

"The year before Granddad passed away, he talked to me

about Anatole and his work," Malik told her. "I thought it was strange at the time that he could only do an email introduction."

"I remember," his grandma said. "That was when he became adamant about knowing where Anatole was living. Your granddad's health was declining, and he kept talking about needing an in-person meeting with Anatole. I wasn't able to orchestrate that, but I did find him."

"Was that the address in Singapore?" Malik asked.

"It was, indeed." His grandmother held up a pair of the Singularity Group vision glasses that Malik had noticed were hanging around her neck. "People treat the internet like it's their diary. This was a big help in finding his family."

Malik was impressed by his grandma's tech savvy. "Excellent sleuthing."

"Why, thank you," his grandma replied with a smile.

Malik's mind flashed back to strolling through the solar powered trees in Singapore's Gardens by the Bay. The Supertrees were easily fifteen stories high. The lush green of the diverse plants that grew vertically along the sides hid the metal poles that gave them structure. At the top, the poles of the Supertrees spread out in every direction, with the look of entangled roots. "Did you know that Anatole's partner was a cellist?"

"I did, though I never heard her play."

"You remember I paid him a visit after Granddad passed?" She nodded, so he continued. "I was surprised he welcomed it, but I think he felt bad about Granddad. Anyway, while I was there, Anatole took me to see his wife in concert at Gardens by the Bay." Malik was silent as he recalled standing with Anatole while his daughter went to meet up with some friends at a mobile ice cream stand before the concert began. The memory triggered a feeling of sympathy for the two. "Who would have thought a few months later, his wife would be gone?"

"It's so awful," his grandma said.

"Do you think he'll ever pick up his work again?" Malik asked, but then felt ashamed. "Is that awful for me to ask?"

"Who knows, but right now, he's focusing on raising his daughter, and I can't imagine that being an easy thing."

"I know. It's just that no one has come close to the breakthroughs that he's made."

"We need to respect his grieving process," she said. "He can't create until he's ready."

Malik nodded, knowing that his grandmother was correct. "He told me he had gotten close."

"Is that so?"

Malik looked at the mass of documents sprawled across the table. "I just... I wondered if I could get there and leave him be."

"There might be another way, Malik."

Malik met her eyes, trying to read her expression. "What do you mean?"

"I've been... no." She sighed and tried again. "You've been... wait."

Malik watched as his grandmother—who was always good with words—seemed to struggle with what she wanted to say.

"You know, I've always wondered how I would tell you this."

"Tell me what?" he asked.

She stared at him for a long moment. Malik leaned forward in his chair, wondering where on Earth this was going. "What I'm about to tell you," his grandma said, "is absolutely true. I need you to believe me. I need you to open your mind."

"Alright," Malik said, as he tilted his chin down toward the ground and leaned his ear toward his grandmother, a method he employed to focus on listening.

"For about," her eyes drifted up and to the left as she counted, "sixty years, I've been traveling to different dimensions... different versions of reality." She picked up a cream-colored journal off the desk. "I've been documenting everything that I've seen to highlight humanity's progress and preserve knowledge for future generations. Because of the role that I've played and because of your character and what drives you, those who I have worked with for six decades would like to offer you an opportunity."

12

THE DEAL OF A LIFETIME

THE ROOM WAS SILENT, AND MALIK STAYED SEATED, STARING INTO HIS grandmother's face. He was waiting for something, but he wasn't sure what.

"Do you remember the strange dream you told me about? The one where I had dementia?" she finally asked.

Malik nodded. "Mm-hm."

"That was a dream to you, but in reality, it was a different version of the world—a version in which some things went incredibly wrong, and you actually helped set things back on the correct course. That's part of why those I have been working with believe in you so much."

"And that was a different reality you traveled to?" Malik asked.

"No, not exactly. That was a version of reality that we had to rewrite. Thankfully, it's no more than a faded memory now."

Okay, he thought. Malik noticed his grandma's hand was still resting on the journal, and images from throughout his life of her scribbling in those journals filled his mind. "But you do travel to other realities, and that's what you've been writing about in all of those." He tilted his head toward the journal.

"I realize it may be hard to believe, but you are anything but a doubter. In this world, I spent a career writing publicly, but even that was part of a greater purpose. I was able to put a spotlight on positive progress and inspire others. And then I also privately acted as a record keeper of sorts. There is so much universal knowledge that gets lost throughout time after conquest and the rise and fall of civilizations. Not every version of reality has achieved the same heights either."

Malik sat back in his chair, trying to process all that he had heard. Malik studied his grandmother's face, waiting for her to crack a smile or give any hint she was teasing him. Nothing. "You're telling the truth," he said.

"Why would I lie?"

"How do you travel to these different worlds?"

"With this." She held up her wrist, displaying a watch. "This allows the atomic structure of my body to hone into different frequencies of distinct realities. Imagine the world is a giant radio and what we see, hear, and experience is just one station of that radio, one channel. Our bodies and minds are programmed to only receive and experience a set number of channels." His grandmother seemed to reconsider that statement. "Now, there are, of course, ways to affect that. We grow, evolve, imagine greater things for ourselves, make choices. We can change our station in life and the frequency to which we're tuned."

"I understand that," Malik said, remembering his grandfather's insistence on being mindful of his thoughts. *"Your thoughts become your reality,"* he would say. "That's easier to wrap my head around, but… what do you mean, distinct realities?"

"That's where it gets interesting." His grandma raised her eyebrows high, and she seemed almost hesitant to say what she was about to say. Then, in a single breath, she said, "Every single outcome for every single event that could have ever occurred has occurred." She then leaned back in her chair. "We're existing in the version of events that the majority have accepted."

"Every single outcome of every event has occurred?" he repeated. "So, you're telling me that there is a world in which Germany won the Second World War?"

"Yes, and the first one."

"But how?" Malik asked.

"Because it was imagined. In that turn of events, people with enough power and conviction imagined it so."

"But not in our world."

"In this world as we know it, the collective *we* decided against it. More people imagined a better world not controlled by division and oppression. There are other realities that have progressed more than our own as well."

"How so?" Malik asked.

"There are worlds where mass genocide never occurred. Versions of reality without slavery. Realities where ideas were accepted and debated, no matter who they came from. Worlds where diverse ideas have been preserved and built upon over time." His grandmother tilted her head and narrowed her eyes at him. "Where do you think some of the Singularity Group's technology came from?" She touched the vision glasses around her neck. "When the technology utilizing dark energy and dark matter launched, ninety percent of the population didn't even know what that was, let alone how to harness it."

"You've been able to visit these places and tap into all of this knowledge?"

"As could you."

Malik's pulse quickened. "So I could finish a cure for solar sickness?"

His grandma let out a laugh. "Oh, you are so focused. Yes, and much more. If you decide to go through this recruitment process, you will have access to an abundance of resources."

"What's the catch?"

His grandma smiled. "Astute question, young man." Malik watched as her gaze drifted toward the window. He turned to see what may have caught her attention, and it was Noah, who was running around chasing fireflies. "Want to get some fresh air?"

OUTSIDE, the family was taking in the evening air. Malik saw his mother sitting on a blanket with Aries while he practiced rolling over from his stomach to his back. Beyond them, Magaly was standing behind an easel, cleaning up some art supplies. "Hey there," she said when she saw him approach.

"Where did you find that?" Malik asked, walking around to give her a hug and see what she'd been working on.

"Jonas found it in storage," Magaly said. She had been sketching the scene of his mom and Aries on the blanket. Aries was on his stomach, pushing up to look at the flowers. Magaly had included a few butterflies floating near him. "I lost the light. There's more I want to do tomorrow."

"It's incredible!" Malik said. "You're getting great at this so fast."

"Thank you." Magaly's bright smile warmed Malik's heart. "I've still got a lot to learn, but I'm really enjoying it."

"Many talents, indeed," said Malik's grandmother as she hooked her arm into Malik's.

"You're kind," Magaly replied with a laugh and folded up the easel. "A baby's face is so much harder than I thought it would be! I'm gonna get it though." She went to finish putting things away.

Just then, Noah ran by, chased by Jonas in a lively game of tag.

Malik's grandmother gently tugged on his arm and led them

over to walk the perimeter of the yard. "Back to your question, then?"

"Yes," said Malik.

"They are the catch. No one outside of your familial unit can know anything about this."

"So I can tell Magaly and the boys?" he asked.

"Yes, but I would have caution with what you tell the children."

"Did Mom know?"

"Sort of, but not really," his grandma laughed. "Nia just knew I had really fun friends. But on a more serious note, Malik, I want to give you all the information so you go into this with full awareness."

"Okay," Malik said. He rolled his shoulders back, bracing himself as if the impact of his grandmother's next words would cause a physical blow.

"If your training is successful, and we all believe it will be, you will develop an ability to create, to manifest, what you imagine faster than most, maybe even instantaneously. Part of what you must learn, and the sooner the better, is that if you are going to own this power, you must be incredibly aware of your thoughts."

Malik cleared his throat. "I'll be careful. But, if that's true... I don't know. How will I be able to become that controlled?"

"It's going to take training, discipline, and time. We all know you to be worthy. Believe yourself to be worthy too."

Malik swallowed and stayed quiet. He already felt the familiar determination rising in his chest.

"The next thing is the boys."

"What about them?"

"Even if you shelter them, they will be likely to witness some incredible feats. Their imaginations will be completely open to all possibilities."

"And that's bad because?"

"It's not bad at all. But they will need present parents who provide guidance, or it could lead to a path of destruction."

"They are our priority, always."

"I know that. But you just need to be aware that your lives will look, feel, and be very different."

"I don't know what to even imagine at this point."

His grandma nudged him and said, "I understand. And while I know I've been stressing the great responsibility, your life will be beautiful. It will be free and abundant. And you will be together."

They came to a stop, watching the rest of the family make their way inside for the evening. Malik stood in silence and gently nodded his head as he considered the proposition. All he wanted was to protect his children, and what future would they be living in if the impacts of the solar flares continued to worsen? "If I have the opportunity to give them a better future, I should take it."

His grandma pulled a folded piece of paper out of her pocket. "If you're going to pursue this path, then it's important that you get rooted."

"What's this?" Malik asked, taking the piece of paper.

"Think of it as pre-training."

13

BE STILL... BE ROOTED

MALIK CONTENTEDLY SIPPED HIS MORNING COFFEE WHILE NOAH gobbled up a last bite of waffle and Aries smeared a banana across the tray of his high chair. Even though Malik knew there was more mess to come, he leaned over to wipe banana mush off Aries's forehead.

"Anything else you need, Malik?" Jonas asked. He had just slid an omelet onto Nia's plate.

"I'm all set." Gesturing down at his now empty plate, Malik added, "It was excellent. Thank you!"

"Ooooh, is there more of whatever he had?" Magaly asked. She strolled in from her workout wearing black yoga pants and a purple top, looking energized.

"Coming right up!" Jonas said, barely able to hide his pride as he reached for more eggs.

"How was it out there?" Nia asked.

"It was incredible!" Magaly stretched her arms in the air and leaned back. "This might become a morning ritual."

"Be our guest! You'll probably have that space all to yourself,"

Nia said before taking a sip of her coffee. "I'm more of an evening yoga person."

As soon as Magaly sat down at the table, Jonas placed a mug in front of her and filled it with fresh coffee. "You like it black, right?"

"You take such good care of us!" Magaly smiled at him. "And that's right. During my residency, I learned I could do without milk and sugar."

"Have you missed practicing medicine?" Jonas asked, moving back to the stove to flip her omelet.

"At times," Magaly said. "But I'm enjoying this break and developing new passions."

"You're quite the artist," Nia said.

"I remember loving to draw as a kid, but..." Magaly sipped her coffee before continuing. "Somewhere along the way, I just stopped."

"Well," Jonas said from the kitchen, "now is the perfect time to pick it back up. It's an excellent way to spend your time."

"Speaking of spending time," Magaly turned to Malik, "what are you doing today?" Malik watched as Magaly leaned back in her chair and inspected him. "Whatcha wearing?"

Malik looked down at what he thought was a presentable but comfortable outfit. "What?"

"Untucked shirt and linen pants, I like this new look." Magaly held her mug close to her lips and winked at Malik.

"Alright you two," Nia said, "that's how you have another baby."

"I want another baby!" Noah shouted.

"We all do," Nia said.

"Enough of that talk. We have a baby right there!" Malik laughed. "I'm going to check out a meditation studio that Grandma recommended. I'm hoping it will help me be more present."

"Nice," Magaly said. "Let me know if you like it; maybe I'll check it out."

MALIK SHIFTED the car into park and double-checked the address scribbled on the piece of paper his grandma had given him. He was at the right place: a two-story brick office complex painted a burned-yellow with dark brown trim. He wasn't sure what he had been expecting, but this wasn't it. It looked dated and, well, commonplace. Malik got out of his car and, per the instructions, walked to suite 783. Before he could knock, the door opened, and a woman appeared, her smile warm and welcoming. She wore a loose-fitting orange linen outfit, and her hair was shorn close to her scalp.

She placed her palm across her heart, bowed slightly, and said, "You must be Malik. I'm Lotus. I'll be your guide for your first part of training." She stepped to the side to invite him in.

"Nice to meet you, Lotus," Malik said as he crossed the threshold. He took in his new surroundings, which were quite breathtaking. Almost the entire left side of the space was enclosed by a tall free-standing screen. Each of the seven panels within the thin black frame was a unique and vibrant mural. The first scene was of a tree with roots that appeared to clasp Earth. A glow traveled from Earth up the roots to the top of the tree canopy, creating a halo effect above the tree.

"Beautiful, aren't they?" Lotus asked.

"I've never seen anything like them."

"Well, have a look around and make yourself comfortable. I'll be right with you." Lotus disappeared around a corner while Malik moved on to the second panel.

His eyes were drawn to the center of the image, which had a black fish and a white fish moving in a circular motion, creating ripples that spread up and down along the panel. *Yin and yang,*

Malik contemplated as he continued walking forward. As Malik was about to take his eyes off the second panel, a flash caught his eye. He leaned forward and noticed there were smaller versions of the same two fish, creating smaller ripples in the mural's background. Whenever ripples would interact, there were flashes of light. "Amazing," he whispered.

The third panel had the outline of two people with no distinguishing physical traits. They were composed entirely of colors, which kept changing, alternating between purple, pink, orange, red, green, blue, and yellow. One body was standing while the other was sitting on the ground. They were facing each other, and the person standing was handing the other a large bowl. *Hmm, generosity? Or empathy?* Malik wondered.

An old wooden ship with large white sails was the central image on the fourth panel. Malik thought about the classic book *The Count of Monte Cristo* and wondered if this was the type of vessel that Edmond Dantès would have traveled on. The crew on the ship were dressed in all-white clothing. The white parts of the mural glowed. *A journey? To where?* Malik noticed the entire crew were staring in the same direction, and he followed their gaze to the fifth panel.

He expected to see an iceberg or a sea monster, but instead, he encountered the fangs of a snarling tiger, crouched down, poised to strike. Its eyes were not on the ship, though; instead, they were trained outward on Malik. The position of the tiger conveyed its power, yet one could also see its control.

Malik approached the sixth panel, where he saw the hilt of a sword with its blade plunged almost completely into a large stone. "I've always liked this story," Malik said to himself, while admiring the artistry. The cross guard of the weapon had intricate geometric shapes that appeared to be shifting and changing, while the grip had seven distinct rings, each with a unique symbol. "Is this Sanskrit?" Malik muttered aloud, and then looked around for

Lotus, who was nowhere in sight. Turning back to the sword, he noticed the image on the circular pommel at the end of the grip continued to change as well, from an open book to a quill to a crown. *Select your weapon of choice?* Malik wanted to continue watching each image, but his eyes were drawn to a bright light on the seventh and final panel.

The center of the seventh panel had a black hole the size of Malik's fist, with a bright violet hue radiating around it. As Malik's eyes fixated on the image, a bright flash of lightning struck, this time sparking motion across the entire panel. The black hole slowly got larger. As it did, Malik noticed along the circumference of that black hole were other smaller black holes. As the image zoomed, more appeared, all connected by what looked like a bolt of lightning. *I've seen this before.* Malik tried to recall where, but he couldn't put his finger on it.

"Ah, the Mandelbrot set." Lotus's voice caused Malik to jump. She leaned close to the panel and quickly glanced at Malik as she breathed, "Interesting." She then directed him toward the center of the room where cushions and teacups were positioned in a circle on the floor. "Please, come take a seat."

Malik settled himself down on a cushion, but his attention was still on the art he had been appreciating. "What technology is that? It looks like paper, but the images aren't static."

Lotus poured two cups of tea. "That paper is made from the pulp of a very special tree. It's incredibly rare."

"Is there a specific meaning to each of the scenes?" Malik was curious to hear more about the intent.

"There is," Lotus said. "Though the meaning can be internalized in unique ways." She took a sip of her tea, and Malik did the same.

"Is that something we'll go through?" Malik asked.

"It can be." Lotus set down her cup, and Malik followed suit. Lotus cast her eyes in the screen's direction and interlaced her fingers. "The first signifies a direct connection with all creation and life." She shifted her hands into a gentle clasp. "The second, I'm sure you surmised, shows that balance in oneself is essential to keeping the connection." Lotus then lifted her clasped hands to her chest. "Ah, the first of the last kind deed." Malik met her eyes as she asked, "What does that mean to you?"

"I—I'm not sure," Malik replied. "I thought empathy?"

"Empathy is good," Lotus smiled. "I see forgiveness, which is important in life, especially on this journey that you travel. And speaking of journeys," Lotus opened her hands and motioned to the next panel, "that ship signifies several voyages are ahead, and how it connects with the tiger tells us we may face battles as well. That's not all the regal tiger has to say, though. Embrace the power and the patience. Turn away from fear and toward faith." Lotus made fists with her hands as she explained the sixth panel. "Excalibur. Only the worthy can pull the sword out of the stone and yield its great power." She relaxed her hands and continued, "I encourage you, however, not to think of this as a weapon, but as a tool. You can choose what kind of tool you wield." Lotus held up her index finger. "And you don't have to choose just one." Lotus stared at the final mural again but only said, "I think that's enough for now. I think it's time we get to why you're here."

Malik wanted to hear about the last image, and what she had found *"interesting,"* but something told him not to push and let her guide the session.

"So tell me. Why do you think you are here?"

Malik gathered his thoughts. *What should I say? What does she know?* Malik shifted on the cushion and decided to keep it vague. "I'm trying to find a solution for a problem, and my grandmother recommended I come and see you first."

Lotus nodded. "Why do you think she recommended you come here?"

"She said I needed to be rooted." Malik shrugged. "I'm not

sure, to be honest. Maybe she thinks I need to improve my meditation." Malik scanned the rest of the room. "That is what you do here, right? You meditate?"

"Here, we focus on being still to be present. Meditation is a way to be still."

"I'm not really great at meditating."

Lotus took a sip of her tea, which Malik had almost forgotten was there. She tilted her head and looked into his eyes as if they held information she was seeking. "You've always been a very busy person. Your mind is constantly working through something. Some problem. Some solution. I've found that, in the beginning, it helps to just focus on your breath. Focus on inhaling in through your nose, as far as you can." Malik watched as Lotus closed her eyes and breathed in, her chest and chin rising. "Then," she whispered as she exhaled, "you breathe out as long as you can, pushing out through your stomach. Focus on closing your mouth and inhaling and exhaling through your nose."

"With my eyes closed? What if I fall asleep?"

Lotus smiled, her eyes now open. "That's okay. Let's start."

"But—"

"One hour," Lotus said. She picked up a small gong and struck it with a wooden rod.

Malik wanted to ask more questions, but when he saw Lotus close her eyes again, he knew he'd get no reply. So Malik closed his eyes.

At first, his mind stayed active with an array of thoughts. *I'm supposed to breathe in and breathe out. For an hour? I don't know how this will help. But it must, or Grandma wouldn't have sent me here. An hour is a long time to sit here and do nothing.* A scene from Malik's latest dream floated into his mind: the thousands of bodies asleep on the streets of New York City.

"Just inhale and exhale," Lotus whispered. "When you focus only on your breathing, you don't have time for other thoughts."

Inhale and hold it… exhale… keep going… inhale… exhale… inhale… exhale… What is that sound? Malik focused on the sound of trickling water. *I don't remember seeing a fountain.* He felt his shoulders and back relax as he shifted and settled into his position. *Inhale… exhale… inhale… exhale.* Malik heard a humming from the ceiling as the air-conditioning unit switched on. *Stay focused. Inhale… exhale… inhale… exhale…*

A GENTLE SOUND from the gong made Malik jerk his head up.

"Well done." Lotus's voice was just above a whisper.

"That's it? That was an hour?" Malik asked, his eyes and body adjusting. He looked down and saw a small damp spot on his shirt from drool. "I think I may have dozed a bit."

"How do you feel?"

Malik first stretched his arms and then his legs. "Amazing, actually. That felt great."

"I'm glad," Lotus said as she put her hands together at her heart and then gave a slight bow. "You have questions. Please, let's step out into my garden."

Lotus led Malik onto a back patio with a small artificial pond and several potted plants, along with a simple wooden table and chairs. Lotus motioned to one of the two seats, inviting him to sit with her.

"So, how do you know my grandmother?" he asked.

"Oh, I don't."

"Then how did you know who I was?"

"Ori told me you'd be dropping by."

"Ori? Who is Ori?"

Lotus leaned in as if she were telling a secret. Did he detect a hint of mischief? "You'll find out soon enough."

Malik mulled over the comment for a few seconds and realized the answer was probably more complicated than he could handle right now. "So, how often do I need to come back?"

"As often as you would like," Lotus said.

"If I don't come back, will I fail this training?"

Lotus rocked back with a laugh he hadn't expected, and her cheeks glowed with amusement. "You are so ambitious! You won't fail this training; it's led by you. It will be challenging, but you will not fail unless you decide to."

Her more animated demeanor enhanced his comfort level, so he didn't hold his questions back. "Why would I want to fail?"

"You would be surprised by the number of people who won't get out of their own way," Lotus said. "I don't want to assume anything, but did something happen? Something that activated your awareness?"

"What do you mean?"

"Something that made you realize... How can I put it?" Lotus looked around the back patio. "Something that helped you see you have a unique seat in the universe? A unique vantage point that belongs only to you?"

Malik recalled trying to awaken the sleeping people in his dream. "How did you know?"

"Ori typically sends people my way when they are on a journey to attain their higher selves. Being present is critical to accomplishing that. But to get there, one typically has to have a moment like that."

She must have sensed Malik didn't know how to respond because she continued, "The universe is always communicating with us... Always." Lotus held eye contact with Malik. Satisfied he had taken her point, Lotus leaned back in her seat. "But most people have busied themselves with so many distractions they are not prepared to receive the messages, which tend to be ever so subtle." Just then, a ladybug landed on the table.

"Hello, there," Malik said as he watched the tiny beetle tuck in its black wings, showing only the orange and black spotted shell.

"See?" Lotus said with a grin.

"My granddad always believed ladybugs were good luck. That is wild timing."

"No, Malik, that is divine timing. That shows you are connected and in flow. The more in flow you are, the more things will happen just as you need them. Learning to be still, through meditating, helps you learn to be present, and that will help you keep an open mind and open energy to receive any message from the universe."

"Are you telling me I'm on the right path?" Malik asked the ladybug.

"That's a wonderful message to receive. Earlier in our session, you mentioned being rooted?"

Malik looked up and nodded. "Learning to be present like this?"

"Yes, and understanding you are rooted in this specific version of reality. All of your manifestations, the dream life you want to experience, will happen here." Lotus pointed to the ground. "Every moment you get, practice your breathing, practice staying present. As you increasingly live in flow, the things you need or request will manifest more quickly. Whatever you imagine will happen, for better or worse. Ego loves conflict, and it rears its ugly head whenever it gets a chance. So mind your thoughts. Only think of the positive."

"I've been getting that advice a lot," Malik said.

"Valuable advice is often repeated. This whole thing, although it's happening to you, it is not about you. You are becoming a conduit. You perform the tasks for the universe. Your reward for this job is whatever life you are bold enough to imagine."

14

CHAOS IN THE MEDIA

"Happy birthday to you, happy birthday to you, happy birthday, dear Noah, happy birthday to you!"

Jessica watched as three generations of her family sang and cheered while Noah blew out the candle on his chocolate cake. She closed her eyes, inhaled deeply, and thought, *I'm thankful to experience this moment.* Her mind flashed back to her sixteenth birthday, which had been one of her most memorable. Jessica's parents weren't the kind of people who went all out to celebrate birthdays, and she was never bothered. Her friend Janice, however, was quite the opposite. Jessica remembered the joy and surprise of walking into that pizza parlor to find that Janice had gathered her closest friends, all wearing party hats, to celebrate with her.

Nia's hand on her shoulder brought Jessica's mind back to the present beautiful moment. "Are you okay, Mom?"

Jessica smiled, nodded, and patted her daughter's hand. She watched Malik hoist Noah onto his shoulders and lead the family in a birthday parade through the house. She stayed seated, resting her knees. With the room to herself, the soothing sound of rainfall on the roof became more pronounced.

All alone, she decided now would be a good time to see what was going on in the world. Jessica placed the pads of the vision glasses onto the bridge of her nose and secured the temple tips over her ears. "Let's see," she whispered to herself as she lightly placed her fingertips on the long, skinny temple on the right side of the glasses before using her index finger and thumb to adjust the rims. "What's the latest news?" she said under her breath.

The lenses transitioned from transparent to dark, and the image of a news anchor appeared. Jessica never understood how people could walk around while watching television programs without crashing into things. *Kids these days.*

"The life expectancy for Americans has dropped for the third year in a row. We think..." *Next,* Jessica thought, and the screen on the lenses changed to her next preset station.

Images of homes and cars submerged in a flood appeared, the red of a stop sign just barely peeking its head above the water. "Severe weather changes are causing problems for insurance companies and nightmares for customers." A man appeared on the screen, fatigue and worry etched into his face, his eyes red and puffy. "I—I don't know what my family is going to do. This..." The man turned back to the chaotic scene in the background with an expression of bewilderment. "Just a month ago, our town was suffering from the worst drought in years, and now this." *Next.*

The White House Press Secretary was standing behind the podium about to have a live press conference. *Interesting,* Jessica thought, as the woman behind the podium pointed to a reporter out of view. "What is the White House's response to the increase in violence seen throughout the nation?" the reporter asked.

"We've received congressional approval to allocate one hundred million dollars of funding across various outreach programs."

"Which programs?"

"That information can be found on our website."

"Is that going to be enough?"

"That's the best we can do. Next question," said the Press Secretary, a trained impassive mask in place.

"There's a belief that the increase in crime is linked to the solar flares. What is the White House's statement?"

"We have not seen enough convincing data to agree with that statement."

"What about the Male Warrior Hypothesis?"

"I'm not familiar with the theory."

"Some experts have suggested that the increase in violent outbursts results from the lack of any large-scale conflict."

"No comment."

"What support will be given to the victims of the violent changes in weather patterns?"

Jessica pulled the glasses off her face, letting them hang around her neck. The rain stopped, and Noah ran in the grass outside. Malik walked into the kitchen holding Aries. He appeared to be searching for something. "What do you need?"

"I'm looking for the baby's walker," he said, referring to the little bamboo table on wheels that Aries had just gotten big enough for.

"I think it was down there." Jessica pointed down the hallway. "It was in the living room last I saw it."

"May I?" Malik asked, holding the baby out.

"Of course!" Jessica replied.

Malik sat Aries in her lap and said, "Be right back."

The baby looked up at Jessica, showing his big, shiny cheeks and toothless smile, which made her heart melt. Jessica smiled back, and a quick movement near the large glass door caught her attention. A hummingbird was hovering there, as though staring inside the house. Behind the small bird, Jonas, Nia, and Noah were playing while Magaly was trying to capture the scene on her violet-covered sketch book.

Malik returned with the walker and placed the baby inside. "Do you need anything to drink, Grandma?"

"No, thank you." Jessica was still gazing at Aries. He gave a couple of low grunts as he put the walker into motion. His heavy head bobbed as he made his way over to the door. Jessica turned her attention back to the glass. To her surprise, the hummingbird was still there, and Aries was fixated on it. *Observant little one*, she marveled.

"Aw, how cute," Malik said as he sat down with a glass of water. "Aries, are you watching your brother play outside?" Jessica glanced over at Malik, and though he seemed to enjoy the moment, his knee was bouncing rapidly.

"How was your time with Lotus, by the way?" she asked him.

"Really good. Better than I expected."

"Have you been practicing your meditation?"

"I have been." As he looked at her, she tilted her head toward his restless knee, which then slowed to a stop. "I guess I have a lot on my mind."

"It'll get easier," Jessica said.

Aries was now cooing and reaching for the door. Jessica saw the hummingbird was now about eye level with the baby.

"That is just the most adorable thing," Malik said. "I should record this." As the words left his mouth, Jessica watched the hummingbird zip higher, causing the baby to crane his neck. When Malik pulled his phone out of his pocket, the hummingbird flew away.

15

POP QUIZ

MALIK SAT BACK IN THE METAL CHAIR AND TURNED HIS CUP IN SLOW circles on the round metallic table. Condensation dripped down the side of the cup, creating a ring of water on the table. Malik slid his thumb up the side of the cup, collecting a pool of liquid before letting it drip down to the table. The shafts of sunlight in front of him suddenly broadened and intensified. Malik shielded his eyes as he looked to the sky to see the only clouds in sight float past the sun, offering no further protection. Malik reached for the sunglasses he expected to be hanging around his neck and touched only the cloth of his shirt. He searched the table, then the surrounding ground, but had no luck. As the sunlight got brighter, Malik felt a wave of panic. He felt his pocket for his phone so he could check his solar flare alerts, but that too was missing.

Malik stood and surveyed the area. *Where am I?* For the first time, he recognized that people with shopping bags were all around him walking in various directions. Malik was in a food court on the bottom level of a seven-story, open-air shopping mall.

As Malik observed the scene, the movement took on a rhythm.

Shoppers were filing in and out of stores, steadily collecting more bags in a way that could have been choreographed. This was happening as far as he could see, up through the sixth floor. Only the seventh floor was quiet. Malik turned in a circle to realize he was the sole customer in the food court, and every restaurant employee had their head down. The closer Malik got to them, the more difficulty he had seeing their faces behind their visors or hats.

Malik stopped far enough from the counter that multiple restaurants were in his periphery. Then as if on a timer, each of the register workers popped their heads up and stared past Malik. *What is happening?* He pivoted and let out a gasp as throngs of people rushed the food court in a rainbow of color-coordinated shirts. *I've seen this before.* Malik's memory flashed to his high school marching band in the royal-blue T-shirts they wore when traveling to games or competitions. Malik looked down and saw he was not only wearing the T-shirt again, but he also had on his backpack.

A voice came from behind him. "It's getting close to graduation. Are you ready for the exams?"

Malik turned around and was facing a standing desk that formed part of a pod. He was inexplicably no longer in a food court. On either side of him, brick walls were painted sky blue along the top and bottom. He was back in one of his high school collaboration areas.

Which exams do I have? He placed his fingers on the keyboard, and the computer screen came alive to display a study guide. Before Malik had time to read it, the bell rang, indicating class was about to start. There was a tablet on the desk, so Malik unplugged the device and slid it into his empty backpack. Malik slung the bag over his shoulder and followed the flow of students. The weight and momentum of the backpack pulled his body backward. Though previously almost weightless, it now felt like it could have been loaded with heavy antique textbooks. Malik tried to hurry, but he could barely move.

A group of students walked past him, and one shouted, "Come on, you don't want to miss the study session!"

Malik struggled to keep up; the students were moving too fast. *I don't even know where the classroom is,* Malik thought, as the group disappeared around a corner at the end of the hallway. Once Malik finally dragged himself to the corner, he had lost all signs of the other students. He could feel his heart pumping harder in his chest, and a lump formed in his throat. *I'm going to fail this test. I must get to that study session.* Malik closed his eyes and attempted to quiet his worried thoughts.

"Malik?"

Malik blinked his eyes open at the sound of his name and glanced to his right and left in search of the source. Malik was the only student sitting in the front row of class. *Okay good, I found the classroom.* He rotated in his seat, hoping he'd recognize someone sitting behind him.

Then the teacher shouted, "Malik!"

He quickly swiveled back to face the front.

The teacher was standing at the board with his back facing the class. He had tufts of white hair fanning out in all directions, and he was wearing a beige sweater with a green chevron pattern. The teacher held a stylus in his hand, waiting to write. "Well, Malik, do you have the answer?"

"Umm... the answer, sir?" was all Malik could manage.

The teacher turned his head slightly and sighed. "How can you not remember the answer? You will never graduate."

"But," Malik stammered, and focused on the equation on the chalkboard. $E=mc^2$. "I—I thought this was a study session."

The teacher shook his head in frustration. "No, no, no, no, no, no, no. You've missed the study session. This is the exam. Where have you been, Malik?"

Malik opened his mouth to answer, but no words came out.

"Where have you been?" the teacher asked again.

"I–I don't know." Malik's heart was racing.

"What?" the teacher shouted.

Malik felt frantic. "I said, I don't know."

The teacher shouted again. This time, his voice was a high-pitched, "Whaaaaaaaaaaaaaaaaaaaaa!"

Malik's stomach twisted in knots. This was one of his earliest nightmares coming to life. He was unprepared for something important. Something he knew, or should have known, would take place. How did he miss this? He did not know what the teacher was talking about. He didn't even know what class they were in. How could he forget his final exams to graduate from high school? He was frustrated and angry, not at his teacher, but with himself. What in the world had he been doing for an entire semester to be this lost? He didn't know what to say for himself. As he was about to say that to the teacher, he remembered something so simple: *I've already graduated.*

Malik opened his eyes and heard the wailing coming from the baby's room upstairs. Malik rolled out of bed. His movement must have woken Magaly because she rolled over, clutching her pillow. "I've already changed him, so he shouldn't need a new diaper. And he nursed too, so he may just need to burp again or be soothed."

Malik leaned in and kissed her forehead. "Thanks, love."

THOUGH IT COULD TAKE A WHILE, soothing the baby back to sleep was often cathartic for Malik as well. Malik slowly lowered Aries into his crib and tiptoed backward out of the nursery. As Malik pulled the door, the hinge creaked. He winced, held his breath, and paused, staring into the crib. Aries shifted and exhaled, but stayed sound asleep.

Malik made his way down the stairs to the kitchen, feeling surprisingly wide awake. He looked at the clock on the fridge, 3:57 a.m. He grabbed a glass of water and turned to head to the office when a dark figure emerged in the middle of the hall. Malik jumped and did everything he could to not drop the glass.

"Boy," his grandma whispered, "why are you so jumpy? No one out here is after you."

Malik cleared his throat before whispering back. "I didn't expect anyone to be awake."

"I can see that. So… what are you about to do?"

"I was going to go to the office and go through more of the notes. Why?"

"I have a better idea. It's time for you to start your training."

"Right now?" Malik asked, looking back at the clock.

"Now is the perfect time. There are fewer people up. It clears the airwaves." His grandma walked past Malik and opened the sliding glass doors that led to the yard. She turned back to Malik and said, "Well… are you coming?"

Malik chugged his glass of water, placed the glass on the counter, and started after his grandmother.

"Hang on," she said. Malik watched as his grandmother gestured to his socked feet, then up to his T-shirt. "You can't go like that. Go put on some workout clothes."

"Forgot I was in pajamas." Malik went back to his room and changed clothes. When he came outside, he saw a dark shadow next to his grandmother that was at least twice her size. Malik heard his grandmother saying something as he approached, and the other person gave a thunderous laugh in return, the large shadow bouncing with each chuckle.

"Malik," his grandma said, "I'd like to introduce you to Vau."

Malik could not make out any facial features. He just saw a tree-trunk-sized arm extend in his direction. "It's nice to meet you."

Malik shook the man's hand, his own becoming completely enveloped in Vau's grip. Malik thought about how Noah must feel holding his hand. "It's nice to meet you too."

"Alright," Vau said, "are we ready to go?"

"Yes, we are," his grandmother said, turning toward the woods. "I'm excited. I've never been this way."

"It's cool," Vau said. "These routes haven't been used in ages."

16

THE TREE OF LIFE

MALIK FOLLOWED THE SMALL AND LARGE SHADOWS OF HIS grandmother and Vau on the moonlit forest trail. The two had an ease about them, walking along together engaged in a casual conversation. Meanwhile, Malik couldn't take his attention away from the ankle-high shrubs that bordered the trail. His head was on a swivel, his eyes focused on the forest.

Just then, he saw movement off to his right a few paces ahead of him, several yards into the trees. He felt the tingling sensation of unidentified fear running down the back of his neck, and he froze, staring toward an oval-shaped figure which shifted again before it, too, became still. Malik's grandma and Vau had continued walking ahead with no worry or hesitation.

Malik inhaled and tried his best to force away the feeling of fear. *If she's not worried, then I shouldn't be.* With that, the old Dr. Seuss story about pale green pants came into his mind. Malik snorted out a laugh and relaxed. As he started to walk again, he saw the shadow extend its wings and fly into the sky, revealing its full shape as it swooped momentarily into the light of the moon.

Vau's voice boomed from up ahead. "A barred owl."

"Really?" His grandma seemed surprised. "Those are pretty rare in these parts."

Malik caught up with her and Vau. "They're pretty common in our woods at home. Noah loves them."

The trio continued down the path, and after a while, the sun started its rise off to Malik's right. His increased ability to see his surroundings comforted him. Around him, the forest's understory was awakening. Birds appeared and sang; squirrels and chipmunks chased one another around. A pair of cottontail rabbits hopped across the path a few feet in front of Malik. He watched as they darted across the forest floor and then broke off with sharp turns when they came across a buck, who then lifted his head and made eye contact with Malik. Steam wafted from the buck's nose as the impressive animal exhaled into the cool morning air— holding his head high, putting his majestic antlers on display. It surprised Malik the deer didn't run, and he turned back to the path, expecting to see his companions observing the buck as well. They apparently had continued on, and there was once again a distance for Malik to cover.

As Malik closed the gap, a fog emerged from the forest, sweeping across the path and temporarily blocking his vision. He waved his hands to fan away the low cloud and, soon, it dissipated. He caught sight of his guides again, and either his eyes were playing tricks on him, or Vau's stature had become even more imposing. *It was dark when I first met him*, he conceded.

Malik had been following Vau and Jessica down the soft dirt trail for some time. His shirt was drenched with sweat and mist, and there was a burn in his lungs. He placed his hands on his hips and inhaled to catch his breath.

Malik's grandma gave a loud laugh and jokingly shoved the mountain of a man, who pretended to lose his balance. This change in his grandmother baffled Malik. *She's seemed frailer lately.*

How is she keeping pace? He studied the ninety-year-old's comfortable stride that had taken on a youthful bounce.

Vau then spoke over his shoulder to Malik. "We are almost there."

"Great, thank you," Malik gasped, and convinced himself to march on. Ahead, Malik saw bright light where the tree-covered trail opened up. His grandma and Vau exited the woods well before he did. When Malik caught up, they were standing at the top of a sizable hill overlooking the forested coastline, which curved in the foreground, the ocean glittering beyond.

"I've never been on that trail before," his grandmother said.

"Each one, unique to the traveler," Vau replied.

Malik bent over and rested his hands on his knees, appreciating the brief break.

Vau approached Malik and gently patted him on the back. "The beginning is the most difficult." Vau pointed off to the left. "Would you like to sit?"

Malik glanced in that direction and saw a green park bench facing the coastline. It looked inviting, but Malik shook his head. "I'm good. Thank you though." Vau nodded and continued leading them forward.

Malik glimpsed his grandma's face as she walked past. Something was different, but Malik couldn't quite put his finger on what. Malik stood up straight and readied his mind for the rest of the trek when he noticed a low buzzing sound— one that sent goosebumps down his arms—getting continually louder. All three of them paused, and then a thick cloud of insects flew into view. A few broke free from the swarm near where Malik stood, but he didn't move. He wasn't what they were after. "Honeybees," Malik whispered, watching one of them land on a yellow flower off the path before rejoining its group.

As the black cloud flew on, Malik looked at his guides and

realized they had been awaiting his reaction. He wasn't sure why, but they seemed pleased.

MALIK CAUGHT his second wind and was now keeping up. The dirt path ran parallel to an estate. In the distance, Malik could see several homes made of stone and timber, and another that could have been modeled after a European castle. Closer in were perfect rows of trees, some of which were bearing fruit.

As if reading his mind, Vau took a detour to pick some fruit from the trees and returned to share it with them. "This orchard is one of the best on the island. Unbelievable apples, pears, plums, quince. Here, try the cherries."

The sweet juice of the fruit was refreshing and energizing. Malik no longer felt the burning in his lungs, nor the strain in his legs from the extensive hike. Overhead, an enormous bird glided into view with its unmistakable white head and brown body. *A bald eagle.* It mesmerized Malik until the raptor soared out of sight, and then Malik suddenly thought, *Wait, did he say island?* "We're on an island?" Malik asked Vau.

"Yeah," Vau said, and looked back at the orchard. "Should we see if any plums look ready?"

"No, thanks," Malik said. "Can we go back for a second?"

Vau turned around, stepped toward Malik, and asked, "You want to go back?"

"No, no. That's not what I mean. I meant, I want to go back to what you said about being on an island."

Vau nudged him and let out a big laugh. "I'm just messing with you. I knew what you meant."

Malik's grandma was bent over laughing. "Don't mind him, he's just Vau."

"You've got to loosen up," Vau said, continuing to chuckle. "Yes, we are on an island."

"But how? We were..." Malik tried to think back about their path. "We didn't cross any bodies of water." He shook his head. "We didn't..."

"Are you sure?" Vau asked.

"Yeah, I'm sure," Malik said.

"You saw everything the entire time we were walking?" Vau asked again.

"I—I mean... It got a little foggy." Malik reflected on their trip. "Yeah, I'm sure. I couldn't have missed a large body of water."

Vau let out a laugh again. "Good, you're right. Trust what you see."

"Then how did we get on an island?" Malik's eyes alternated between his grandma and Vau.

Vau tilted his head toward Malik's grandma. "He asks a lot of questions, doesn't he?"

She spoke to Vau as if Malik weren't there. "Oh, he's always been that way. He is my grandson, after all. But ever since he was a child, he has needed to know how everything works."

"Malik, I wish I could tell you the how, but there are some things we aren't meant to know," Vau said. "All we needed to know today was if we walked down that path, we would get to the Point."

"The Point?" Malik asked.

"Yes, that's where we are now." Vau cleared his throat. "And, listen. Back there, you showed an ability to not worry about the how. I encourage you to keep that mentality. Focus on the what, not the how."

"What do you mean 'back there'?" Malik asked.

"You know," Vau shrugged. "You didn't worry about *how* you got to the food court, or *how* you got to the classroom." Vau chuckled and used his fist to cover his mouth. "I mean, you freaked out about the test."

Malik felt his stomach contract. "How do you know about

that?" Vau didn't answer though. He started walking down the path, beckoning them to follow.

Malik searched his grandmother's face. "I just had that dream last night. How could anyone know about that?"

His grandma took his hand. "Baby, listen. What you are about to experience will blow your mind if you let it. Vau and the others, they aren't like us. They're celestial beings. They have gifts that allow them to do certain things."

"Vau can see my dreams?"

"In a way, yes. But don't worry, it's actually a good thing. Dreams are a way for them to communicate with us. A way to send help when we need it."

"You two seem close." Malik's question came out more like a statement.

"We worked together for a long time," his grandma explained. "Also, that's another one of his gifts. Vau is excellent at connecting with people. You'll see." She tugged on his hand. "Let's go. We're almost there."

Vau had disappeared down the trail, which narrowed once more. Malik's eyes were drawn from the brown dirt path up to the sky, where he saw what he at first believed was a tower. It took a second for him to realize that it was the largest tree he had ever seen in his life, the top of which disappeared into the clouds.

"Yes." His grandma's voice interrupted Malik's thoughts. "That is where we're going."

"Is that a tree?" Malik asked.

"Yes, it is. Now, come on. They are expecting you."

This narrow part of the trail led to an enormous dark cave. Vau was standing outside the mouth. "Uh, where we going?" Malik asked.

"In there," Malik's grandmother said before walking in side by side with Vau.

Malik considered his options, then chose to suppress his fear and proceed. Once inside, Malik paused momentarily to allow his eyes to adjust.

He heard his grandma's voice calling back to him. "Keep moving forward. Your eyes will adjust just fine."

Malik did as instructed, and with each step he took, he noticed neon green light radiating brighter all around him. "Bioluminescence," Malik whispered to himself and smiled at a memory of sitting with Noah while watching a nature program and learning things himself about all the living things that can emit light.

Malik marveled at his surroundings, taking everything in until he caught up with his grandmother and Vau, who had been patiently waiting. The floor transitioned from a soft surface to what felt like slick marble before they walked into a black glass elevator. He looked around to see the bright pink, yellow, and white fluorescent strands that he first observed in his grandfather's office bathroom at the Singularity Group. "Is this dark energy? How did you guys install it here?"

"We didn't install the dark energy here," Vau said. "Ori deployed this technology out there."

Malik had another question on the tip of his tongue when the elevator doors opened to reveal an office.

"Welcome to the command center," Vau said.

Malik's grandma smiled back at him as she walked out onto the floor. "I like to think of this place as the Tree of Life."

"This tree," Vau continued as he ushered Malik out of the elevator, "is connected to every dimension and reality with plant life, which I'm sure you realize human beings need to survive." Vau led the way to sliding glass doors, which revealed an octagonal room beyond with a round table in the middle. "And this is where the magic happens."

Several people were already in there, and Malik quickly recognized one person. Her hair was short on top and shaved on the sides. She looked like the person who had worked on special projects with his grandfather. He thought to himself, *There's no way that's Jordan. She hasn't aged a bit. But could it be?* "Jordan? Is that you?" he asked.

"Hi, Malik," Jordan said in reply. "I'm glad you made it."

"Welcome," a familiar voice said. It was like it came out of Malik's own head. He looked over and saw a man who stood a head higher than he was.

"Déjà vu," Malik whispered.

"This is Ori," Vau said.

"I—I've seen you somewhere... You were in my dream," Malik said slowly, his rational mind resisting what he was experiencing. He turned to his grandma. She was next to a woman with curly brown hair who was wearing a long, flowing, white dress. An image of that woman standing next to him in a crowd and then tugging his arm, flashed into Malik's mind. "You're Evelyn." Malik then looked at the one person still sitting down at the table. "And you, you're a mechanic, right? Tony?"

"Mm-hmm." Tony smirked.

Malik snapped his head toward Vau. "And you! You were the one driving the tow truck."

"That's right." Vau smiled, then looked at Ori. "His connection is happening fast."

Malik faced Ori once more. "Why do I have this urge to call you Coach O?"

"That was a part I needed to play in another version of your reality. And in the tree," Ori motioned around them, "your connections with your various existences are strengthened."

"How is this possible?"

"The short and fast answer is that a combination of the tree's connection to all relevant existences, along with the integration of dark matter and dark energy, allows us to tap into all frequencies. And you, Malik, like all other living things, are an energy field with your own frequency. Your body vibrates at its own frequency, as does your mind. Starting from the smallest atom up to the entire planet, everything has a vibration."

"And here," Tony chimed in from the table, "we can observe and strategize."

"Strategize? Really?" Jordan said.

"What? I like that word. It's a good word."

"If you say so," Jordan said.

"Don't mind them," Evelyn said, her voice calming the chatter. "The main thing for you to know now is that this is where you will conduct a portion of your training."

"Okay," Malik said tentatively. "What will that portion of training be?"

"You will have a series of dreams," Evelyn explained. "Once you wake, you will come here for analysis and next steps."

"And there's good news already," Ori said.

"What's that?" Malik asked.

"Based on your last dream, we don't have any doubt you will complete your training."

17

TRAINING PROGRAM

MALIK FOLLOWED EVELYN TO A DIFFERENT ROOM, WHICH HAD ONLY A single desk in the middle, though it was more like a live edge piece of wood elevated off the ground. Evelyn walked to the center of the room and turned around to face Malik. "This is where you will conduct the classroom portion of your training."

The room was round and dark, with a row of lights running the full length of the wall. It reminded Malik of an observatory. He then heard his grandmother's voice behind him. "I've never been in here before." Malik turned to see that she had walked in behind them with Ori.

"We specifically tailor each training to the individual recruit," Evelyn said. "Daylight please."

As soon as Evelyn finished saying the words, the walls changed. Malik felt like he was in a spacecraft with neon green and pink nebula clouds zipping past, or was he zipping past them?

"This is fancy," his grandma said, watching as a small bright circle began quickly getting larger. Malik recognized the image as a star.

"That's not just any star," Ori said.

Malik kept watching as the image of the ringed planet passed by. *Saturn*, Malik assumed, as the screen continued to zoom toward a bright blue planet.

"And I know you know what that is," Ori said.

Malik nodded. *Earth*. "This is amazing. Were you able to get footage from the James Webb Space Telescope? I thought they were keeping it private."

Malik watched as Ori and Evelyn exchanged smiles. The room was now bright, and the room looked as if they were in a grassy field on a partly cloudy, but beautiful, sunny day.

"Will this be enough light?" Evelyn asked.

"Uh, yes," Malik said.

"Great," Evelyn said. "Now, before we leave you to it, there are a few ground rules that we need to cover. For your recruitment, we call what you will go through your training, but it is more of a process that has been personalized just for you by a deep part of you. This process, when completed, will allow you to achieve your higher self. It's a serious commitment, and if you are going to do it, you must go all the way, which is why we have a few rules."

Malik looked at his grandmother, who had moved close to the door. She smiled and nodded at Malik, encouraging him to go on. He turned back to Evelyn and said, "Okay."

"First, you must never discuss with anyone out there," Evelyn pointed a finger in the air, indicating the outside world, "what you do and learn in here."

"Got it."

"Second, you must commit to this process fully. You must go all the way, no matter how long it takes."

No matter how long it takes? Malik contemplated this before asking, "How long do you think it will take?"

"It could take several years," Evelyn said.

Ori stepped forward. "With focus and dedication, a few years is feasible."

"I—I don't know if I have that kind of time. I don't want to lose years with the boys and Magaly," Malik said.

"Oh, you wouldn't," Evelyn assured him. "That's not what we meant."

"How does that work then?"

"A portion of your training will be in the subconscious. It will be an almost dreamlike experience where you will come here to debrief. And similar to a dream, time will move differently. It will feel longer than it really is. Your lifestyle can influence that as well." Evelyn nodded her head toward the door. "You are living a very present life. Time feels like it moves slower when you are focused on the current moment and not worried about tomorrow, next week, or next month. That will be reflected in the subconscious time you spend here, making it less likely to impact your time out there."

"And the other portion of training?" Malik asked.

"Yes," Evelyn said. "The other portion of your training will require your physical and mental presence. For that, we encourage recruits to begin early in the morning, like today, before others are awake."

"That's how the boys won't really notice any change," Ori said. "They will be asleep."

"And Magaly?" Malik asked. "She notices every time I get out of bed."

"She understands more than you think," Evelyn said.

Ori stepped in front of Malik, looked him in the eye, and placed a hand on his shoulder. "I guarantee that if you go all the way on this, you will be able to access the answer to any question you ask." Ori's dark brown eyes changed, his pupils dilating until the iris was completely black. Then there was a bright flash of gold, momentarily blinding Malik. After the stars in his eyes faded, he saw Ori's eyes had returned to normal.

"What was that?" Malik asked, not sure if he was imagining things.

"As a sign of good faith," Ori continued, ignoring Malik's question. "We have already set into motion a way to protect people from the solar flares. And I will place information key to completing that plan in your possession."

"What?" Malik said.

"But," Ori continued, "you will not be able to understand it until you complete this process. So, is it worth it to commit this time?"

"I can commit."

"Third," Evelyn started again, "you cannot reach out to anyone outside of your immediate family or other recruits, not until you complete the process."

"But what if people need me?" Malik jumped as a loud, heckling laugh rang across the room. "What was that?"

"That was the ego," Evelyn said. "I said that you can't reach out to anyone. I didn't say that people can't reach out to you. If someone needs you, they will call you."

"Okay," Malik said. "I'll do it."

Evelyn clapped her hands together. "Wonderful. Your first instructor will be in momentarily. We'll see you later."

Malik watched as his grandma and Evelyn exited the room, with Ori close behind. *Where are they going?* Malik wondered.

Ori paused at the door and turned back to say, "We need to check on other recruits." With that, he vanished like the others.

MALIK PACED AROUND THE ROOM, awaiting the instructor. Though it felt like a perfect day with blue skies and a warm sun, Malik was aware that he was inside his "classroom." He approached the desk in the middle of the room and strolled around it. Malik ran his fingertips along the curvy edges and sat in the chair. He shifted to settle in before inspecting the underside of the desk, finding nothing there. He then realized there was also no paper, no books, just the chair, the desk, and a view of a grassy meadow.

"So, you are my trainee, huh?" A voice came from the door.

Malik turned to see a woman with straight black hair pulled back into a ponytail. She was wearing cargo pants, boots, and a black T-shirt, and her attention was on her watch. She walked distractedly past Malik to the front of the desk and said, "Sorry for being late. I just got in from a mission."

Malik slowly rose from his seat. "Callie?" he whispered.

"Yeah," she said, and took her eyes off her watch to face Malik. Callie's eyes widened, and she rushed around the table to give him a big hug. "I'm so happy to see you," she said. "I wasn't sure if or when you would get here."

Malik couldn't help but evaluate his friend. "You look—you look so good."

"Thank you, so do you," Callie said.

"I—I mean..." Malik tried again. "How is this possible? The last time I saw you—"

"Was in a dream," Callie said, cutting Malik off.

Malik was silent. That was not what he was going to say. "Wait..." He thought back to Callie appearing in the bedroom, right around the time he heard the mosquitoes.

"It's all coming back now?" Callie grinned. "Yeah, dreams are more than just dreams."

"But," Malik scanned through memories, "before that, the last time—"

Callie interrupted him again. "Now is not the time to relive the past."

"Okay. But you're here now... in the present."

"I told you I had a job that I was interviewing for." Callie chuckled.

"You did?" Malik was confused. "When?"

"In the car, on your way to…" Callie paused and slowly nodded. "Ah, I see."

"What?"

"You don't remember that. Well, never mind." Callie spread her arms. "Welcome to the Point of Singularity." She surveyed the room. "Um, was this Evelyn?"

Malik didn't know how to answer.

Callie continued, "Let's switch this up. Can we get a couch?"

Malik watched as a large gray U-shaped couch materialized in the room. Malik walked around the couch, looking up at the ceiling and down at the floor. *Where did this come from?*

"Do you need this?" Callie stood next to the desk and was pointing at it. Without waiting for Malik to answer, she continued her redesign. "It seems formal. Can we get rid of this and…" Callie seemed like she was thinking, then she snapped her fingers, "get one of those old school rolling televisions."

"What are you talking about?"

"You know, the ones that they used to roll into the elementary school library on rainy days when we couldn't go outside," Callie said, as it appeared. Malik gawked at the thick box with faux wood side panels and a bulging glass front, which was sitting atop a narrow metal cart.

"I've never seen one of these in my life."

"Maybe not this version of you," Callie said. "Alright, that's more like it." She flopped on one side of the U-shaped couch and threw her hands in the air. "You ready for your first training session?"

"Ready as I'm gonna get," Malik responded.

"Alright, so you can ask me anything as we go along. I'm sure you will have a lot of questions. I know I did. But, mind you, there is a good bit we need to go through."

Malik nodded.

"First off, Evelyn covered the three rules about training, right? You know, you have to complete it, no talking about it…"

"Yes, she told me."

"Cool, she always does. Okay, so next, I give you a rundown of how this goes."

"Wait." Malik asked, "How long have you been here?"

Callie's eyes tightened as she thought. "You know, I can't remember. Time is a funny thing here. I've been on so many missions now, through all different points in time and existence, that it all just blurs together. Good question though."

"Will that happen to me? Will I lose track of time?"

"In some ways, yes. But you have two unique ways to watch time change."

Noah and Aries, Malik thought, calling to mind an image of his elder son planting vegetables in the garden with Jonas.

"Okay, so after all our introductory stuff this time, you'll have a session in the lab to get your assessment. That's essentially where they run a bunch of tests on you to understand what types of assignments you can go on."

"Assignments?"

"Yes, once you complete the process, then you will become a Universal Citizen. To maintain your citizenship, you must fulfill the Conduit Requirement, which will allow you to act as a conduit for the universe as either a teacher, guide, or guardian. We never know which role we will be asked to play until the assignment comes around. For people like us, we are most often asked to be a guide. Some who have been Universal Citizens for a while are teachers. Usually, the more tenured citizens are called upon to be guardians for special missions."

"What's the difference?"

"Well, each role has a different level of interaction with non-citizens. Teachers spend more time, guides may exist for a moment, and guardians may never be noticed. Your training will prepare you to perform successfully whichever role, or roles, is the best match for you."

"They said that something within me dictates my training."

"Your subconscious," Callie said. "And it communicates what you need to learn through a dream, then we here interpret that dream." Callie motioned her hand to the antique television set, which turned on as soon as she looked at it. "Then someone is selected to run the training."

Malik looked at the screen, and he got goosebumps. On the screen was a first-person account of his dream last night. He was at the metal table. He saw his brown fingers collecting the condensation off the cup. The image moved quickly, everyone was walking and moving faster—as if someone had a remote control—and it froze on the image of the teacher standing at the board.

"This is my dream," was all Malik could say.

"Yeah, from your perspective. That's why I wanted to start you on this silly television screen. If I were to have done it on the wall, it's kind of a trip, like you're having the dream all over again. I've found it better to do it this way first. It's easier on the mind."

"Thank you," Malik said, and meant it. He couldn't fathom how his dreams were easily broadcast in this place.

"I know what you're thinking," Callie said. "Just remember that here at the Point, all the laws and rules that we learned about how things work don't necessarily apply." Callie turned back to the screen. "We use this pre-training dream to give you an idea of how things will work, okay? So, pay attention to your dreams, but the team is here to help you."

"Will you be here for all the training?"

"I'm not sure, but probably not. I've just been giving a lot of the introductory sessions since I'm one of the newest citizens. Alright, are there questions?"

"Not right now."

"Alright, on to the first thing." Callie grinned at Malik and arched her eyebrows. "You are a rare one."

"What do you mean?" Malik felt a sense of excitement building in his stomach.

"Look at this." Callie turned back to the screen. "I mean, you have the trifecta."

"What's the trifecta?"

"You dream in color, in first person, and with sound." Callie's hands waved with excitement.

"Doesn't everybody?"

Callie's brow furrowed. "No, they definitely do not. Those are three variables you'll need to be aware of." Callie held up her index finger. "Is the dream in color or black and white?" She continued counting on her fingers to make her point. "Is the dream in first person or as an observer of oneself? And last, is it silent, or is there sound? So, don't be surprised if you experience something different. Got it?"

"Got it," Malik said.

"Make sure you are paying attention. There will be a quiz later."

"Really?"

She smirked and shrugged. "Maybe." Callie turned back to the television screen, which was frozen on the teacher and the equation on the board. "But here, let's get back to this. Do you know what this is?" She gestured to the $E=mc^2$.

"A little Einstein."

"Yep, that's right. It is the equation that shows the relationship between mass and energy. Do you know why it appeared in your dream right before training?"

"I have no clue."

Callie smiled as she leaned in and whispered. "I think this is kind of cool." She rocked back and continued. "This equation essentially states that every single thing in existence that has mass —so anything made of matter from a rock, a table, a chair, to your body—has energy in it. The more mass it has, the more energy it has. So, your body has an incredible amount of energy in it. Look how large you are."

Malik looked down at himself and said, "I guess I'm taller than average."

"Most people," Callie said, "don't consciously know how to control it. What you'll learn through your training is just that. How to tap into and use the abundance of energy that makes up your entire being. And to do this, you must learn the first and most important lesson."

"Which is what?"

"How to stay grounded. You should have been assigned a teacher to help you stay grounded."

"Lotus?" The meditation studio flashed into his mind.

"Cool. It's important that you learn how to channel your energy and stay present. As a Universal Citizen, you will travel throughout time and the multiverse." Callie took a beat, which made Malik focus. "The only way to always find your way safely back to where you're rooted is by strengthening your connection to that reality."

"What happens if I'm not grounded enough?"

Callie shook her head. "Then your rational mind might not make sense of what belongs to which reality. It's not a good look."

"It takes its toll on the mind." Jordan's voice came from the back of the room, catching Malik off guard. He wasn't sure how she had come in so quietly, but she was standing by the door peeling an orange.

Callie was unfazed. "She's not wrong. That's why it's important for you to practice the art of meditation and being still every day, which you should be doing already. Now, you just better understand why it is important."

"Wait, what about you? If my reality…"

Jordan spoke up again. "She died in the realities you remember. But there are several realities where Callie is very much alive and well. In one of those, like you, she ascended to her higher self."

Malik turned to Callie and smiled. "Are we best friends in those realities?"

Callie tried to smile, but Malik could tell there was something she wasn't saying.

"You are to her," Jordan's voice said, "as she is to you."

Malik let the words sink in. *I died?* Malik turned to Jordan for confirmation, but all he saw was the door sliding shut.

Malik faced Callie again. She smoothed her hair back and looked away, but he could see that her eyes were watery. She gave herself a little shake, then said, "Enough of the sad talk. I'm happy we're all here now." She cleared her throat. "Where were we? Oh yeah, staying grounded. Although your training is tailored to you, you will also learn how to identify and contact other citizens. Let's see what is next. Oh, the library."

"There's a library here?"

"Sure, but that's not the one I'm talking about. You have been granted access to an extensive library. The reason for this is that there are three fundamental ways to travel to any point in the multiverse. Traveling through your dreams is the vehicle first and most used by recruits and Universal Citizens. The books in your library, when read, especially right before you fall asleep, will transport you to that time and place."

"My library?"

"At Jessica's place."

Malik remembered what he discovered when he climbed the ladder in the office. "The journals at my grandma's house?"

"Those journals are specifically assigned to you. The books have locations and times where you or a version of you exists. That way, when you go there, your consciousness will take over that version of you."

"There are quite a few of those." Malik heard the surprise in his own voice.

"Yes, that's right. You exist in more realities than you might have imagined, which is part of the reason you are a great recruit. Your karmic behavior—on a very large level—has enabled you to have an existence that is suitable for travel." Callie leaned over and winked. "Well done to the many yous throughout the infinite versions of existence."

"Thanks, I guess," Malik said with a laugh.

"A word of caution, though: Ori hasn't been able to confirm all your existences. The books are mainly the ones where you have taken steps toward a better version of yourself. Where you are on that journey differs, but you will all be in an excellent position. The books with the black spine are realities in which, at the time of our interaction, that version of you has yet to decide."

"Has yet to decide what?"

"Whether to pursue your higher self. Without that, it is very difficult to tap into the universal flow, which is what you will be consciously using. Make sense?"

Malik nodded, signaling for Callie to continue.

"Now, dreaming is the preferred way for you to travel. While you are in the target location, it will all feel real, and you will understand your role. There may be times when you won't fully know your aim, but if you stay true to your role, it will all work out. Then, when your mission is complete, you will awaken in your bed and go on with your day in the physical world. Questions about dreaming?"

Malik shook his head.

"Perfect," Callie said. "Now, I'll quickly cover the other forms of travel. Once you're ready, you will be assigned this." Callie held up a wristwatch, then extended her arm to give him a closer look. It was a skeleton watch with two circular sub-dials. The timepiece was easily one inch thick, and Malik watched as several layers of gears turned. One sub-dial displayed a large number 8, while the other displayed the number 7.81.

"This watch allows you to program your grounded location and several other target locations. Each existence functions at a different frequency that is connected to the hertz frequency at which Earth resonates. It's sort of like tuning a radio. This timepiece will tune your atomic structure to the target frequency. There are some things you have to be aware of when your physical body actually travels to the target location. For instance, you need to know if a version of you already exists there. You don't want to run into yourself; that would cause interference. If you existed but no longer do, you need to make sure that all recognizable memories of you have been wiped clean from the shared knowledge of that civilization. Tony helps with that so we don't create chaos."

"Sounds complicated," Malik said.

"Yeah. So, you will get a watch only once you are ready." Callie sighed. "I know, this is a lot, but that's it. Questions?" Callie laughed. "Of course you have questions."

Malik opened his mouth to begin, but a tap at the door interrupted his thoughts. They both turned to see that his grandma was back. She had a patient smile on her face. "I think you are going to have to wait for your questions." She took a few steps into the room and spoke. "Can you show the woods, please?" Instantly, the walls changed from the peaceful, sunny meadow to the wooded trail behind his grandma's house. Malik saw Noah race past the screen.

"Someone's awake!" Malik said, standing up. "I better get back."

"Evelyn and Ori want you to stop by the house on your way back. If we head there now, we can still get back and meet Jonas and Noah before they're done adventuring."

"Well," Callie spoke again, "I'm so glad you're here." She stood up and hugged Malik. "You guys are going to love this life." Callie's watch vibrated, and she released Malik to check her wrist. "Oh, man, I've got to go."

Callie jogged to the door, then turned back quickly to shout, "Good luck with your assessment! I hope I'll be able to see you again soon."

Callie disappeared before Malik could respond.

18

A SHOW OF GOOD FAITH

MALIK AND HIS GRANDMOTHER LEFT THE COMMAND CENTER HOW they had come, through a narrow trail that opened up to a wide dirt path with the coastline on one side and the orchard on the other. Instead of continuing toward the woods, his grandma led them through the orchard to a stone house that had seemed modest in the distance, though the closer they got, the more impressive it became. Beyond the orchard was a stone path—only wide enough for single file—that was lined with vibrant green shrubs of varying heights, all meticulously trimmed into perfect, curving shapes. As they walked under a wooden pergola, Malik couldn't help but admire the draping of delicate purple flowers with the sunlight filtering through in such a beautiful way.

They followed the stone path to the left, where it circled around the building to a spot with French doors that were propped open. They faced a wide field of grass framed by trees on either side. On the far end, the field opened to a view of the coastline. Malik noticed a bench there and thought about what a peaceful spot that must be.

"Malik," Evelyn appeared just inside the French doors, "please take a seat. Jessica will be right back." He hadn't realized it, but his grandma must have gone inside for something. Now Evelyn left the room as well.

Inside, there was a couch, a love seat, and an armchair, each positioned to have its own view through the open doors and large windows flanking them. Malik chose the chair, which was even more comfortable than it looked. He settled back into it and felt so relaxed, his eyelids became heavy. He was feeling the effects of his early wake-up.

He forced himself to sit up straight and surveyed the landscape for anything to keep him engaged. Just then, a red flash flew by the window and perched on top of a nearby shrub. As Malik gazed at the cardinal, he also noticed more bird songs floating in from outside and thought of Magaly. This was one of their favorite parts of the morning, and when they had a chance, they loved to have their coffee on the deck to watch and listen to the birds.

Malik stood back up, walked to the door, and leaned on the frame, scanning the bushes and trees, when something caught his eye off in the distance. *Is that a soccer ball? That seems out of place.* Malik felt movement behind him and turned to see Evelyn reenter the room.

"How was your first day of training?" she asked as she sat down on the love seat, with one foot on the cushion, the other on the floor.

Malik made his way back to the chair. "It was— There is a lot I have to wrap my head around."

"Yes, it can be a little overwhelming at first, but it will begin to feel more natural. And we'll all be there to provide the help you need."

"That's right." Ori appeared from a hidden hallway, holding what looked like one of Malik's grandmother's journals. She walked back in, right behind him. Ori extended the book to Malik. "This is for you." Then he joined Evelyn on the love seat.

"Thank you," Malik said as he placed the book on his lap.

"Well," Evelyn smiled as she glanced back and forth between the book and Malik, "aren't you going to open it?"

Malik opened the book and saw more small handwritten lines of zeros and ones. *I don't know what they expect me to do with this,* he thought, staring at the strings of digits.

"That sign of good faith I mentioned?" Ori said. "This is part of it."

"The part I won't be able to understand until I complete the process?" Malik asked.

"Yes. In that book, you will find much of what you need."

Malik thumbed through the pages, his mind trying to crack the code. *Maybe I can scan this and find a software that could read it. That shouldn't take…*

"There are no shortcuts," Ori said, interrupting his thoughts.

Malik looked up to find them all watching him with an amused expression. "He can hear your thoughts, by the way," Malik's grandma said.

"I knew it!" Malik laughed.

Evelyn leaned forward. "But really, Malik, try not to focus on the journal. As you progress in your training, your connection with source energy will be so strong you will be able to read and interpret signs that come to you, including that book. We know how badly you want to solve and fix things, but this is something you cannot fix alone. Your job now will be to understand what is happening and why and to act as a facilitator in the service of others."

"But to do that," Ori said, "you must be of great service to yourself. That is why it is critical for you to learn to control your energy. Your next training session will not come to you until you are fully living in the present and have achieved the enhanced awareness that comes with that."

"I am working on it," Malik said.

"You've made a great start, taking a sabbatical to be there for your family. Stepping away from the Singularity Group also shows an awareness of ego and your ability to contain it," Evelyn said. "That is one of the key steps to reaching your higher self. Another is accepting the role that the universe has carved out for you to play, whatever that is. You're seeing things others aren't seeing. Over time, you'll understand why."

"And when you do, you become a conduit," said Ori.

"A conduit," Malik whispered under his breath.

"Indeed," Ori said. "Answers will be channeled through you that will help serve others."

"Like a solution to help protect people from the harmful impacts of the solar flares," Malik said.

"Correct," Ori said.

"Why is this happening, anyway?" Malik asked.

"To help rewire the way the world thinks. When people ignore the planet, the very thing that sustains you, then what does that do for that life you sustain?" Ori extended his arm and pointed to Malik's stomach. "It's all connected."

"I'm not sure I follow," Malik replied.

"Well, let's see," Ori said. "The existence you're rooted in is seven point eight three hertz." As Ori placed a finger on his watch, the face turned a metallic black, revealing gears that were a variety of vibrant, bright lights. "At this moment, your reality, which is leading all realities in overpopulation, is at seven billion, eight hundred and sixty-nine million, eight hundred sixty thousand, three hundred and forty. Oh, nope, four hundred and fifty. Wait, five hundred." Ori looked up and over at Malik. "With over seven billion people, the world doesn't work as efficiently as it was meant to. A universal process has kicked in to get the population back down to a sustainable number. It's all about what you feed the tiny little beings that own your body. As I believe you already understand from some of Anatole Patterson's research, when exposed to harmful solar flares, the most dominant bacteria in one's microbiome aggressively multiply for eighteen minutes and twenty-five seconds."

"People are impacted by what they consciously and unconsciously consume," said Evelyn. "When possible, conscious decisions such as the quality of one's diet can help offset harmful things like pollutants. Unfortunately, that's not possible for everyone depending upon where, when, and how one lives. There are countries and versions of your world in which broad choices have been made to minimize pollutants, protect the environment, and ensure as much of the population as possible has access to foods with high nutritional value. And then there are those where that is not the case."

"So for everyone, it comes down to a combination of circumstances and choices?" Malik asked. "And then the dominant bacteria leads to dangerous or violent behavior?"

"Not necessarily," said Evelyn. "It interferes with mental cognition and decision-making, and what happens after that seems to be dictated by lifestyle. For some, the brain fog does not result in something extreme."

"The extreme aggression seems to happen for those who consume a great deal of content that is very high in conflict, violence, and death," Ori said. "It depends upon your programming."

"There are many people we won't be able to save. And without our help, humanity as a whole is at risk. But with your help, we have a plan to help humanity overcome this event and ensure there's a lasting civilization."

. . .

MALIK and his grandma started their walk back in silence. The weather was so pleasant that it seemed to quiet his mind, and his grandma had such a peaceful look on her face, he didn't want to interrupt. She walked at a quick pace on their way into the woods, and Malik thought, *At least I'm getting my exercise.* Under the shelter of the trees, as before—from out of nowhere—a white fog billowed around them, limiting Malik's visibility.

As the cloud lightened and disappeared, Malik felt his grandma's hand on his elbow. "I don't move as fast out here as I do in there," she said, tilting her head back. "Do you mind?"

"Not at all."

They took their time as they walked down the trail toward her home. Malik watched as his grandmother closed her eyes and held her chin up high, taking in deep breaths of air and exhaling. "I love it out here," she sighed.

A high-pitched voice came from somewhere in front of them. "I found another one, Opa!"

Malik immediately searched for Noah, as he sounded nearby.

"Oh," his grandma said calmly, "there's still a bit of time before we'll see them. Now that you've established your route to the Point, your connection with these woods is amplified."

"Here's another, and another!" Noah shouted again. "They are all over the place."

19

ICE CREAM AND DREAMS

MALIK'S KNEE BOUNCED UP AND DOWN AS HE WAITED FOR THE VAN door to open wide enough for him to jump out. He heard his mom shout, "You better make sure you changed out of your cleats!"

Malik looked at his white tube socks and cleats, stained with the red clay dirt from the baseball fields. While he changed his shoes and slipped into flip-flops, his teammate, Ronnie, hopped out of the van and looked pleased with himself for having already switched into his tennis shoes. Something was strange about the scene as Ronnie ran ahead in what seemed like slow motion, with his shoelaces trailing behind him.

Before following his friend, Malik turned to his grandma, who was sitting quietly on the other side of him with her chin tilted up, appearing to enjoy the warm sunlight on her face. Malik felt bad interrupting her moment of zen, but he didn't want to leave her out. "Grandma, do you want me to get you anything?"

"I'm alright, baby," she said. "I already told your mom what to get me." She then turned toward him, her eyes sharp. "Just make sure she doesn't get me any of that fat-free nonsense." Her expression softened as she winked at him, and Malik couldn't help but laugh.

"Will do! It's blistering hot out here though. You sure you don't want to come inside?"

Her smile seemed forced, and Malik believed he might have seen a tear in her eye. *It may be from the glare,* he reasoned.

"I'm sure. That's the beauty of having kids and getting older." She leaned in. "Nia wants to do everything for me, so I'll let her. We're just gonna keep that air on full blast."

"Okay, Grandma," Malik said, and he pressed the button on the inside of the door and watched it slide closed.

When Malik turned around, Ronnie was only now reaching the ice cream shop. He swung the door open, creating a blinding glare. Malik quickly averted his eyes, and that's when he saw the bright red, oversized sports utility vehicle with a vanity license plate on the front that read B16-E60. Everything else got hazy, and Malik's stomach knotted up. He didn't know why, but he couldn't pull his eyes away from the vehicle parked in the middle of the street, facing their direction. *You've got to have money to be comfortable doing that,* Malik thought.

"You coming?" Ronnie called, still holding the door to the ice cream parlor. Malik trotted inside the building. The combination of the sweet smell of sugar and the cool refrigerated air made the ice cream shop Malik's favorite place to visit during the summer.

"What are you going to have?" his dad asked as he took two scoops of chocolate ice cream in a big waffle cone from the server.

Malik's dad took a big bite of ice cream and pointed Malik to the person working behind the counter. Malik approached the glass counter to peruse the varieties, but with each step, the counter got taller. *Am I shrinking?* he wondered as he stood on the tips of his toes. Malik heard a rattling sound and spotted the stacks of paper ice cream cups on a shelf behind the server. Malik watched as the cups kept shaking, then noticed the framed poster on the wall was vibrating too. Then the walls themselves seemed to pulsate. Malik scanned the room. All the patrons seemed unaware, including his parents, who were focused on their frozen treats, laughing between bites of ice cream.

Malik turned back to the counter—which seemed to return to its normal height—to see a person with straight black hair that was short on the top and shaved on the sides. He knew her from somewhere but couldn't recall where or how. *Were we in the marching band together?* Malik wondered until a name popped into his mind. "Wait, you're Jordan, right?"

She didn't respond, nor did she return his friendly smile. Her serious demeanor made him slowly back away from the counter.

"Mom!" Malik tried to shout, but no sound came out. His parents were engaged in a conversation he couldn't hear. All had become silent. Malik pivoted back to the counter. Jordan wasn't there. A lone cup of ice cream now sat on the counter where she had stood. Malik knew it was his. He collected it to find his favorite—one scoop of chocolate chip cookie dough and one of mint chocolate chip. Malik brought the spoon to his lips, but he couldn't taste a thing.

In what seemed like the blink of an eye, the shop was empty. Everyone was gone. He looked toward the door and saw the person he recognized as Jordan standing on the other side of the glass door, her back facing Malik. She was completely still, staring off at something. Malik felt a knot move from his stomach up to his throat.

He heard a voice shout from behind him in the store. "Wait for me!" He had thought no one was there. Ronnie jogged past him and out the door. Malik stepped outside and watched his family piling back into the van. Right before he reached them, Ronnie tripped on his untied shoelaces.

"Man, sh—" Ronnie yelled, before Malik's mom jumped in.

"Boy, you better watch that mouth."

"But I dropped my ice cream." Ronnie pleaded, "Can I get another one?"

While they were caught up in the discussion, Malik's attention was once again pulled down the street. He sensed the chaos before he heard it.

"Get your hands off me!" a man screamed. A crowd surrounded him, but he was pushing his way through to climb into the oversized vehicle. The man was shouting and waving his hands frantically. "I'm sick and tired of this. It ends now." The man slammed his car door. The engine was silent, but the screeching sound of the tires was something out of a nightmare.

Malik's focus swiveled between Ronnie—standing outside the van negotiating to get a new ice cream cone—and the B16-E60 of the large vehicle, which had peeled out and was racing in their direction. As soon as Malik's brain caught up to what was about to occur, he lurched forward to warn his family, but his arm was yanked back so hard that the next thing he knew, he was lying flat on the ground, staring up at a couple of white cirrus clouds brushed across the blue sky. The force of the collision sent shockwaves through the ground, and the screeching sound of metal on metal pierced Malik's eardrums.

He clinched his eyes tightly shut. "Please wake up! Please wake up!"

MALIK OPENED his eyes and felt immediate and immense relief to find the ceiling fan of the guest bedroom in his grandmother's house. He gave a big exhale and glanced over to the other side of the bed, where Magaly was sound asleep, her mouth slightly ajar. A white flash brightened the room, and Malik looked out the window as the glow of lightning vanished. He was thankful that the tremble he soon felt was from thunder this time. His chest still felt tight from the stress and emotion of his nightmare. Malik's throat was dry, so he sat up and reached for the glass on the nightstand—which only had a swallow left—and gulped what water remained. His thirst unquenched, he pulled back the covers and crept out of bed.

From the kitchen, Malik saw his grandmother stargazing by the sliding glass door, her frame illuminated by the full moon. Malik filled his glass and then tiptoed over. "Will I always be awakened with such intense dreams?"

His grandma laughed, though she probably wouldn't have if she had known the details. "I'm not sure. I haven't gone through what you're going through."

"Really?" Malik asked. "What did you go through?"

"Well," she took half a step back and assessed Malik before continuing, "you should go change first. I'll tell you on the way."

"On the way?" Malik asked.

"Yeah, you're getting your assessment today."

20

THE ASSESSMENT

IT SURPRISED MALIK HOW COMFORTABLE THE TEMPERATURE WAS IN the woods for such an early morning hour. "It's always so comfortable in here."

"Mm-hmm," his grandma said. "This forest has its own microclimate."

"So... why didn't you ever have to get this assessment done?"

"Well, they recruited me to be a Scribe. You know, to document everything that I witnessed and experienced."

"All your journaling certainly makes more sense now," Malik said. He had grown up knowing his grandmother was a journalist, and had assumed, by the ever-present notebooks, that she was very dedicated to her work. And so she was.

"Everywhere I went, someone on the team accompanied me. I believe they give assessments to any citizen who will need to travel, physically and unescorted, to a reality that is outside of the one in which they are rooted. This assessment will help calibrate your body."

"What do you mean, calibrate?"

"If, for some reason, you get stuck someplace you aren't meant to be, atomically speaking, then the assessment will help buy you time until someone comes to bring you back."

MALIK'S GRANDMA led him to a different section of the command center. This area was less busy than the place he visited during his first trip. A door opened, and she pointed for Malik to enter. "You'll be alright," she said as she nodded for Malik to go ahead.

Malik walked into a white room so clean he could hardly tell where the walls met the floor or ceiling. There was a silver table with a matching chair in the middle of the room. On the chair was a black sleep mask.

"Please, take a seat." The voice came from the back corner of the room.

Malik jumped. "Oh, I didn't see you there."

The person continued, "I'll be administering your assessment today. If you would please take a seat, we can get started."

The administrator was wearing an all-white jumpsuit with white boots, gloves, and a mask that covered their hair, mouth, and nose, leaving only their eyes and a little skin on their cheeks visible. Their eyes were amber, and as Malik stared into them, he could have sworn that the tiny specs and shapes in the iris were rotating around the pupil. He couldn't look away as their amber irises glimmered and shifted. The administrator broke the spell, motioning again for Malik to sit in the chair. "Please, take a seat."

Malik did as requested while still observing the person, apprehensive about what was to come. They touched a place on the wall, which opened a rectangular panel, and pulled out a clear container.

Malik picked up the black eye mask in front of him and placed it on his lap. He watched the administrator as they moved around the room—accessing different panels camouflaged into the white walls—collecting different containers and then placing them into several black boxes on the table.

Malik twisted around in his chair but could not make out what was being done. Now directly in front of Malik, the administrator cupped a small jar in their hands. "We are about to conduct your pre-assessment calibration. The first step is for you to smell what's in this container and do your best to describe what you smell. After that," the administrator glanced back at the table of seven black boxes, "we will conduct the broader assessment."

Malik held up the black eye mask. "When should I put this on?"

"After the pre-assessment calibration."

Malik motioned his head toward the table. "What are in those black boxes?"

The administrator pulled an item out of one box and held it for Malik's inspection. The item was a stone shaped in a perfect sphere. Malik noticed there were small pores all over the stone. After displaying the object, the administrator returned it to its box. "These stones will help us test your sense of smell."

"Oh, this is a smell test?"

"Of sorts, yes. We first calibrate how your body reacts to this." The administrator held up the jar.

"What is that?"

"This is a hormone called androsterone. There are three," the administrator shook their head and corrected themself, "four potential reactions. Depending on what you smell, we then adjust the stones in those black boxes to align with how your body perceives smells." They held the small container close to Malik's nose. "Inhale."

Malik inhaled deeply and quickly regretted it. "Augh!" He coughed and forced back a gag. "That smells like urine."

The administrator placed a lid on the jar and put it on the table. "Great, thank you."

"What do other people smell?" Malik asked. The person was moving from box to box, tinkering with something on the back out of Malik's view.

"Some smell urine, some smell sandalwood, and some smell nothing at all."

"That's three," Malik said. "You said that there are four reactions."

"If you were in the fourth group, you would not be here. The fourth group would have smelled feces." The person glanced up at Malik. "Surviving here is very challenging if you're in that group."

"Why is that?"

The administrator locked eyes with Malik. "You will soon learn that in some realities, smell is one of the most important senses for survival. Now, put on your blindfold. We are ready to start the assessment."

Malik placed the cover over his eyes. With everything black, he suddenly recognized how cold the room was, and the buzzing sound from the bright white lights seemed amplified.

"Are you ready for fragrance number one?" the administrator asked.

"Sure."

Malik heard the soft, muffled steps as they came near, and he felt more warmth as they stood within inches of his face.

"Inhale please."

Malik inhaled again, hoping for something better this time. It was as though he felt something more than smelled it at first. He thought of sitting on the back deck of his house, the morning dew glistening on the grass as the sun rose in the distance, a warm cup of coffee still steaming in his hands. He could hear the deck door open, sensing that Magaly was about to join him. "I smell coffee," Malik said.

"Okay, thank you."

After more soft footsteps, the process repeated. "Please inhale again."

As Malik inhaled again, he saw himself running and weaving between the trees in the woods near his childhood home, pretending to be a superhero, saving the world. "I'm smelling citrus."

"Great." A moment later, they asked, "How about this one?"

This time, a spicy smell made Malik move his head and nose back. "I smell cinnamon."

"Okay." Malik felt the administrator pull the container away.

"That was surprising," Malik said.

"Yes, that one often is, especially for people with powerful personalities." Malik felt the administrator move away before returning. "Try this one."

Malik was hesitant as he moved his nose forward. "That's honeysuckle," Malik said. The scents were coming more quickly now. This one evoked a memory of the day he first saw Magaly.

"Okay, just a few more."

Malik sniffed. "Is that mint or… yeah, it's mint."

"Good, and how about this one?"

Malik inhaled and coughed. Images of sailing throughout the Virgin Islands on a fifty-four-foot sailing yacht flashed into his mind. "I smell the wind and the ocean breeze." Malik felt the administrator pull the container away, yet the smell was still around him. His body felt relaxed, as if floating on the water, drifting with the gentle waves. Malik had a moment of panic but reminded himself he could be at ease with wherever this current was taking him. The scent faded, and Malik was brought back to the sterile room.

"Is the scent gone?"

Malik inhaled again and couldn't smell anything. "It is. I don't smell it anymore."

"Great. Now, this is the last one."

Malik was excited to see the results of this assessment. He inhaled and got light-headed, imagining himself standing in a large grassy field surrounded by vibrant purple flowers. He could feel the sun warming his thick hair, but his scalp was still cool. "Lavender," he whispered.

"Well done. Now, take a few cleansing breaths before removing your eye mask and opening your eyes."

Malik took deep breaths. He still stood in the large open field, but on the horizon was a tree larger than any he had ever seen. It covered nearly the entire horizon and reached far up into the clouds. At this distance, Malik couldn't identify an individual branch or any leaves. As he focused a little harder, he saw a slight purple glow emitting off the top and around the edges of the tree like a force field.

"Malik."

He heard his name being whispered.

"Malik, take a few more cleansing breaths and come back."

Malik did as instructed and felt himself seated again in the room.

"Well done," the administrator said. "You can take off the mask. I'll be right back."

When the administrator came back in, they handed Malik a circular container small enough to fit into his pocket. It was heavier than expected and intricately engraved on top. The design spiraled out from the center, with a pattern of triangles, pentagons, and five-pointed stars that got larger each time they appeared. The container had seven small squares on the side, each with a different color dot that seemed to follow the sequence of the rainbow.

"This is your pack," the administrator said. "Keep this on you at all times, especially when you are traveling outside of Zone Seven. You shouldn't need this, especially once you get your watch, but you'll want to have it just in case."

"Okay," Malik said, feeling the need to show he was paying attention.

The administrator held one black box. "Each color is tied to your assessment. Will you sniff this?"

Malik glanced inside the box. To his surprise, he saw nothing there. He shrugged and inhaled. Malik's stomach rolled so strongly it was as if he ate something bad during an earthquake. Malik grabbed his stomach. "I smell mint."

"Good, now which of these colored dots do you have an urge to press?"

Malik eyed the blue dot, but was second guessing his decision.

"Don't hesitate. It's based on your intuition."

"The blue one," Malik said and pressed his thumb on the square with the blue dot. A wedge popped open, revealing a small circular blue pill with a spiral design like the container.

"Has anyone explained how the pills work?"

Malik shook his head.

"Your physiology is rooted to an existence where reality resonates at seven hertz. As long as you are there, your body will function properly, assuming that you take care of it. But if you ever spend time in a different zone, then your body may have trouble functioning."

"Don't the watches help with that?"

"They do. That is correct. However, if you stay in a particular zone for an extended period, then your atomic structure will want to change to adapt to the environment. These pills will help in case of any emergencies when your physical body is outside of Zone Seven. If one of your seven programmed smells hits you at the same time as that uncomfortable feeling in your gut, then take a pill."

Malik placed the pill on the tip of his tongue and felt it disintegrate. "That's it? It didn't taste like anything."

"It's not meant to. When you experience a smell accompanied

by that strong feeling, take the first pill that comes to mind. For someone like you, you'll probably most often crave the red pill, which smells of coffee, or the blue pill, which your mind will associate with mint. These two will help temporarily root you into that reality and allow you to communicate." The administrator stood up and walked to the door.

"What about the other pills?" Malik asked as he followed them to the exit.

"You should never be away from your reality long enough to need the others." The administrator opened the door.

Then why give them to me? Malik wondered. "Great, thanks," Malik said. "Also," Malik held the container up, "what is this made of?"

"That's iridium and platinum."

"It's beautiful."

"It's a common design for people from the seventh. We designed it to look like an antique that is pretty enough to return to the owner, but not nice enough to want to steal."

Malik turned the corner and saw his grandma leaning against the wall. There was something different about her. Malik studied her as she lifted herself off the wall and started walking.

"So," she said, "now that your assessment is finished, you are on to the hardest part."

"Which is what?"

"Being patient."

"Meaning?" Malik asked, still trying to understand why his grandmother looked so different.

"Now, all you can do is work to strengthen your connection with source energy. Only once you're ready will you receive instructions for the next phase of your training."

"Practice being present, meditate, do yoga. Is that it?"

"It's about living in the now and becoming aware of your mind so that you are really intentional about what you imagine."

"I think I am intentional." Though even as Malik said it, he felt nervous energy around the idea of being able to manifest anything.

"Well, then perhaps this process will progress quickly for you."

"But… but what if it doesn't?" Malik shook his head. "I wish I could read the journals."

"A few more words of advice?"

"Go ahead."

"Trust the process," his grandma said. "I know you want answers, and I know and appreciate what you are trying to do. Evelyn, Ori, and everyone, they've always done exactly what they've said they would do. You can trust them and this."

Malik said nothing, but he searched her face, then nodded.

"I'll show you out," she said.

"You aren't coming with me?"

"No, I'm going to hang around here for a while."

Then Malik realized what it was—her hair. His grandmother had always aged well. Her skin was smooth, and she kept to a strict exercise regimen, always walking, swimming, or doing yoga. The only way people could guess she was older was through her white hair. But now, her hair was mostly black again, with just some streaks of white, mostly along the bottom.

"Your hair," he said. "It's different. Did you dye it?"

His grandma snorted. "Child, please. Since when do I dye my hair?"

"But…"

"My body first came here when I was pretty young, so whenever I hang around here long enough, my body goes back to that anchoring point."

21

THE CONDUIT REQUIREMENT

MALIK STARTED TOWARD THE PATH HOME BUT WAS FEELING ANTSY about not knowing when his training would progress. *I'm supposed to go back for who knows how long and try not to think about what's next?* This restless energy would not help. He saw the park bench overlooking the coast and decided to have a seat and try to center himself. The view was incredible. Malik watched an eagle soaring in the distant sky until it vanished behind a mountain on the far side of the bay. As he let out a sigh, he noticed the wind creating ripples on the water, which sparkled in the morning sun.

"How was your assessment?"

Malik turned to see Jordan walking up to take a seat next to him.

"Uh, good, I guess." Malik reflected on the unusual experience. "I mean, let's be real. This is all very far out there. I mean... right?"

Jordan laughed. "For you, yeah. Welcome to my world. I go through this so often."

"How do others cope?"

"Most people never take the first step, you know, to see their Lotus."

"Oh, huh."

"Yep. But if they do that and they come to the Point, I guess they just learn to embrace it. Anyone who comes here finishes the program."

Malik felt relieved. "That's good to know." Malik recalled the dream from the previous night. He could smell the sweet sugar in the air like he was in the ice cream parlor and got a deep feeling of sadness in his chest. "I hope the dreams get better."

"I know last night's was rough, Malik."

Malik felt his heart rate increase. "I knew it was you. Why didn't you say anything?"

"There was nothing for me to say. That dream was meant to show you that there are several frequencies impacted by the solar flares, some worse than others."

Malik swallowed. "So that wasn't just a dream?"

Jordan shook her head. "I mean, to this version of you, it was. But not to the other you." Jordan took a breath. "Be happy and grateful that this is the reality in which you're choosing to be aware."

An image of Anatole's daughter running to the mobile ice cream stand flashed in Malik's mind. "The car accident that took Anatole's wife..." Malik paused. "I read that a man under the influence slammed into her while she was parked. Is that how it happened?"

Jordan stared into the distance. "Something like that."

"That poor kid," he whispered, feeling an even stronger sense of compassion for what Anatole's family had gone through.

"Empathy is a powerful thing, isn't it?" said Jordan.

Malik let that sit with him for a minute. Then his mind drifted again to what was ahead. "These dreams seem more and more intense."

"They are probably going to continue that way. Did you get your container?"

"Yeah, I did." Malik pulled the container out of his pocket and ran his thumb along the spiral design. "Why are there seven colors if I'm only going to use one or two?"

"Wait," Jordan said. "Can I see that?"

Malik handed it to Jordan, who inspected the different sides, and then bit her lip before handing it back to him.

"What is it?" Malik asked.

"I knew this would happen. With your background, I figured you and your family would be prime candidates."

"Knew what would happen?"

"It has been a long time since someone from your version of Earth has had an assessment and been assigned all seven pills. It typically only occurs for citizens who go to realities where there is harmful karmic interference with someone who is ready to ascend. These citizens act as guardians."

"Callie mentioned guardians but didn't really say what they do. She just said that they are usually longer-standing citizens."

"Usually, yes," Jordan said. "You can think of them as the anonymous Good Samaritan who saves the day and disappears, or as someone who sets a positive chain of events in motion. If you are destined for that, you'll have missions that ultimately lead to others having profound moments of awareness."

"Why would they already be thinking of that for me?" asked Malik.

"I could think of a couple of reasons. Perhaps it's because you're a legacy recruit."

"Is that rare?"

"Rarer than you might think. In your case, in what seems like a faded dream, you have already helped humanity in ways that you'll probably never fully understand. As a reward for that willingness to help, they granted you special access to beneficial manifestations."

"Did you just use past tense? What beneficial manifestations?"

"Typically, when someone wants to manifest something in their life, it takes time for it to appear in physical form. How long it takes depends on the person's beliefs, thoughts, words, actions, habits, and character. The bigger the gap between…" Jordan moved her hands in a circle, as if thinking of how to express the idea. "The gap between how their being vibrates now versus the ideal frequency of a person who has already received that manifestation dictates the time it takes for the wish to be fulfilled. That's true for you as well, Malik, but they've given you a well-earned advantage."

Malik narrowed his eyes at Jordan, unsure of what to make of what she was saying.

"Haven't you ever noticed that anytime you had a problem you wanted to solve, no matter how difficult, you would have a breakthrough? You'd find inspiration from a news headline or something you read or watched with your child, and then the solution would just unlock?"

"Except the solution to solar sickness," Malik replied.

"That's not a problem you can solve on your own. But your genius seeking the solution is a big part of why you're here right now. That dream you had of being back in New York, do you remember?"

"How could I forget?" Malik's mind went to the sleeping bodies sprawled out as far as the eye could see. "Wait, how did you know about that?"

Jordan tilted her head and gave him a look that said, *Really?* She leaned in. "You are the only one in your world who not only understands that what's happening is solar sickness, but you have been actively searching for a way to overcome it. And look, now you're going to be part of solving that problem too. You've been given a gift that's just going to get stronger. You'll need to protect it."

"By being mindful of my thoughts?"

"Well, yes, but what I meant was limiting who you and your family are exposed to."

"Ah, right. Don't talk to anyone about what I experience here," Malik said.

"You realize that doesn't stop after training? You'll need to be living a life where you really only interact with your family and other Universal Citizens."

Something dawned on Malik for the first time. "So, I would never go back to the Singularity Group?"

"Not actively, no."

"Wow."

"That's the Conduit Requirement. You'll need a lifestyle that limits the chances of receiving requests that are harmful to your family and others," Jordan said. "You gotta remember, solving everyone's problems is not your job. In fact, that creates more chaos. It's easier to remember that when you live your life this way."

"From a sabbatical to the start of a new life." Though he hadn't thought of it this way before, he knew it was right.

The two sat still as Malik thought about all Jordan had said. Instinctively, he took a deep breath and slowly exhaled.

Jordan laughed. "It's kind of funny when you think about it."

"What's that?" Malik asked.

"It's pretty common knowledge, now, that all the physical material you know of makes up just five percent of everything in existence."

"Hmmm." Malik waited to see where she was going with this.

"Do you think the air you breathe is part of the five percent or the ninety-five percent? Is it possible that when you breathe, you're inhaling the same matter that is connected to the entire universe?"

Malik looked up at a blue patch of sky between the clouds.

"Something to think about while you're practicing being still."

"I should probably go get started on that," he said.

"The universe has heard your request. It has given you the answer. Be patient. Stick to the script. Trust the process, and it will all work out."

Malik let her words soak in and nodded his head. The two continued to sit for several minutes, listening to the birds singing in the fruit tree grove behind them.

"Besides," said Jordan, "with your little citizens, I think you'll have plenty of beauty to keep you in the moment."

22

BE THE FLOW

THOUGH MALIK KNEW IT WOULD TAKE TIME FOR HIM TO BE ABLE TO read the journal Ori gave him, he couldn't help but try. He had gone back to disappearing into the office when the kids were asleep for the past couple of weeks. His efforts were futile so far. Malik realized this didn't suit the whole aim of being present, but it distracted him from waiting until he received his next dream and could continue training.

As Malik prepared to take a break for the day, a small body zoomed past the windows. "Nap time must be over," he said to himself. He heard Noah laughing between high-pitched squeals and went closer to the window to see what the family was up to.

"Keep counting!" Noah shouted. "I'm not ready yet."

Malik surveyed the backyard through the floor-to-ceiling glass and saw Jonas covering his eyes by a tree, while Noah tried to hide behind some wild blackberry bushes.

"Ready or not, here I come," Jonas said, pretending not to see the small boy. Malik laughed as he watched Jonas—who was a few feet in front of Noah—spinning around in a circle, calling, "Where are you? I can't find you."

Jonas continued walking until Noah jumped out from behind the bushes. "Here I am, Opa! Since you didn't find me, I get to hide again."

Malik joined them outside to find his mom and Magaly lounging on a blanket with Aries, who was comfortably sitting up by himself, holding a board book in his hands. It seemed like he had just gained this skill a week ago, and now it was hard to remember a time when he couldn't sit by himself.

"He emerges from the cave," his mom teased as he approached.

"Do you wanna show Daddy your book?" Magaly asked the baby.

Malik kneeled next to Aries and tapped the book. "What do you have, little one?"

The little book had a cutout of an owl on the cover, making it easier for Aries to hold. He clutched the cutout, shook the book, and gave Malik a big smile.

"Dad!" Noah came running over. "You should come and check out the garden! We have a lot of tomatoes. I mean a lot, a lot. Like, one million. Right, Nana?"

Nia stood up and said, "Yeah, let's show him." She then addressed Malik. "Noah has been a big help in the garden."

"I'd love to see," Malik said, looking at Magaly to see what she was thinking.

"You guys go ahead," said Magaly. "I'll probably need to feed this one soon anyway."

Now sure that Nia and Malik were close behind, Noah turned and sprinted to the garden. There might not have been a million tomatoes, but Malik could see why Noah was so excited. There were red grape tomatoes all over the vines, looking ready to be picked. "Wow! I am impressed!" Malik meant it.

"If you want to pick some, I bet we can incorporate them into dinner," Jonas said, walking up with a wicker basket in hand.

"I want to pick them, Opa!" said Noah, reaching for the basket, which Jonas handed him with a broad smile. Malik watched as his mom guided Noah around the garden, helping him select tomatoes that were ready.

"This is Nana and Noah time," said Jonas. "You taking a break from work?"

Malik let out a heavy sigh. "I need to. I'm not making much progress."

"Feel like a walk?"

"Sure," Malik said, and the two began a leisurely stroll through the rest of the garden and around the side of the house.

"You know," Jonas said with a sly smile, "I've tried what you are doing now." He exhaled sharply. "Hell, I've been where you are."

"Wh—what do you mean?"

"You know, in my old life, well, in one of my previous chapters, I was a mathematician. I love numbers. There's a real beauty to them, especially fractals. I was recruited out of school into a job that needed a brain like mine." Jonas puffed his chest out and stuck his nose in the air before he let out a laugh and deflated. "A job where we had to solve the problems that no one else could solve. So, I spent a career in an unmarked building, solving super-secret problems." Jonas leaned toward Malik. "And I was one of the very best. I could solve anything. Just leave me alone with my thoughts… Your mom mentioned that you and I had that in common." Jonas squinted as he stared up at the sky, deepening the wrinkles in the corners of his eyes. "I could never decipher those journals in the library."

Malik was silent as he considered what to say next. He was afraid to admit that's what he'd been working on, because he couldn't share why, and he didn't want to lie.

Jonas didn't seem to need confirmation. He continued, "It just looked like simple binary code, albeit a lot. I actually scanned and converted pages and thought I'd be able to translate the code relatively easily. The results made no sense though." Jonas glanced over at Malik. "Either the code is not as simple as it looks, or it changes."

Malik had been encountering the same thing, but again held himself back from saying so. Instead, he asked, "So, what did you do?"

"I realized I was forcing it, and either those journals weren't meant for me, or I just wasn't ready to read them," Jonas said. "I decided not to obsess about them and focused instead on living in flow."

"Living in flow?" Malik asked.

"Yes. First, you just go with the flow and don't force things. And then you've got to learn to be the flow."

"How do I do that?"

"Well, think about what all of it is for. What's your ultimate goal, and what does life look like for you when you've achieved that? Then you live in the end every day."

Malik saw the spark in Jonas's clear green eyes and could feel how much he believed in what he was sharing. "What was that for you?" Malik asked.

"I had been forging a career that put logic on a pedestal above all else. I was lacking connection, emotion, beauty, and I wanted to live a life filled with those things. So, I left that line of work. Instead of being inside an unmarked building every day, I spent my days outside. I read extensively about nature, philosophy, and astrology. Then I just walked through open doors and listened."

"Listened to what?"

"You receive messages in the most peculiar, yet wonderful, ways. And before you know it," Jonas held his arms out around him, "you are living a life where every moment is filled with peace." Jonas looked back at Malik. "It's fascinating really."

"Oh, yeah?"

"It was one decision to listen to something that was calling to me. It took follow through, of course, but it's as though I changed my frequency. Shortly after that, I met your mother, the love of my life." Jonas had led them to the front porch, and as he took a seat in a rocking chair, he extended his hand toward the other, inviting Malik to sit. "Every day is filled with connection, love, beauty. I think we are all connected to this... this source of energy, this life."

"I think I know what you mean," said Malik. "I really see it when I watch the boys. Time doesn't really seem to exist to them, and they just revel in whatever is happening at the moment."

"Oh, absolutely," said Jonas. "I was just talking with your mother about that."

"I mean, when Noah was two or three, the only concept of time was before nap or after nap. That was it. There's no tomorrow or next week. And Aries, I think he fights us so hard during bedtime because he may not have learned yet that tomorrow will come."

"And they bring so much joy to everything."

"So true," agreed Malik.

"It's not exactly the same, but I try to live similarly," said Jonas. "I believe that understanding the universe is a matter of understanding time—to realize that it exists and doesn't exist all at the same time. If you learn to be wise with your time, then you get more of it."

Malik liked that. As the two men fell into a companionable quiet, Malik rocked in the chair and enjoyed the view.

After a moment, Jonas said, "I better go see what bounty our gardeners brought in so I can start dinner. I'll see you inside in a bit?"

Malik nodded and stayed seated, allowing his mind to wander. He reflected on what Jonas had said, "Think about what all of it is for." *For me, this is all for the future, for my children's future, so they can be happy and safe, and so they can become their best selves. If that's my goal, then I should live every day with and for them.* He thought about how fast they're growing and changing, and how much they had already changed him. *Noah.* Malik could hear the squeals and laughs from the backyard, even here. *My first born. Having him has made me go back into my past to understand how it formed me. And Aries, my infant and wise counsel. Observing how he lives completely in the present keeps me open and curious about the world. Noah and Aries will help me stay in a state of flow. And I get to experience it all with my partner and guardian, Magaly. With them, I can be patient.*

23

A GLIMPSE OF THINGS TO COME

JESSICA LAY AWAKE, UNSURE OF THE TIME. SHE GAZED OUT HER bedroom window at the silhouettes of the trees bordering the yard. The light from the sky was just bright enough for her to make out a dark figure swoop down, perch on a distant branch, and blend into the shadows. Her mouth and throat felt dry, so she reluctantly pushed herself up to a seated position and reached for the glass of water on her nightstand. The refreshing liquid cooled her mouth and wet her throat as it made its way down to her stomach. She drained half the glass before returning it to the nightstand.

Jessica slid her feet into her soft slippers. Her knees were not yet warm, and she grimaced as her body and mind worked through the stiffness that had accompanied her age. Jessica paced around her bedroom, keeping her lips sealed as she took a series of deep breaths. She filled her lungs, held her breath until she felt her heartbeat on the left side of her head, flexed her stomach, and slowly exhaled through her nose. With her breathing rhythm established, she strolled through her room until her knees felt limber, her body awake and ready for the day.

The sun had risen just enough for Jessica to see that the creature who had occupied the tree outside had moved on. Feeling a sense of calm, Jessica walked to her nightstand, took a few more sips from the glass of water, and hung her vision glasses around her neck. Jessica sat down in her armchair and braced herself. She liked to know what was going on, but she could never watch for long anymore. Jessica placed the rims over her eyes and secured the pads on the bridge of her nose. She touched the temple and watched the lenses turn dark before displaying an image of a funeral procession.

Jessica slid the ear buds into her ears in time to hear the commentator say, "The general's contributions to ending centuries of war in the Middle East won her a Nobel Peace Prize. Leaders from every nation are in attendance to honor the person who some say is responsible for bringing peace to the Middle East."

Jessica smiled as she thought back to her childhood, when she and her friends would repeat the phrase "Peace in the Middle East" without knowing what it meant. Jessica touched the temple of the frame again. *Next*, she thought, and the image changed to a split screen showing three commentators.

The person on the left side of the screen—a fresh-faced young woman with big, brown, curly hair, wearing a slim fit, blue blazer —was speaking when the feed connected. "The problem is we are continuing to see a rise in deaths from vehicular-related accidents. It's putting a strain on our society, the families of the victims, the automotive industry, as well as the insurance companies. Now is the time for our country to have serious discussions about building our public transportation infrastructure. It's good for the environment, and it will give more people access to higher paying jobs in the city."

On the right side of the screen, another woman had a less formal persona. She had styled her hair in one long, thick braid that rested on the shoulder of her burgundy blouse, right next to a chunky pearl necklace draped around her neck. "These tragic events are, like my counterpart has said, putting a strain on society. Fewer people are buying vehicles, which means fewer people are paying for automotive insurance, so the insurance companies are shelling out enormous sums on these claims, which are disproportionately expensive because they all deal with serious injury. But we need to get to the core of the issue. The question we really need to understand is, why don't people want to get behind the wheel? And the truth is fewer people want to drive for fear of being sued by the family of someone who is injured."

"You mean the family of the victims?" the person on the left interjected.

"Are they victims?" the person on the right asked.

The person in the middle, who must have been a moderator, stayed quiet.

"They are pedestrians, they have the right of way."

"But not if they decide to walk on—"

Jessica touched the temple. *Next,* she thought, and the screen changed to a woman exiting a store, her hands filled with at least a dozen shopping bags. The woman wore sunglasses that covered most of her face. Her jet-black hair was pulled into a tight bun. The scene changed to the same woman, in a red cocktail dress with her hair curling down her back, at an event where someone threw a drink at her. "What is this?" Jessica whispered. *Has someone changed my presets?* The images faded, and the woman was now sitting on a sofa across from a talk show hostess. The woman's green eyes, which seemed wise beyond her years, scanned the hostess, then the crowd, before flirting with the camera. *Not a wrinkle or spot on her,* Jessica mused. The celebrity guest smiled at the crowd, a smile which, though bright, had a practiced look and didn't quite reach her eyes.

"Are you happy that you are retiring and leaving moments like that behind?" asked the hostess.

The woman nodded hesitantly. "I think it's time for a little privacy. You know, I never set out to do this show. In fact, I was really against having people witness every moment of my life. But my life was crazy enough, all the time, that I didn't really have to do anything but let the cameras roll. Once I embraced it, it offered me so many more opportunities than I ever dreamed."

"I'll say. Your show, *The Real Life of Why?* is the most viewed series of all time."

The studio audience applauded and cheered as the interviewee smiled, cupped her hands together at heart center, and bowed.

"What are you going to do first?"

The woman laughed. "I'm going to spend a lot of time somewhere well out of the reach of technology and just unplug."

"Well, you've earned it. Right, folks?" The studio audience cheered again. As the camera panned across the people in the crowd, Jessica's attention was pulled to one person who wasn't cheering or clapping; they were just standing there. The woman had long, dark hair and freckles on her cheeks. *It can't be. Janice?* Jessica thought in disbelief. Before the camera moved on, it looked like the woman was about to crack a smile.

"Wait, please go back. Rewind," Jessica said. But the vision glasses didn't comply. She watched as the reality television star stood up, shook hands with the interviewer, waved at the crowd, and exited the stage.

THE KITCHEN AREA was bustling by breakfast. Jessica could barely keep her eyes on Noah as he ran from room to room, imitating some superhero that she had never heard of before. She considered asking Nia, but she smiled as she realized the child probably had so much going on in his mind, it would be a full-time job to keep it all straight.

"GG," Noah said as he put his hands on her knee. "Did you see that? Did you see my super-speed?"

"Yes, baby, I did!"

"Zoom," Noah said, and darted away again.

Jessica watched the boy disappear around the corner, and then she felt a slight tug on her pant leg. She looked down to see Aries, with a hand full of her pants, trying to pull himself up to a standing position. "Good for you, little one," Jessica said, as she touched the baby's soft hair.

"Look at you!" Magaly cheered. "So strong."

Aries turned to see where that voice was coming from before he flashed a proud smile.

"What's happening?" Nia asked from the other side of the kitchen.

"Aries is pulling up on GG, aren't you, baby?"

"Good job, little one!" Nia beamed at the baby.

Aries's attention was back on Jessica. He reached for her watch and kept touching it with the tip of his finger. "Oh, do you like this?" Jessica asked. "It is really quite shiny." Jessica leaned in as much as she could, which wasn't much, and whispered, "It's also special. One day, you'll have one too."

Aries looked up into her face and smiled once more.

"You understand me, don't you?" Jessica said. "I know you do."

Aries continued touching her watch as she caressed his hair and surveyed the room. Nia and Magaly were chatting and drinking their coffee while Jonas was cooking away, making them something delicious. Jessica spotted Malik outside on the porch, sitting on the floor with his legs crossed. She could see his back elevate, pause, then lower. Elevate, pause, then lower. Jessica, without thinking, inhaled deeply, held her breath, then exhaled until her breathing rhythm was in sync with Malik's. *Just be,* she thought, as she watched her grandson embrace the peace, beauty, and everyday abundance.

"Roaaarrr!" Noah snarled as he jumped in front of her, dressed in a tiger costume. "GG, did you see what Nana and Opa gave me?"

"Isn't that something?" Jessica said, watching Noah crawl on his hands and feet toward the porch.

24

A YEAR OR SO LATER... A TIMEPIECE IS GIVEN

IT HAD TAKEN ABOUT THREE MONTHS, BUT MALIK HAD FIGURED OUT his perfect day. He did not obsess about the journals or worry about when training would continue. Every morning, he woke up early to exercise, meditate, and write in his journal until the kids woke up. He helped prepare breakfast, after which the family took part in some outdoor activity, often selected by Noah. There were so many options on the grounds and in the woods. Once back, while the boys would spend time with Nia and Jonas, Malik and Magaly would read or relax. He had also begun helping in the garden, constructing garden boxes, setting up a new greenhouse, and composting. Each night, the family would cook and eat dinner together, reflect on their favorite parts of the day, then share one thing they looked forward to for the next day. Noah usually had multiple things to share. A year passed this way. Noah leaned out. Aries was walking around, getting into everything. And one morning, Malik went out for a run, and at the edge of the path was Vau.

"Well done," Vau said, as Malik approached him. "How does it feel to own your time?"

"It's pretty beautiful," Malik replied.

"A valuable currency. You look good, friend."

"Thanks, but I still haven't had any more dreams."

"Soon," Vau said. "I don't want to interrupt, but after your run, come to the command center."

"Okay, will do." An extra surge of energy made Malik's run go by faster today, and he finished it at the Point. At the command center, he went to the same room where he'd had his first session with Callie. It seemed to be back on Evelyn's settings.

Tony walked in with a wooden box in his hands. He placed the box on top of the elevated desk. "Alright, Malik. Glad to see you back. Today you get to spend time with none other than," Tony used both thumbs to point to his chest, "this guy." Tony lifted a jet-black bangle out of the box. "Today, we will cover the most important things to understand about this."

Malik leaned forward to get a better view. It was polished to a shine, and at first, Malik believed what he saw was light reflecting off it. Upon closer inspection, he realized that the light on the bracelet was moving along and through it. Unsure if they were electric volts or something else, Malik stepped back.

"Don't worry, it won't hurt you," Tony said as he used both hands to stretch the bangle out so it was flat, like an old snap bracelet they used to give out as carnival prizes. "Your wrist, please?"

Hesitantly, Malik extended his left wrist. Tony raised his hand with the bracelet up and swung it down fast. Malik clamped his eyes shut, expecting a painful impact, but he felt nothing.

Malik opened his eyes to Tony grinning at him. "You need to relax."

Tony gently lay the bracelet on Malik's skin, and the cool sensation was soothing. It stayed flat, resting there for several moments as vibrant pink, violet, and blue strands streaked across the black. Then Malik watched it melt and wrap around his wrist. Once secured, it became transparent, allowing Malik to see the brown of his skin through the nearly clear wristband.

"It's almost done calibrating," Tony said. Then it became black again and the smooth edges morphed to appear like a standard rubber watch band. There was also now a watch face, and Malik studied it as Tony continued to speak. "Ah, it looks good. Your timepiece is for beginning travelers. You have two sub-dials, one dial that roots you to your home location, the other for where you need to be for an assignment. As you learn more about other locations and as you travel more, additional dials will be added."

Malik compared his watch to Tony's, which had four sub-dials. Both watches had the glistening gears and radiating lights he had seen on his grandma's and Callie's watches. "How does it work?"

"There are thousands of lightning storms happening at any point in time on the planet. If you were to zoom out and see Earth in its entirety, you would see forty to fifty lightning flashes per second. All this electrical activity creates electromagnetic waves between Earth's surface and the ionosphere. There are infinite realities that you'll have access to along a vibrational frequency between seven and eight hertz."

Malik was familiar with resonant frequency, so he nodded Tony along.

"So, for the watch, first, you enter the frequency of the destination." Tony tapped his finger on the sub-dial that was sticking out of the top right corner, then twisted the bezel that wrapped around the face of the timepiece. He held his hand out to show Malik the face of the watch, which now displayed the number 7.11. Tony pulled his watch back and continued, "Then you confirm that your rooted location is accurate. For you, that's seven point eight three." He tapped on a different sub-dial and twisted the bezel again. "Once you have confirmed those things and are in a nice secluded green space, then you press your finger anywhere on the face, inhale deeply, and wait."

Tony followed his own instructions and whispered as he exhaled, "If you have a visual of where you're going, that helps too. Make the image as vivid as possible. If there are landmarks, see them up here." Tony—his eyes still closed—pointed to the side of his head near his temple. Thick white clouds filled the outside edges of the room, rolling closer toward Tony. As they reached his feet, Tony removed his finger from his watch and opened his eyes. "That's about it." The clouds evaporated in a split second.

"Now," Tony's tone became serious, "it's important to be firmly rooted to a location. That way, if something goes wrong, for whatever reason, then you will go back to that location by default. That's why you went through your assessment and why you needed to establish ownership of your time." Tony pointed to Malik's watch. "What's on your wrist is not just a tool to tell time; it's a timepiece. This mechanism adjusts your atomic structure so your physical body can travel to the frequency your mind desires. It allows you to travel to where and when you want to go. And this is not the only way that you'll travel, so I probably ought to back up."

"Okay. My grandma and Callie have only told me a little, so I'm all ears."

"There are three safe ways to travel to a reality other than your own. The first way is through your dreams. In the beginning, this was really the only way to travel. Well, for most people. The second way to travel has been through some man-made mechanism."

"Like a time machine?" Malik asked.

Tony frowned. "It allows more than just traveling through time. We are talking about the multiverse…" He paused and tilted his head to one side, as if contemplating an idea. "I guess you can think of it like time travel, since some versions of reality are at different stages of progression than others. So, yes, for the sake of simplicity, let's just say a time machine. And third, a direct connection to the network."

"What is that?"

"Don't get too excited. I haven't seen it happen in my time with the team. Thousands of years ago, your brains could hone into other frequencies of existence at will. Over time, that reduced to a small percentage of people, mainly artists. Now, people seem to have lost this ability altogether. But there are life-forms that exist simultaneously in multiple dimensions, like fungi and other microscopic living things that are critical for life on the planet. It's possible for people to connect through that."

"Through consumption?"

"That's one way, which is why in some ancient civilizations, like Egypt, only royalty could consume fungi. Anyway," Tony continued, "those are the three potential ways to travel, but it's really two: through dreams and through some form of technology. They tasked me with creating a better piece of technology because older versions were clunky, attracted a lot of attention, and sometimes failed, stranding travelers."

"This is pretty slick," Malik said, admiring the timepiece.

Tony looked like he was trying to hold back a smile. "There are advantages and disadvantages to both types of travel, so we will talk about them and which form of travel to choose, depending on the situation. Let's talk about dreams first, which require access to information about your destination."

"Is that what the library of books is for?" Malik asked.

"Exactly. You will use those to gain insight and detail about different locations."

"I'm still unable to understand them."

"Yeah, that takes a while. Once you are ready, it will happen. You can't rush that."

"Alright," Malik said, giving an affirmative nod.

"Before you read, you set your intention of being in the target destination. Remember, it's all about the details. As you read about the place, you will fall asleep, and your conscious and subconscious mind will transport you there."

"So, the library is for dream travel?"

"Actually, reading the texts and researching the destinations are critical for both forms of transport. You've got to know what to expect. You'd stand out if you didn't have a basic understanding of shared knowledge. But, if you travel via dreams, there are several things to note. One, it is critical that you do not make physical contact with anyone there, anyone who is not wearing one of these." Tony held up the watch. "If someone tries to touch you and they realize you don't have a physical body, then your cover is blown."

Malik nodded in understanding.

"The other thing about traveling to realms via dreams is that if you are killed or die publicly, then when you wake up, it will feel like an awful nightmare. That energy will impact how you feel and how you are in the reality where you are rooted. If you are in danger, it's better to wake up rather than stay to defend yourself."

"Why can't we defend ourselves?" Malik asked.

"You can, but it takes training to manage that well. Your minds are so powerful that trying to defend yourselves could create too much attention." Tony narrowed his eyes. "Imagine if someone were to fire a weapon at you. You might instinctively throw up your hands to shield yourself. Your subconscious would interpret that as not enough. I've seen someone pull an entire brick wall in front of them to stop a bullet." Tony shook his head. "That was a lot of cleanup... Got it?"

"Got it."

"Now, let's talk about traveling into someone else's dream."

"Is that something I might do?"

"Yes. And for this, it's all a matter of brain frequencies. The trick to it is that you have to find the best frequency to travel to. Once you have that, you plug it into your destination sub-dial, then you drift off to sleep."

Something about this made Malik nervous. He remembered some of them appearing in his dreams, but it hadn't occurred to him he might do that too.

Tony's voice brought Malik back to the lesson. "If you are going to enter someone's dream, you must be sure to get the exact frequency where they are most likely to cooperate with and be accepting of your presence. The subconscious is very protective and will attack."

"How will it, uh, the subconscious, know?"

"Whatever you think about while in someone else's dream will appear in the dream. Their subconscious will realize something is off and move to rectify things. That is why recruits are first taught to clear their minds and be present. When in another person's dream, if your thoughts intrude, just focus on your breath. That's the best way, in my humble opinion, to clear your mind. Got it?"

"Yes, I believe so. But where do I find a specific location for someone else's dream? Are they in the journals as well?"

"Ha, no way. They are always changing, and there are literally infinite possibilities. Certain beings high," Tony held his hand above his head to illustrate his point, "and I mean high, up there have them."

"Okay."

"Cool." Tony continued, "One last thing on functioning in the dream state. If you decide to engage, just be aware that it is incredibly taxing on your mind. The more engagement, the more fatigued your mind will be when you awaken. If you do this too often, it will impact your ability to function in the reality in which you are rooted. This could impact the strength of your connection and how well you are rooted. That's where your capsules come in."

Malik reached into his pocket and pulled out the circular metal container with seven colored dots.

"That's it," Tony said. "Depending on what you smell, take the corresponding color."

"Okay, so when would I travel in a dream state?"

"Only when you need to observe things or act as additional inspiration. Never when you need to have physical interaction. When that's needed, we have these." Tony pointed to his watch. "I made these watches from a special compound that is no longer found on the planet. When you adjust the dial to the destination frequency, the compound of the watch combines with the energy that your body naturally has and sends signals through the earth itself. Your atomic structure at your resonant frequency comes apart and then is reassembled to the frequency of the destination. This process consumes a lot of energy and can be hard on the body, which is why we require a moist conductor like the mist of the forest or a nearby body of water. We also prefer you not to travel to a place where the forest and waters are depleted."

"These timepieces not only allow your safe travel to other dimensions, but they also allow you to identify other citizens. You get to choose what people see when they look at your wrist." Tony passed his hand over his watch. The gears, bezel, and sub-dials of the skeleton watch disappeared and were replaced with a black rubber band and a calculator. "This doesn't attract any attention, but it can become whatever you imagine. The point is, you can conceal it from people."

Tony clapped his hands together. "So, what if you need to physically travel to a place to guard or protect someone? These are usually special missions that have been approved by the Council and assigned. The advantage here is you won't have to worry about physical interaction rules and all that stuff. If anyone remembers anything, then we can clean all the details. It is much easier to operate when you don't have to worry about being exposed. Although, we ask that you try not to do something wild in front of a large crowd of people. If there's no way around it, let me know, and I can disrupt all electronic devices."

"To make cleanup easier?"

"People love to record everything. Disabling devices in advance is more efficient."

"Got it."

"You've got a family, so the next thing is big. Travel takes place between three o'clock and five o'clock in the morning where you're rooted. Sometimes you can go as early as two o'clock. You'll have two to three hours to handle what you need, which is plenty of time. One hour equals one day with physical travel, and most missions are less than two to three days. So, the world that you are rooted in shouldn't know any difference. However, if something happens, and you are detained for any reason, then you won't be home when your family wakes up in the morning."

Malik's chest tightened as the severity of this lifestyle sank in. He never imagined a scenario in which his family would expect him home, and he would not be there. "Okay," Malik said. "How do I make sure that never happens? I need to make it home every time."

"Do all the right prep and planning, and it should never be an issue," Tony replied.

"And what if I need to do something outside of those hours?"

"You can make a special request to Gabriel and Aja, and we'll establish an appropriate cover for your family." Tony held up his finger. "Again, if you think you are going to be on assignment longer than the two hours or outside of that window, make sure you take your supplements. The same rules apply. They will help keep your mind, body, and spirit together until you can get back to the place where you are rooted."

"Do you ever encounter others on these missions, besides who you're traveling with?"

"We could assign you to correct someone who is interfering with others. Those people typically stay up late or sleep very little."

"Will they be able to identify us?"

"Only other people with watches will identify you until you let someone know who you are."

"If other recruits or citizens can identify us by these, are we at risk of them telling others?" Malik asked as his fingertips felt the cool, sleek watch face.

"No one who can see these will jeopardize your identity."

"How do you know?"

"Because it's the law of nature," Tony said.

Malik raised his eyebrows, unsure of how that applied here.

"If someone wishes something that you don't want for yourself, then that goes back and happens to them," Tony explained. "If you don't want to be exposed and someone tries to expose you, then any secrets they are hiding, no matter how tightly concealed, will be revealed. The universe has your back," Tony said with a smile. "Okay, what next?"

"Are you still not done?" Malik heard Jordan's voice from behind him and turned to see her waiting in the doorway.

"Almost," Tony said. "Why?"

"Vau needs you."

"For what?"

Jordan shrugged.

Tony rolled his eyes. "You know he's just doing this to mess with me, right?"

Jordan grinned. "I know."

Tony looked back at Malik. "One last thing. Right now, since you haven't learned how to decipher your library, you won't be able to travel with intention through your dreams. What you can do is this: Within the first few minutes after you wake up, glance down at the two locator sub-dials. You will recognize which one you are rooted to, then it's always fun to see where your mind traveled to."

"You *would* call that fun," Jordan said.

Tony shook his head and sighed. "Alright, class dismissed."

25

THE SHIP

THE SUN'S GLARE OFF THE WATER WAS BLINDING. MALIK RAISED HIS hands to get relief from the bright yellow light. *Where am I?* he questioned as beads of sweat collected on his forehead. He shifted his body forward, but something was gripping him in place. Malik glanced down to see that he was wearing a seatbelt. *Breathe,* Malik coached himself as he inhaled deeply and exhaled slowly. *What is the last thing I remember?* Malik's mind locked onto the glass of red wine he had while sitting on the back deck watching the sunset. He rubbed his fingers together as he remembered the sensation of the cool, slender stem. Malik could see Magaly throwing her head back, laughing as they talked. *I went to bed last night. This is a dream.* Malik relaxed a little with that realization.

"Good," a voice came to him as Malik surveyed his surroundings. He was sitting in a parked car on top of a steep cliff that overlooked two large concrete domes. They stood around two stories tall, and the blinding light was reflecting off the ocean in the background. *Is that the old nuclear facility near San Clemente?* Malik guessed. *San Onofre?* Malik saw several workers walking around below. *Impossible.* Malik studied the area. *Those were decommissioned, and the domes were demolished when I was a boy.* Malik remembered it vividly because his father had worked on the project for so long that Malik and his mother had flown out for an entire summer. He had fallen in love with the California weather, but that was also when he saw the cracks in his parents' marriage.

The voice spoke to him again. "Good, Malik. What else do you see?"

"Who are you?" Malik asked, moving closer to the speaker on the door.

"It's me, Ori. I'm not in the door. Also, you don't have to speak aloud. You don't want people to pay you any unnecessary attention."

"So, you're just a voice in my head right now?"

"And as usual, I can hear your thoughts."

"But why are you so loud? It sounds like you are in this car with me."

"Because," Ori explained, "your senses and your connection with the universe are amplified when you are functioning outside of where you are rooted. But listen, this dream is important for your training. Stay focused."

"Okay."

"Practice not speaking."

Oh, right.

"Better," Ori said. "Now, listen. I'll also come around if things get very intense and you need some guidance. You are doing well so far. Just be patient and observant."

What do I do after that?

"Don't worry. It will happen to you. Remember, we are still in a diagnostic phase, meaning this will tell us the other areas in which you need to be trained. Now, focus."

With those words, Malik sat back, took another deep breath,

and noted everything he saw. In the passenger seat, he noticed a laptop bag with a laminated document on top, which, upon inspection, appeared to be some marketing material. Malik turned to see several boxes in the back seat and a navy-blue sports coat hanging from a hook above the passenger side window. Seeing the coat reminded Malik of how hot he was. He extended his finger to press the button to start the car and was surprised to feel a set of keys there, hanging from the ignition.

Strange. Malik turned the key and was thankful for the gust of cold air being pumped from the dashboard. There was a new car smell to the vehicle, yet it was using a key for the ignition. He also noticed there was a fuel gauge and no battery charge status.

Okay, maybe the global warming regulations have not been implemented here. Malik glanced back toward the gigantic domes, but they had vanished. In their place was a large cargo ship. And Malik was no longer parked on a cliff in California, but was now in a shipping yard.

Malik spoke. "Wh-what is—"

Ori's voice rang out again. "Random scene changes are common in these dreamlike states. Your rational mind doesn't fully comprehend, but your subconscious mind knows what to do. To strike a balance, first your mind will take you someplace the rational part can make sense of. If you are patient enough, you will then be pulled to the appropriate location."

As soon as Ori finished those words, Malik saw movement out of the corner of his eye. There was a man wearing black pants, a white short-sleeve shirt, and a black tie. The man, who was maybe in his fifties, had gray hair, a thick mustache, and black-framed glasses.

"Dave?" Malik whispered, not sure how he knew that. He unbuckled his seat belt and opened the door to greet the man.

"Malik, we are so glad you could come," the man said as he extended his hand to Malik.

Malik was about a head taller, but he got a look at the man's credentials—which were attached to a strange black belt—to confirm that his name was, in fact, Dave.

"How was the trip here? I'm glad that you could come. All these guys can talk about are those smoothies."

Smoothies. Right. Malik nodded as a sales pitch came to his mind. "The trip wasn't so bad. I'll take any reason to get near the water. What are you guys working on these days? Still top secret?"

"Oh, you know it," Dave said with a smile. "This ship just got in yesterday, and the first thing my team of engineers asked for was to get more of your company's smoothie powder."

"I brought several boxes with me." Malik opened the door to the back seat and then pressed a button on his key to pop the trunk. "I even have more in the trunk."

"This is great. Yeah, we have to ship back out as soon as we can." Dave turned and nodded over to a young man with matching attire who was waiting off in the distance. Taking his cue, the young man pushed a cart over to the car, and in a matter of minutes, unloaded all the boxes and disappeared near the ship.

"Would you like to come aboard?" David asked. "My boss has been asking to meet you."

"Sure…" Malik said. His vision instantly blurred, and he found himself in an office, standing across from a dark brown desk and a black chair that was facing away from him. Those were the only items of color in the otherwise white room. Malik suddenly felt uneasy about being on this strange vessel, not knowing how to escape. He heard a loud cackling laugh that seemed to come from the walls. Then a different man Malik did not recognize turned around in the chair.

The nameplate on the desk simply said David. He reclined in the chair and put his feet on the desk. His demeanor seemed both hostile and suspicious. "So you are the sales rep, huh?"

Malik forced a smile. "That's right, I am."

"It's a great product," David said. "My crew is hooked on the stuff." He pulled his feet off the desk and leaned forward, now placing his elbows on the desk.

Malik didn't know what to do, so he simply nodded his head and glanced around the room to avoid direct eye contact.

"What's in it?"

I have no clue, was Malik's first reaction, but as he opened his mouth to speak, a string of rehearsed lines about vitamins, minerals, organic, and sustainable spilled out.

David stared at Malik without saying a word. The door behind Malik opened, and he felt movement on both sides of him. The loud cackling laugh rang out again. Puzzled, he was about to ask David if he'd heard that sound until the man spoke again. "Out there, my guys are exposed to many elements, and those solar flares do something to them. But," David reached down under the table and pulled out a clear bag of turquoise powder, "this smoothie mix keeps them strong."

"That's good news, right?" Malik was hesitant as he shifted his gaze to view the two bodies standing in his peripheral vision.

"It's better than good," David said. "My guys have had so much energy that we've started a new pastime. Do you fight, Malik?"

"Excuse me?" Malik asked, and before he knew it, he was in a cafeteria filled with men, all dressed in black slacks, white shirts, and black ties. The men were huddled around a circle, and Malik could hear the punches. Suddenly, as if they all felt Malik's presence, the men stopped and calmly turned his way. Two sprinted toward Malik, and when they were a few feet away, he thrust the palm of his hand up toward the men as if it were a shield. The two men were thrown through the air, clear across to the far end of the mess hall. The crowd watched the flight trajectory, and then turned their attention back to Malik, and the entire group sprinted toward him.

"That's enough," a voice called out, and Malik saw flames burst out of the kitchen area to his side. Malik's body vibrated as if there were an explosion, and everything went black. Malik opened his eyes and immediately checked his wrist. One sub-dial displayed the number 7.83; the other showed 7.81839.

26

DEFENSE TRAINING

Malik enjoyed having his morning coffee on the covered patio overlooking the valley below. The boys were already outside. Aries was toddling along, doing his best to chase his big brother around the playground equipment that Malik and Jonas had installed. Noah climbed up the jungle gym and was preparing to go down the slide, while Magaly patiently moved behind Aries, ready to spot the fearless child who was constantly testing his climbing abilities. As Aries placed his hands on the round metal ladder, he stopped midstep with his head tilted toward the sky. Aries pointed and Malik followed the toddler's fingers to identify what caught his attention.

"Fa," the boy uttered.

Magaly kneeled behind him to gain the same perspective.

"Fa, fa," Aries said again.

"That's right, I see the falcons too. Very good." Magaly encouraged him.

Then the pair of raptors came into Malik's view as well, at first circling above, then swooping down into a pine tree that bordered the yard.

"I haven't seen them in a while," said Malik's grandma, joining him on the patio. She sat in the open chair next to him and looked out at the trees. "You may want to finish your coffee. It looks like someone is waiting for you."

Malik looked down under the canopy and saw Jordan there, barely visible in the shade of the trees. They rarely came this late in the morning, so he wasn't sure what to expect. He finished the last of his coffee and started off to meet with Jordan.

"Daddy," Noah yelled as he slid down the slide and ran to Malik's side. "Are we going on a walk today?"

"Not this morning, buddy."

"Ah, man," Noah said in disappointment.

Malik squatted down to be at eye level. "When I get back, we'll do something extra fun."

"Can we watch live animals?"

That was Noah's way of asking to watch nature documentaries. Malik hugged the wriggly five-year-old. "Of course we can."

"Hey, no hugs. I'm a big boy now."

"My mistake," Malik said as he let the boy go.

"Daddy." Noah looked around, something he did when he was stalling, trying to think of a question.

"Yes?" Malik waited patiently as his son surveyed the area, looking for inspiration.

"Did you see that ant mound?" Noah pointed to the ground behind Malik.

"I did not," Malik said. "That's a big one."

"Do you think those are fire ants or leaf-cutter ants?"

"I can't be sure."

"We should watch something about ants soon."

"Sounds good to me. Can you do me a favor?" Malik spotted Aries making his way toward them. "I need you to go distract your brother."

"I can do that! See ya later, Dad!" Noah darted past Aries. The toddler turned too quickly as his brother passed by and fell on the grass. Malik watched long enough to see Aries push himself back up onto his feet and give chase.

As Malik got within earshot of Jordan, he asked, "Should I have come to the command center this morning?"

"No, you haven't missed anything. We analyzed your dream though," Jordan replied.

"Wait, don't I need to be there?"

"No, we always look at it ahead to prepare." She seemed to stare up at the two Merlin falcons still perched on a branch in the tree. "I guess it is what it is."

"What does that mean?"

"It means you get defense training. Sorry it couldn't be earlier in the morning."

"Sounds good, and that's okay." Malik was actually relieved, given his dream last night.

"It's been a long time since someone was allowed to have defense capabilities directly taught to them." Jordan turned and led Malik in a new direction.

Malik treaded behind her, sensing she didn't want to talk today. When they exited the woods, they came to a set of metal bleachers next to a lush green field.

"Wait here."

Malik called after her. "For how long?"

"Be patient!" she yelled over her shoulder before she disappeared into a white cloud.

Malik sat on the bleachers and waited for someone to show up. For a moment, he half expected a pickup game of football to start. To take his mind off the waiting, Malik watched the tops of the trees sway as the wind picked up speed. When he remembered the mob of men running toward him, his body tensed. The whistling of the wind brought his attention back to the treetops. It was odd because he felt only a gentle breeze on the field, but the trees were bent at a forty-five-degree angle by what must have been much more powerful gusts of wind.

Then Malik heard the loud cackle from his dream and from somewhere else he couldn't place. He turned around, expecting to see someone behind him, but he was all alone. When Malik was facing the field again, he spotted someone he didn't know in the distance. The man emerged from the woods that bordered the far end of the pitch and walked up to the bleachers.

The man came to a stop in front of Malik and stood in a parade rest position, with his legs shoulder-width apart, elbows bent, hands behind his back. "Malik, my name is Silas. Today, you will learn how to defend yourself. The reason I've asked you to come out to this pitch is twofold. One, you will get a feeling for the best terrain for defense mode. Two, when going up against the ego, there is a high likelihood of some embarrassment. Here, there won't be many witnesses. Now," Silas paced along the front of the stands, his arms still behind his back, occasionally making eye contact with Malik, "typically, recruits are assigned another teacher to help develop their physical strength."

Another teacher? Malik felt slightly panicked, wondering if he had missed something.

"If you haven't been given any…" Silas searched for the words, and continued, "opportunity to receive strength and conditioning training, that means your current routine is sufficient, and you are encouraged to continue doing what you are doing." Silas returned to his parade rest position. "Your commitment to developing physical strength, flexibility, and mobility is not a suggestion, but mandatory. Body, mind, and soul. Now, get up and face me."

Malik stood up and held his chin up like he had seen in movies, doing his best to imitate a soldier in basic training.

"Learning to defend yourself is a critical part of your training, given your dream. It will come in handy in the physical worlds you will visit, as well as in any dreams you'll need to enter."

I hope that's not the norm, Malik thought, still able to feel the hostility.

"In most physical worlds you visit, there are rules, beliefs, ideals, norms that a society lives by. There are systems in place to ensure that everyone lives and functions according to what is believed to be acceptable. Anyone who behaves in a manner outside of the agreed-upon standards is likely to be attacked. This attack could be carried out by individuals or by the entire system itself. In a previous life, that's how I was used."

Malik watched as Silas stared down at the ground in front of him, lost in a memory. Silas grimaced, then regained his composure.

"Dreams, Malik, are not so different. Your subconscious, which runs the dream world, allows things to happen based on the rules and knowledge established by each person's belief system. When you enter a dream, the people, the buildings, the locations, all of that will be created based on what the dreamer has witnessed in waking hours. But your subconscious is infinitely more powerful than the waking mind and cannot be bound by the limited perspective of the conscious mind. So our dreams, no matter how rationally programmed a person is, can be so surreal. That gives room for flexibility. However," Silas raised his index finger, "you must remember each person is their own creator. The subconscious mind is the conduit for all creative ideas. If the subconscious mind senses an outside force interfering with its ability to create, then it will attack."

"What would be considered interfering?"

"Telling it what to create. Ego sum."

"Pardon?"

"I am," Silas replied. "That obnoxious laugh you heard before I arrived? That wasn't the first time you've heard it, was it?"

Malik shook his head. "No."

"I saw your dream. You heard it once you boarded the ship, correct?"

"That's right."

"You and I have something in common," Silas said. "We both gained our awareness in realities where the ego, that very core part of each being, loves and feeds on conflict. For you to be successful, it is important to be aware of the ego to control it. The very nature of your work will spark excitement in not just your ego, but also in the minds of those with whom you interact."

"How so?"

"Think about how much attention is paid to things that are wrapped in controversy and drama. A great movie wouldn't be great without pain and conflict, right?"

"I—I don't know about that."

"You don't have to believe me. Your dream said it all. Without even knowing it, there is a part deep inside of you that expects drama. And because you expect it, you will find it. You will overcome it, of course, but that's why we have this training."

"What can I do to avoid unnecessary conflict?"

"Becoming aware of it is the first step."

"And then?"

"Anytime you feel yourself expecting conflict in a situation that hasn't happened yet, change your thinking. Imagine that things will go smoothly. Acknowledge to yourself that your mind, your ego, is causing unnecessary drama."

"Hmmm, and that works?" Malik asked.

"Why don't you practice it and see?" Silas tilted his head forward slightly. "Don't imagine the worst potential outcome. It's rarely ever that."

"And if I master that, will I still need defense training?"

"It will still be beneficial. Many beings have not learned this lesson and are unaware of how powerful the ego is. This is also why we never tell a target what to do or what to create. We only plant ideas into someone's mind."

"Provide inspiration?"

"That's right. Then trust that their subconscious and conscious mind recognize the relevancy of the clues and are moved to nurture that idea and create." Silas motioned for Malik to move to the side of the field.

"Okay, so don't expect conflict, and don't tell someone what to do or create," Malik said to show his understanding as he walked to where Silas had shown. "But just in case, you'll still prepare me for something like last night?"

"Yes. That dream was grounded pretty firmly in reality, but a dream attack could look like anything. Especially with all the dark images some people consume." Silas inhaled sharply. "That's why we must get you ready, starting with the basics." He stood a few feet in front of Malik. "Put your fists in the air in a defensive pose."

When Malik's fists were up, Silas gave his next command. "Focus your eyes on me and tuck your chin into your chest."

Once Malik did as instructed, the surrounding scenery changed. The air became thick and somehow tangible. "Elbows up," Silas shouted.

Malik's elbows were already up, but he flapped his arms out as if to loosen his shoulders. In reality, he wanted to test a theory. In trying to lift his elbows, Malik felt a slight force against his arms, requiring more engagement from his back muscles. *The air, it's resisting my movement.*

"Good idea, Malik," Silas said. "Try to move your arms and shoulders. Do you feel that? What does it feel like?"

Malik grunted. "It's like trying to move in water, but less dense."

"Yes, when you get into a defensive position, your body can physically tap into and manipulate dark matter. That's what you're feeling. Now, focus your eyes on me."

Malik locked his gaze on Silas's chin. For a moment, Malik's vision went dark before vibrant strands of color appeared. Malik thought of his first arrival at the command center, as well as his former office at the Singularity Company.

"Just breathe," he heard Silas say. "It will be back soon."

As Silas finished his sentence, Malik's vision returned, but it was now dramatically enhanced. He could make out every detail of Silas from the patches of gray in his stubble to the insect that had just landed on the side of his neck. Malik could even see the red thorax of the tiny fruit fly. Although Silas was clear, there was a hazy aura around him.

"You probably notice that everything but your perceived threat is now slightly blurry. You've successfully synced into your defense network. Any time there's a threat, this is how they will appear to you."

"What if there's more than one threat?" Malik asked.

"All threats, regardless of the number, will be identified." Silas turned from Malik and took twenty large paces away.

Malik's field of vision widened as the distance grew. Silas then assumed a position with his back foot pointing off to the side, dug into the ground by about an inch, while his front leg was pointing toward Malik. *He's bracing himself for impact*, Malik thought.

"Alright, with an open palm, feel the force that is the dark matter. Allow your rational mind to grasp that this is now something you can manipulate."

Malik made small circles with the palms of his hands and saw what looked like ripples of clear water with every circular motion.

"Good. Now try to slap me on the chin."

With Silas several meters away, Malik wasn't sure what to do.

"Don't overthink it. Just take a swing at my face," Silas barked.

Malik shrugged and whispered, "Alright." He loosened his right shoulder, made another small circle with that open palm, pulled back, and then threw his arm forward, not holding back. His pectoral and shoulder muscles burned with the strain, as if he were at the end of an excruciating workout. Malik watched as the ripple he created actually struck Silas on the chin, though Silas didn't budge. To make matters worse, the ripple ricocheted back and hit Malik's hand with a startling force. It spun him to the side and had him bending over, squeezing his wrist between his legs to dull the pain.

Silas had come to his side and patted his back. "The pain will go away shortly. Sometimes, the best way to learn a lesson is by experiencing it firsthand. If you try to attack someone unprovoked, there are repercussions. Only in missions where you have received explicit approval are you ever able to strike someone without aggressive provocation. But even then, you must do so intending to cause the least amount of harm possible. You will feel all that you put out there, which is why your strength and conditioning are important. Regardless of where you are or when you are, tapping into and using dark matter is taxing on the body."

With the pain now gone, Malik stood up. "How do I use this, then?"

"Good question," Silas said with a smile. "Don't let me get close to you."

With that, Silas jogged to the far end of the field. He then broke into an all-out sprint toward Malik, who panicked, trying to figure out his options. Silas was only a few steps away when Malik lifted his hand from his side up in the air. A chunk of earth flew up from the ground, connecting with Silas's chin, elevating him several feet into the air before he flopped on the ground.

Malik ran over and extended his hand to Silas, who shook his head and laughed as he sat up. "Great job, Malik. You can use anything to prevent the threat from reaching you. Using a part of the scene, like earth, or concrete, or something lying around is great because it requires less cleanup for Tony. It's important to be creative. Your goal is to not be noticed."

"Wouldn't even this look unnatural?"

"Only citizens will really see what actually happened. Anyone else will explain it away. Maybe there was a hole in the field, or a rock they didn't see." Silas shrugged. "Who knows what their minds will create? It's only when you don't use parts of the scenery do people get suspicious. Then you are exposed and have to abandon that role."

"And that applies whether I'm in another reality or in someone's dream?" Malik asked.

"Yeah, and when you've entered a dream, situations like this should only arise with other characters in the dream. You never want conflict with the dreamer themselves."

"Can they be hurt?"

Silas stood up and dusted himself off. "No, but if the impact is strong enough, then they would wake up. That means the game is over for you. The dreamer's subconscious will deem you as a threat, and that makes it incredibly difficult to accomplish anything. Remember," Silas continued, "our job is to play a role, one that is in the background. To the people out there," Silas waved his hands past the field's tree line, "think of yourself as an extra in their movie."

"Why?"

"Because it is their world, their reality." Silas pointed at Malik. "You trying to be a main character is someone else's life is an opportunity for the ego to run rampant, and we know where that gets us."

"Unconfined ego." Malik turned to see Jordan walking out of the woods. "It causes people to do unthinkable things."

"You're back?" Silas asked.

"I'm here with instructions. Tomorrow morning, we're gonna see how Malik does at tracking and evading."

What does that mean? Malik looked back and forth from Jordan to Silas, hoping that someone would explain.

"I'll meet you in the woods early tomorrow," Jordan said. "Time to see how well you move."

27

REVERENCE AND MOUNTAIN LIONS

THE NEXT MORNING, MALIK DID HIS EARLY MORNING YOGA AND meditation and then ran into the woods before dawn to meet Jordan. Yesterday had been physically taxing, and he wanted to make sure he was loose for whatever training was ahead of him. Jordan met him at the trailhead, and if he didn't know better, he'd think she was looking forward to today.

He greeted her with a "Morning!"

"Mmm-hmmm," she said. "Are you ready?"

"I think so. Where are we headed?"

Jordan ignored his question and squared off in front of him. He felt a warm sensation across his chest, as if he were standing in front of an oven. She then circled around him. "Every creature gives off energy. Warm-blooded creatures give off heat signals."

"And cold-blooded creatures give off cold signals."

"That's right."

Malik tried to keep eyes on Jordan as she stalked around him.

"But, as with everything in this new world you're entering, there is an additional layer. Intelligent beings that are rooted and meant to exist physically in the world in which you are present also give off warm energy."

"Okay."

"That heat you are feeling, that's your brain picking up my signal. I, too, am rooted here."

Malik felt a burst of cold air on his back and pivoted around to see Callie.

She winked and gave him a big grin. "What's up, Malik?" Her hair was braided down each side, and she had on a black outfit with reflective stripes.

"And cold air," Jordan continued, "is emitted by beings who are not rooted in that version of reality. So, Malik, you ready for a little hide and seek?"

"Sure," he replied. He had a lot of practice with hide and seek, but he had a feeling this would be a touch more difficult than playing with Noah.

"You feel Callie's energy? If you focus on her, you should be able to follow it to wherever she is," Jordan said.

"I've got the coordinates. Should I go now?" Callie asked.

"Yes, please," Jordan replied.

"Good luck. I'm fast," Callie taunted. She then sprinted off, out of sight.

"Malik," Jordan said, "see her energy?"

See her energy? Malik thought about the cold sensation on his back and then thermal vision goggles came to mind. "Can I see like that?"

"Imagine that you can."

Malik closed his eyes and inhaled deeply. *I can see thermal energy. I will see thermal energy.* Malik opened his eyes, and his surroundings were slightly darker, as if he were wearing sunglasses. He now saw a light blue streak about chest high that disappeared further into the woods. Malik used his eyes to trace the blue light as it weaved in and out of the trees. The blue light closest to him faded, along with the cold sensation.

"Hurry, Malik," Jordan said. "Don't lose the trail."

Malik chased after the streak at a normal speed at first. Then he thought of yesterday's training with Silas. He imagined himself piercing seamlessly through the dark matter, and he picked up speed. He focused on Callie's wake, and the wooded area around him flew by in a blur. He was moving at a speed he would have never thought possible. He looked off the path for a moment, but that made him feel off balance, and he turned his attention ahead just in time to avoid crashing into a tree. The trail disappeared at the top of a mountain. Malik slowly walked around, searching for any sign of his friend, but he didn't feel or see her energy. Then the opposite happened, and Malik felt heat behind him. Instinct made him cautious, and he slowly spun around. Halfway through his spin, he caught a pale-yellow hue about waist high in his peripheral vision. It was a mountain lion.

As Malik faced the animal, it hissed and growled with its ears back. His heartbeat raced, and his legs trembled. The mountain lion was nearly thirty meters away, but it was in the direction that Malik would need to run, blocking his escape route. The cat's muscles flexed as it advanced toward him. Panic activated a fight-or-flight instinct in Malik, and he shouted and raised his arms overhead, making himself big. "Raaaaa! Get! Get out of here!" The animal backed up a few steps, but then paused, still hissing. Malik did it again, his adrenaline going strong. "Aaaahhh! Go! Go!" The mountain lion took a few more steps back, apparently startled, but Malik's actions weren't enough to force it to leave.

Malik was panting as he tried to assess the animal's body language. *What do you see?* The mountain lion still had its weight forward and did not appear to be considering retreat. *A fierce cat looking for its next meal.* He again thought back to yesterday and noticed a heavy rock off to the left. Malik inhaled deeply, focused on the rock, and lifted his hand, elevating the rock off the ground. As he exhaled, he looked back at the cougar one more time and paused. *What do you see?* The mountain lion's belly was swollen and hanging lower than one would expect. He looked more closely to discover the signs of a nursing mother. *She recently had cubs, and her den must be nearby.* He lowered his hand to put the rock back down on the ground. *She's not after me, unless I'm a threat to her cubs.*

She had backed Malik into a corner, and he didn't see a way out. "Just breathe," he told himself. *This has to be a test.* He locked eyes with the mountain lion and could see his reflection in the animal's eyes. He looked wild himself. As they stared at each other, time seemed to stop. He calmed his breath, his posture relaxed, and he let his arms rest by his sides. "Don't be afraid," he whispered, more to himself than to the cat. Malik watched as the muscles in the mountain lion relaxed as well. *Imagine the outcome you want.* The mountain lion sat back and now seemed more curious than anything. Malik closed his eyes. *I am reverent.*

He then experienced the most incredible feeling of warmth and comfort. His eyes were still closed, but all around him was a kaleidoscope of light. As the rainbow of geometric shapes danced by, he could have sworn every cell in his body was smiling. He lingered in the moment, connected and present, weightless and without fear. *I can decide. I choose respect.*

When he opened his eyes, the mountain lion was off to the side by the shrubs, lying with her paws crossed. Beyond her, there were movements in the grass where her two cubs were wrestling. She glanced around in a leisurely way, comfortable with Malik's presence, leaving a clear path for him to make his way home.

28

WALKING THROUGH OPEN DOORS

"Rrroaarr," Malik growled while crawling on his hands and knees, chasing after Aries. The toddler wobbled around the room, giggling and trying to get away.

On cue, Noah climbed onto Malik's back and shouted, "Not this time! I'll stop you from eating my brother."

Malik let out a snarl. "How dare you attempt to come between me and a tasty meal? I'll just have to eat you instead." Malik rocked from side to side, pretending to throw Noah off his back. Then he reached back and slowly rolled over to ensure Noah landed gently on the floor. Malik tickled the little boy and said, "Hmmm, I wonder what you'll taste like. I'm guessing ice cream!"

"Noooo!" Noah yelled and laughed as he attempted to roll away.

Just then, Aries crawled between them. "Ahh!" he squealed before belly flopping on top of his big brother.

"Aries says, 'It is I who will save you, brother!'" Malik said with a laugh, knowing Noah would get a kick out of it.

"He does?" Noah asked, giving his little brother a hug.

"That's what I heard," Malik replied.

"Time to settle down, you guys." Magaly's voice came from the doorway. Malik hadn't known she was there.

"Your mom is right. We have to get ready for quiet time."

Aries shook his head no, while Noah said, "I'm not tired at all!"

"You think that now," said Magaly. "But we have to give our bodies and minds a little rest so we can feel our best this afternoon and continue all the fun."

Malik conferred with Magaly. "Want me to take Aries or Noah?"

"You actually have a visitor. Your mom can help with Noah."

"A visitor? Who?"

"Ori. He's out back."

Malik walked to the back door to find Ori wearing joggers, running shoes, and a hooded water-resistant jacket. "Hi, Ori. I wasn't expecting you. Would you like to come in?"

"Oh, no, thank you. I was hoping that you would come and take a run with me."

"Uh, sure. I'll just need to change."

"Sounds good. I'll meet you at the trailhead."

WHEN MALIK APPROACHED the entrance to the trail, Ori was staring at the sky. Without looking at him, Ori spoke. "I hope you don't mind. I know it's been a few days, and I didn't come at the usual time. Today's training is better in the daylight, and I figured I could grab you while your children were napping."

"I don't mind at all," Malik said, as he bent down to stretch his legs. He stood up and continued to stretch different parts of his body. "What will the focus of this training be?"

Ori, still staring at the sky, said, "Today, we are going to focus on awareness and fear."

Malik followed Ori's gaze and saw a kettle of hawks soaring in circles overhead. He had never seen so many, though he had heard they sometimes flew in groups like this when migrating. One broke away, swooped down toward them, and perched on a high branch of the tree that bordered the trail entrance. The gigantic bird turned its head, as if evaluating Malik, before flapping its heavy wings and returning to join its group.

Ori chuckled. "Alright, I guess we should get going." He started at a slow jog, and Malik trotted along with him, matching his pace. "Your last training session was quite spectacular, Malik. It has been a very long time since any recruit has connected so deeply with nature."

Malik felt a glow of pride, but kept his reply simple. "Thank you."

"Typically, with new citizens, we ease them into roles. But based upon how your training has been going, we believe that something bigger is calling to you."

"Bigger? Like what?"

"I'm not entirely certain just yet. But we need to cover all our bases with your preparation."

"Okay, that sounds good to me."

"During your last sessions with Silas and Callie, you noticed how fast you could move, right?"

Images of scenery flying by him came back to Malik's mind, and he flinched when he remembered just barely avoiding a collision with a tree.

Ori didn't need any words spoken out loud to know what Malik was thinking. "Yeah, you need more practice with that too." He then slowed down to a stop, and Malik followed suit. "May I please see your timepiece?"

Malik extended his wrist to Ori. The look he had chosen, a platinum band and black face, was one to match the watch Magaly had gifted him for their first Christmas together.

"Nice design," Ori said as he placed his index finger and

thumb on the outer rim of the watch's face. That transformed the timepiece to show three sub-dials.

"Wait, that wasn't there before," said Malik. "I thought I only had two sub-dials."

"A new stage in your process, and today's training relates to that as well. As you know, one sub-dial shows where you are anchored. The second shows where you are planning to go. This…" Ori tapped his finger against the third dial. "This third sub-dial tells you your current location. A third sub-dial means a citizen may need to take detours. And since we do not know what those detours could look like, we need to be prepared."

"How do we prepare for that?"

Ori broke back into a jog. "The detours can be to anywhere for any purpose. It can feel like a dream, the scene and objective changing often. The rational mind will want to kick in to protect you from what it believes will cause you harm. The aim of this training is to prevent that from happening." Ori's stride opened up a little more, and Malik felt the burn in his lungs. "So, the way this works is, I'll lead you through a series of trails before you take the lead."

"Alright," Malik said, a bit winded.

"At that point, the trails are single file. It will be on you to decide which way to turn."

"How will I know?"

"That's where your awareness comes into play. Every path speaks. It communicates with the traveler. One is given clues. You have learned to listen; you just don't know what you've learned to listen to. This exercise will make sure that you are aware and can identify the clues. Take that path, for example." Ori pointed to a small dirt trail off to the left. "What do you think?"

Malik quickly studied the path, which became covered with shadows from the tree canopy before it disappeared down a hill. "What do you mean? What do I think?"

"First thoughts when you consider going down that path?"

"Well…" Malik turned back to look at the trail, but it was now far out of sight. He inhaled deeply, partly to catch his breath and partly to prepare to speak. "I probably wouldn't take that path now. My joints would be upset going down that steep hill. And it looked pretty narrow."

"Tell me more."

Malik revisited the trail in his mind. He saw the shrubs on each side of the path, growing so close to each other that they were touching at the top. "Yeah, it was a clear path, but the brush was making it tight." In his mind, he could see the deep grooves in the center of the trail. "I'd guess it's popular for mountain biking. It could be risky to be on there without a bike."

Ori took a sharp turn onto a path that went uphill. The forest floor became covered with English ivy on both sides, leaving little room for Malik to run next to Ori. *Is this where I will take the lead?* Malik wondered as he fell behind and searched ahead for a place to pass.

"Not yet," Ori called over his shoulder.

Malik followed Ori down trails that wound all throughout the woods. *I've never been this deep in this part of the forest*, Malik thought, and his chest tightened. *I hope I'm not asked to find my way back.*

THE TWO HAD BEEN JOGGING for nearly half an hour by the time Ori stopped. When Malik was caught up and by his side, they were at the top of a hill lined with pine trees. He could make out a boardwalk path down below. "Check the bottom dial of your watch to make sure that you are anchored in 7.83," said Ori.

Malik did as instructed. "Where should I set the destination?"

"Leave it blank."

"But…" Malik hesitated. "I thought that we always need to have a clear destination before we travel."

"That's true. If you don't, do you know where you will end up?"

Malik sensed there was a simple answer to this. "Where?"

"You'll end up where you are anchored, right back where you started." Ori glanced over at Malik. "You can speed up time by always focusing on what's ahead. Or you can slow it down by staying present in the moment. When you run, you focus on your breath and your stride. You're forced to. This slows down your mind and allows you to make much more aware observations. You want to keep that up. Remember to breathe and take the paths that speak to you."

"Okay." Malik felt his nerves kicking in.

Ori pointed down the hill past the wooded path. "Do you see that?"

"The building with the green door?"

"The power that you are gaining, to travel to different realities and into people's dreams, is intended to only be used for the greater good. The universe has created a mechanism to ensure that only the selfless can access and maintain this ability."

"What is the mechanism?"

"Fear." A voice came from behind Malik. He turned to see a man he didn't recognize walking up the hill behind them. "Fear of the unknown can cause people to give up on attaining something. Maybe that something is meant for them, and maybe it isn't."

"Carlos, thank you for joining us," Ori said.

"My pleasure." Carlos smiled and said, "Malik, I'm glad to see you."

Malik nodded in return. "Nice to meet you."

Carlos stood beside them and looked down at the building in the distance. "Fear and doubt are a natural part of this journey. You cannot stop these feelings from occurring, which is why you must learn to recognize them and come to terms with the idea that they are not real. If you can identify what is causing the fear, you can address it and proceed."

"Malik," Ori said. "Soon, you will interpret the text in your library and unlock your ability to travel. I'm afraid that the third dial on your timepiece means the powers that be may need you to take a detour before arriving at your target destination."

"Sometimes those detours are pleasant and other times, not so much," Carlos added. "Malik, your next lesson is through that green door down there. I do not know what's behind it, only that you will face fear and doubt. Keep moving forward, finding the open doors, and walking through."

Malik looked back and forth between Ori and Carlos, and knots formed in his stomach. "Why does this feel dangerous?"

"It may be," Carlos said.

"Can I be hurt?"

"Not if you keep going," Carlos said.

"Why do I need to do this?" Malik asked.

"The universe always gives tests."

Ori spoke up. "You can turn back now if you want to. No one would blame you."

"What would happen if I were to turn back?"

"Then you would lose your third dial, and the destinations you could visit would be limited," Carlos said.

"Would I be able to protect people from the effects of the solar flares?" Malik asked.

"I'm not sure," Ori said. "This test revealed itself for a reason."

I can't risk it, Malik thought. "It sounds like I don't have a choice."

"Malik, you always have a choice," Ori said. "You've earned your time. No one can ever take that away. What you've done for yourself and your family, the time spent, the habits formed, that will never go away. You are winning."

"But what about the others?" Malik asked. "They need a chance to win too."

Ori looked at Carlos, who shrugged and grinned. "I knew I liked him." Carlos met Malik's stare. "As soon as you walk through that door, just react. Don't overthink. Be flow."

Malik nodded and looked off at the green door again. "But what if I—" Malik glanced back and realized that he was now alone on the hilltop. "Well, I guess that's that."

Malik jogged down the hill and was at the door faster than he expected. Malik grabbed the golden handle and pulled. The light was so bright that he covered his eyes as he stepped through. Once both feet were across the threshold, the light dimmed, and Malik could see again. He was standing on a dirt path that split in three directions. One road was paved and disappeared up a hill shaded with tree canopies. Malik turned to his right to see the second road was a dirt road that quickly curved and disappeared out of sight. Behind him was another paved road that ran parallel to a large pond. Malik held up his wrist to check his frequency. His timepiece displayed 7.83, confirming that Malik was in his own version of reality.

There was something familiar about this location. He closed his eyes and let the memory come to him. Noah was running down the dirt road, and then Malik heard the waterfall up ahead. Malik knew where he was. *I'm at Lullwater Park.* Noah used to love running along those trails and identifying all the birds. Malik stood there listening to the rushing water when he heard someone addressing him.

"Hey! Mister Malik?" Next to the pond was a man with a white beard, unkempt hair, and tattered clothes. The man sheepishly pushed his hair back off his face and dusted off his clothes. He made brief eye contact with Malik before he shifted his eyes to the ground. "You—you know it's not safe to be out in the sun, right?"

In that instant, Malik recognized the man. It was the former groundskeeper from Noah's daycare. "Mr. Howard? What are you doing out here?" Malik asked.

Malik noticed as the thin man—once stocky and strong—slouched and shrunk a little. He rubbed the back of his neck, his eyes still downcast. "I—I've been having a hard time finding work ever since..." Mr. Howard peeked up at Malik. "Well, ever since, you know."

Malik's heart went out to the man. "I—"

Mr. Howard continued in a rush of words. "You know I cherished those children." His eyes were darting from side to side as if searching the ground for some answer. "I just don't know. I can't explain what happened. You know I'd never hurt Noah." Mr. Howard peered up, tears rolling down his cheeks. "I haven't found work since, and I've nowhere else to go."

"You're a good man, Mr. Howard. I know that." Malik tried to console the man.

Then the bushes across from the pond shook, and they both pivoted to determine the cause. A different man, whose appearance suggested he may also have been living in the park, emerged from the shrubs shouting, "This is the last time. This is my area! Mine!" The man advanced toward them, then seemed to notice Malik. He waved his arms and shouted more. "You, get back! All of you, get back!"

All of you? Malik turned back in confusion to see a couple of police officers approaching.

"Please, remain calm," one officer said. Malik recognized him as the same man who used to patrol the area when Malik's family would explore there and recalled a conversation they once had.

"Yeah, since we're next to the Veterans Affairs building, we have some displaced individuals who have set up camp in here. We try our best to peacefully relocate them."

The tense situation continued, and Malik took a few steps back.

Out of the corner of his eye, he saw a small pool of water glow. Malik was pulled over to it, where he was captivated by an unusual swirl of color. At that moment, Malik felt in his pants pocket and found keys there. He knew what to do. Malik looked back in time to see one officer tackle the hostile man, while the officer Malik knew was taking Mr. Howard by the arm.

"Excuse me, officer," Malik said to the one with Mr. Howard. "You may not remember, but we met a long time ago. My home is just up the road." Malik held up his keys. "My family has recently moved, but I came back here to find him." Malik gestured to Mr. Howard. "He's an old family friend, who I recently discovered is down on his luck." Malik pulled the house key off the ring and extended his arm to offer it. "Mr. Howard, I have some work around the house. I'd really appreciate you looking after the place while we're away."

The officer studied Malik before he took the key and turned it over in his hand. The officer let Mr. Howard's arm go and handed him the key. Just then, a door appeared in front of Malik, and he walked through. *It's not about you. It's not your movie; it's theirs.*

HE FOUND himself close to where he was before, down the road and out of sight of the chaos. In his hands, Malik held a paper bag full of bread. The earth between two trees that bordered the small body of water had washed away enough for Malik to see exposed roots reaching out like bent fingers. From an opening between the tree roots, a goose appeared and waddled up onto the grass, pecking away at the ground. The goose took a few steps toward Malik, but it was still about thirty meters away and paying him no attention. Malik could see another two geese beyond the tree roots, preparing to exit the water as well. He reached inside the bag, broke off a small piece of bread, and tossed it near the first goose. It glanced at the piece of bread, then promptly turned its attention to Malik, as did the two behind it, and about four more that were now walking up onto the bank as well. Malik reached back into the bag, pulled out a full slice of bread, and threw it toward the geese. They ignored it and all waddled toward him, their numbers growing.

Malik pulled out another slice. This time, he tore off a corner of the bread and tossed it to the goose up front. The goose ate it this time, but then moved even faster than before. Now backpedaling, Malik's hands shook as he tore at the bread and threw his offering to the geese, but they didn't seem satisfied. It now appeared the entire flock was a few feet away, their sharp beaks open, their eyes locked onto the bag in his hands. Malik stumbled as he tried to get farther away from the waist-high birds. Malik did the only thing he could think to do: he threw all the remaining bread into the air and ran.

A large metal door with a rod bolt appeared in front of Malik. He quickly spun the wheel and stepped through. *Your connection to the source will keep getting stronger. Trying to solve every problem will only create chaos. You must access your gift with caution and moderation.*

MALIK WAS NOW in a darkened room. After several seconds, his eyes adjusted, and he noticed light reflecting off a well-polished metal counter that ran alongside a commercial oven. He heard shouting coming from nearby, and he followed the sounds out the open kitchen door. There he saw the back of a man frozen in place as a large mob—wearing white shirts and black ties—charged in his direction. *My dream?* Malik wondered. He glanced down at his watch and every sub-dial was displaying the number eight. *What is going on?* The men were charging in slow motion, and Malik instinctively stepped back. He bumped into some pots, sending them crashing to the floor. The loud clanking made him cringe. No one seemed to notice.

The scene was happening as before, still in slow motion. *How is this possible?* He suddenly heard a hissing sound and glanced down to see that, without knowing, he had glided across the kitchen, and his hand was on the knob of the burner. Malik had turned the gas on. He eyed the other burners, all turned to their highest setting. *I started the fire,* Malik realized, as he found a box of matches in his hand. He struck the match, and the flame sparked and spread, as the men got close to the dreaming version of himself. Then a bright yellow door appeared. Calmly, Malik walked past the flame and opened the door. As he reached the other side, he felt the heavy bump of an explosion. *Trust you are equipped to handle conflict. When attacked, your higher self will do whatever it can to protect you.*

THERE WAS A GUST OF WIND, and Malik was back outdoors, inhaling the scent of pine trees. He checked his watch, which was now back on 7.83. He assessed the setting and recognized he was back on top of the mountain where he encountered the mountain lion. This time, he was watching as the mother was leaving the den, when a cold blue streak passed right in front of him. Malik gave chase.

Callie checked her tail and did a double take, shocked to see him there. "How did you catch up to me so fast?"

"I have no idea!"

He saw Callie get that determined look he remembered so well before she turned away and sped up.

"Okay, let's do this," Malik called out, staying locked in on her back and pushing himself to keep up. The landscape flew by so fast that everything outside of Malik's tunnel vision became almost white. He stared intently at the blue until it consumed more of his vision. He was getting close. Then a black dot appeared and ate away at the blue. Malik thought about stopping as the black overtook the blue, but it was too late. Before he could react, he was out into the dark unknown. He felt as if he had become still, but he couldn't be sure.

A glow of blue light reappeared and split into beams that shot out and illuminated a series of doors. Malik finally felt his legs back under him and heard the tapping of his own feet walking across a hard floor. Each door was made of solid gold and had an engraving of the sword and the stone. Slowly, Malik examined each door, hoping for clues as to which one to open. Each door, at first, appeared exactly the same. Each stone was identical, as was the angle of the swords. There were jagged corners and smooth sides.

He thought of Lotus's words at the start of this journey: *"You can choose what kind of tool you wield."* He knew where to look now: the design inside the small circular pommel at the end of the sword handle. He looked at each door to find a blade, a plume pen, an open book, a bag of coins, comedy and tragedy masks, a crucifix, a hammer and a chisel, and then one with no design at all.

"Which will you choose?"

Malik would know that voice anywhere. "I could really use your help right now."

"Ah, King Malik, you don't need my help." Malik's granddad stepped forward out of the black and stood right next to him. "You want to help the world, now you get to choose how you do it. Just pick a door."

Malik stepped forward, then stopped.

"Don't worry. There's no wrong answer. Do you trust yourself?"

Malik was silent for a moment and took a deep breath. He thought of his family. He thought of the mountain lion. He thought of the beauty in this journey. "I do."

"And you believe it?"

"Believe what?"

Malik's grandfather put his hand over his heart.

Under his granddad's steady gaze, he didn't have to think. "I am worthy." Malik walked to the door with the blank pommel.

"Good choice, my boy," his grandfather said.

Malik placed his hand on the doorknob, but then paused, wanting to ask his granddad one more thing. He turned his head. "Why didn't you tell me about all this?"

"I didn't? Well—"

Before his granddad could finish, the door opened, and Malik was pulled inside.

29

DEATH OF A MALIK

THE SUN WAS WARM ON HIS FACE, FEEDING HIS SOUL. A FEW WHITE clouds were lightly brushed across an otherwise blue sky. He was standing in a field with grass just high enough to cover his ankles. Malik saw no landmark to help him understand where he was. He swayed on his feet, realizing there was a slope to the ground, and he was on a hill of sorts.

Where am I? Malik questioned as he stood in place, waiting for the situation to reveal itself. Malik took a few steps forward, and his body felt lighter and more limber somehow. There was no hint of the subtle aches in his knees and back he usually experienced as an adult turning the corner to forty years old. There was a pleasant breeze on the grassy hill, and Malik reveled in the beautiful day.

Suddenly, Malik's heart rate increased, and he felt his chest tighten. It became hard for him to breathe. He collapsed to one knee, overwhelmed with a feeling of fear. Of what, he didn't know. Movement near the bottom of the hill caught his attention. There was a large black cable swinging around wildly, like an unmanned firehose. The sight triggered a flashback of being in some fast-moving vehicle, witnessing streaks of lights zip past, before everything stopped abruptly, and Malik was jerked forward, then back again.. *Was I in a wreck?*

Malik, still on one knee, scanned the skies at the bottom of the hill. He paused once he found what he was searching for. There was black smoke, just enough to confirm there had been an accident. A high-pitched ringing sounded in his ears, making him realize for the first time he could hear nothing. He rubbed both ears and shook his head, hoping in vain his hearing would return. When that did not work, Malik stood back up and focused on the out-of-control cable.

I know this... Malik saw a two-story home, all black and sleek, looking like two giant glass boxes stacked on top of each other. He now recognized the cable as a downed, active power line. It must have been connected to the house, but where? As Malik concentrated on the house, the image morphed. Those two boxes became two octagons, which were then flattened and elevated off the ground.

What the... Malik thought, but a voice came out of the sky.

"Stay present and let it flow through you."

"What?" Malik replied, looking up above for someone to address.

A throbbing in his temple brought Malik's eyes down again as he held his head. The octagonal shape then evolved further into a long, cylindrical spacecraft. More came back to him. Malik had boarded a private craft with his parents. "We need power," he said to himself. Malik had a memory of the flashing red indicators on the control panels, warning them that something was wrong. He could hear his dad explaining to his mom they needed to land at specific coordinates to connect to a power grid.

"That's our power source." Malik ran down the hill toward the wild cable, and as he did, his hearing came back. Screaming came from behind him. He turned to see his parents waving frantically at the top of the hill. "What?" he mouthed, before losing his footing and tumbling down the hill. Before he knew it, the cable was wrapped around his right leg. His instincts told him to freeze. He heard his mother's screech from atop the hill, and though he forced his mind to remain calm and his body to stay still, his heart was thumping. As he glanced down at the sparking cable, he knew that even like this, it was only a matter of time before it electrocuted him. His mother and father were running down the hill toward him, and his mind raced, trying to think of ways out of this. In an instant, a large, dark body appeared by his side, blocking the sun.

"It's okay, Malik. This is going to happen," the voice said. "But don't worry, when you wake up, you'll be with me at home."

Malik squinted and said, "What? Who are you?" As he leaned up, an inch off the ground, he felt the jolt of electricity enter his body, causing all his muscles to lock up. Just then, the face of the kind stranger appeared, and Malik couldn't believe his eyes. He saw himself. But he was older. He had a salt and pepper afro; the strands of white seemed to shine in the sunlight. Malik relaxed, and as he peacefully lay back down, everything went black.

Malik opened his eyes again and was relieved to be in his bed. Magaly was sound asleep beside him. There was a red cardinal outside his window, and its song urged Malik to roll over to face it fully. His movement must have woken his wife, because he felt Magaly's soft, warm hand on his back.

"Is everything okay?" she asked.

"I just had a strange dream. I—I think that I may have just…" Malik thought about what he may have experienced.

"May have what?" Magaly asked, pushing herself up to look at his face.

He smiled. "It's nothing. I may have seen an older version of myself."

"I bet he was cute." Magaly chuckled and lay back down.

30

THE LAST LESSON

MALIK WASN'T SURPRISED WHEN JORDAN MET HIM IN THE WOODS THAT morning. Last night's dream warranted a debrief, and he was glad he didn't need to wait. He finished his run at the command center, where he found Evelyn, Ori, Carlos, and Jordan viewing his dream and having an animated discussion.

"Zoom in there," Jordan said. The image of the electrical cable froze and became enlarged on the screen. "He recognized what it was…"

"Jordan," Ori said, nodding toward the door.

Carlos turned and saw why Ori had paused the discussion. "Ah, Malik, please come and join us." Carlos pointed to an open seat next to him. "We have a seat for you."

"Thank you," Malik said as he sat down, staring at the screen.

"We were just finishing our preparatory discussion," Carlos explained.

"I didn't mean to interrupt, but I guess I am eager to hear your assessment," Malik admitted.

"Well then," said Ori, "can we please start from the beginning?" Malik watched as his entire dream moved backward rapidly. "We'll look at specific parts of this in a minute, but I think we should start high level. Jordan, do you want to give it a go?"

"Sure," Jordan said, as she turned toward Malik. "Okay, so dreams are a lot of things for many people. They can be a window into an alternate reality. For most, a dream will be a premonition of things to come or a sought-after answer to a question."

Evelyn spoke. "This is why we often encourage people through their subconscious mind first, in dreams. Then, if needed, in their conscious mind, with cues in the physical world."

Jordan nodded in agreement. "Effectively functioning in someone else's dream can be challenging. We can use your dreams to help prepare you for this, and you'll understand how to tell what type of dream you're in."

Malik studied the screen. "Okay, what am I looking for?"

"First," Jordan said, "did you have a first-person or a third-person experience?"

Malik remembered feeling his legs under him. "I think it was in the first person."

"How do you know?"

"I was in my body. I couldn't watch myself doing anything. Everything felt like I was a part of it."

"Did you recognize where you were?" Jordan asked.

"No, but somehow that wasn't alarming until I saw the power line. Though I didn't realize that's what I was looking at for a minute." Malik paused, reliving the dream and seeing his mom and dad standing on top of the hill.

"What is it?"

"My mom and my dad were there, together."

"And?" Jordan said.

"They divorced when I was a kid. But in the dream, I knew they were married, and it felt like real life."

"Then what happened?"

"There was this massive structure. At first I thought it was a house, but then it kept transforming, right before my eyes."

"You mean this?" Jordan sped forward to show the part where the boxes of the house changed into a hovering octagon and then into a cylindrical spaceship.

"That's it. What was that?"

"This is the point when your mind realizes that this is a dream and not happening in the physical world."

"This also helps your mind understand what world this scene could play out in," Tony said, strolling into the room. "Hey, guys, my bad for being late."

"No worries," Evelyn said.

"Can we freeze it on the ship?" The screen did as Tony instructed. "Whenever your mind takes you to a world, pay attention to the technology. That will give you a sense of what is and is not possible. Also, you never looked down at your watch."

"Oh. I've been trying to do that, but for some reason it didn't occur to me," Malik said as he grabbed the watch on his wrist.

"It's more difficult to remember in dreams at first. Don't worry, you'll get to where you do it by instinct," Tony said.

Evelyn spoke up. "What this part of the dream is saying, Malik, is that your mind would expect an object of this size to have been a house. Then it walked you forward, slowly morphing into the actual object in that reality—a personal space craft. Your mind couldn't comprehend it at first to be something that you and your family would use for travel, because it didn't exist in your rooted world at that age."

Jordan took over again. "Something to remember: If things change and then stay one way, that means your mind is getting used to an alternate reality. If things continue to be glitchy, like the setting keeps changing or the people around you change unexpectedly, that means you are likely in a dream."

"If it glitches once, then stays, I'm in an alternate reality. If things continue to glitch and change, I'm in a dream. Got it." Malik nodded his head.

"Because one thing transformed," Jordan said, "but you recognized your parents and everything else felt, looked, and seemed like it could really happen, you can be sure it was a glimpse of an alternate reality." Jordan studied Malik, then turned back to the screen. "In this reality, your family was in trouble, and you were too ambitious and eager to please, which is why you sprinted head on toward that cable."

"I—I," Malik tried to figure out how to explain what it had felt like in the dream. "I didn't think about it like that. It was as if a solution to the problem came to me, and I just had to run toward it. The danger didn't occur to me."

Jordan nodded. "This is the universe giving you a simple reminder that you don't have to be the hero. Your job will be to influence others to fulfill what they are meant to do, then move on to the next mission."

"I know with this work, it's not about me. It was just hard to step outside of myself in the dream, and it all happened so fast."

"Dreams happen fast, even when you're experiencing an alternate reality, and it can feel like you aren't able to think through things. You have to find a way to slow it down and take your time." Jordan's voice was gentler than usual. "Some lessons have to be learned from experience. At the beginning... Rewind it a few panes. Okay, play it back." The screen panned from the sky to the green grass of the hill. Malik remembered the feeling of the sun on his skin. "Stop here. Malik, this is your subconscious trying to get its bearings. It was working to understand where and when it was. As long as there is nothing chasing after you, it is important to be patient. You were at first, but then everything sped up after you saw the power line in the distance. You'll need to stay focused on breathing and being present to keep things within your control."

"Your backstory was filling in when you saw the ship," said Tony. "If you had given it more time, the rest would have come, and you may have made a different decision. Well, theoretically speaking."

"Why 'theoretically speaking'?"

"That version of you died."

"Because of me?" Malik's stomach lurched.

"No, not really because of you. But you didn't change the outcome. And theoretically, you could have."

"Wh—" Malik felt a new weight on his chest. *Should I have known? Could I have changed things?* Then he felt a hand on his shoulder.

"Don't let that consume you," said Carlos. "You are in this position because you have so much more life to give. This dream came to you for your training, for multiple reasons. One of the most important, in my humble opinion, is to teach you not to fear death. If you embrace the possibility of death, you can live truly in the now. The universe communicates with you in the present. You will thrive in this role by staying open and in the moment, receiving your cues directly from the source."

"And," Ori said, "now you see what happens."

Malik's mind conjured that moment at the end of the dream, and again, he calmed down. "Was that me?"

Ori smiled. "That was the absolute best and highest version of yourself. The person who is fully aware of being and completely tapped into all the grace there is. The person who you are becoming, with a power so great you can connect to every version of yourself throughout all existence. And with that power, deliver wisdom, comfort, love, all that you need when you need it. The divine you."

31

MEETING REQUEST

"Fo!" Aries's triumphant shout woke Malik with a startle, and he jolted upright on the sofa. He glimpsed down at his wrist and was happy to see this was not a dream.

"Bring that back, Aries. That's Daddy's phone," Magaly said as Aries scampered away, holding the device over his head. The little guy was getting quicker on his feet. Malik let him enjoy his success for a moment before hopping up and gently retrieving the phone.

Thankfully, Aries wasn't too upset. He trotted right over to the glass door and pointed outside at a cardinal perched on the railing, saying, "Re birr, re birr!"

Malik looked at his phone, realizing the battery was dead. He walked to the desk and plugged it in to find he had multiple missed calls and text messages from Ronnie. Ronnie had been busy with his job in the Atlanta mayor's office and a set of triplets at home. It had easily been two years since they had spoken. *He does not know we've been out here,* Malik thought as he scanned through the messages.

"Is everything alright?" Magaly's voice was calm and curious.

"I'm not sure," Malik responded. "Ronnie's been trying to get a hold of me."

"Did he say why?"

"No, he just asked for me to call him. He wouldn't call this many times if it weren't urgent."

"Hope everything is okay," Magaly said as she picked up Aries and took him outside.

Malik tried Ronnie, and he picked up immediately.

"Hey, Malik," Ronnie seemed out of breath, and Malik could hear several people talking in the background. "Thanks for calling me back."

"Hey, Ronnie. What's up? Everything okay?"

"Malik…" Ronnie's voice was drowned out by people shouting and screaming.

Malik plugged one ear with his finger and was straining to hear. "I can't make out anything you're saying," he finally said.

"Give me one second," Ronnie said, and the phone instantly went silent.

Malik turned toward the kitchen, feeling like someone was watching him. His grandma was calmly staring at him with a cup of tea hovering in front of her mouth. Malik could see the steam drifting in front of her face.

"Malik, can you hear me?" Ronnie's end of the phone was quieter now.

"Yes, that's much better. So what's going on?"

"I can't tell you over the phone. There's someone in DC who is asking to meet with you."

Malik felt a knot build in his stomach. "Why?"

"It's best to talk in person."

Malik shook his head.

"Hello… Are you still there?"

"I'm here, but I'm not going to DC."

"I thought you might say that, but I had to ask. What if I meet you in Atlanta?"

"I'm not there right now."

"Well, where are you?"

"We've been away, spending time with family."

"Is there any way you could meet me in Atlanta?"

Malik stared at the floor, remembering something Evelyn had said. *"If someone needs you, they will call you."*

"Malik? It really is important."

"Okay, I can meet you in Atlanta."

"Tomorrow?" Ronnie asked.

"Why not?"

"Should I send a plane? Where are you?"

"Don't worry, I've got it. Just meet me at the airport."

"Which one?"

"Dekalb-Peachtree."

"Thank you." Ronnie's voice sounded relieved. "I owe you big time."

"Only for you, Ronnie," Malik said.

"I know, I know. I'll fill you in tomorrow. Send my love to the family?"

"Will do, and you do the same."

As Malik hung up, he looked out the window at Aries, who was picking blades of grass while Magaly and his mom watched from the deck chairs. He felt someone approach his side and turned to see his grandmother.

"And so it begins," she whispered.

"You think so?" Malik asked.

"I know so."

MALIK STEPPED off the Gulfstream jet, and as expected, Ronnie was waiting for him at the bottom of the stairs. "This guy," Malik said, as he laughed and walked down the stairs toward his childhood friend. "What are you wearing? Three pieces?"

"Do you like it?"

"I mean, you look nice, but a little fancier than I was expecting."

"Hey, not everyone can just take a sabbatical from their high-powered job and wear sweat suits and joggers all day." Ronnie pointed at Malik's head. "You grew it out? Nice."

Malik ran his hands over his hair. "You know, I honestly haven't been thinking about it. It just feels like me. But," Malik raised his arms out to the side for Ronnie's inspection, "I put on a sports coat just for you. Count that as a win."

"Oh, I'll take it," Ronnie said and gave Malik a hug.

"So, why do I now have a vague lunch meeting invite on my calendar?"

"You're a man in high demand."

"Ha! No one has tried to get a hold of me since I left."

"That's because you left the company in very capable hands."

"Very true. But for real. What's the deal?"

"I was planning to fill you in on the way. This is supposed to just look like two old friends grabbing lunch together."

"So, it's safe to assume that's *not* what's happening?"

"I'm sorry to say it's not." Ronnie paused, which made Malik more apprehensive. "Senator Whitman asked me—no, begged me—to set up this meeting."

Malik sharpened his gaze. "Virginia Whitman? You know I haven't always seen eye to eye with her."

"She was insistent."

"That's why you're wearing that suit."

"You know Virginia—" Ronnie corrected himself. "Senator Whitman is connected. A three-term United States senator has the connections I need if I'm going to get to Washington."

"Still wanting to become a senator, huh?"

"Or president."

Malik noticed the beads of sweat collecting on Ronnie's forehead. "You're hot, aren't you?"

"No one said looking this good was easy. Come on, the driver has the AC on full blast."

INSIDE THE CAR, Ronnie grabbed a black case several inches long and a few inches thick and handed it to Malik.

"What's this?" Malik asked, inspecting what he now saw was a glasses case.

"The background for the meeting."

Malik opened the case and slid the vision glasses onto his face.

"They only programmed them for you to read, so I don't even know what's on them," Ronnie said.

As soon as Malik touched the temple of the frame, several electronic files appeared on the lenses. Malik opened them one by one and swiped through what turned out to be mostly emails.

"They told me everything is organized in chronological order," Ronnie said.

Malik reviewed the correspondence between White House officials, the Centers for Disease Control, and the World Health Organization. "They're seeing the connection now."

"The connection?" Ronnie asked. "Actually, never mind. Let's save it for the meeting."

"Alright, then."

"On a different note, where were you coming from?"

"Out West. I don't know if I told you my mom and stepdad moved in with my grandma?"

"After your granddad passed?"

"Yeah, not too long after. Anyway, we've all been out there, and the kids love it. I mean, it's beautiful."

"Sounds like more than a visit. What made you guys go?"

"Things had gotten a little intense, and Noah saw something happen at the zoo that was pretty upsetting. He asked to visit his Nana, so we did, then we just sort of stayed."

"What happened at the zoo?"

"Uh, do you remember hearing about someone getting hurt in the lion habitat?"

"When…" Ronnie opened his mouth to speak but stopped. "Oh man. Did Noah see it happen?"

"He saw enough. And between that and the incident at his daycare, the change of scenery has been good for us all." They rode in silence for a while. Malik was lost in thought until he noticed there was more traffic than usual. "Excuse me?" Malik leaned forward to get the driver's attention. "Do you know what's going on with all this traffic?"

"I heard on the radio that more people jumped into traffic on I-85. The police have been slowing down all the traffic, and I guess everyone is trying to take the surface roads."

Malik sighed and shook his head as he rubbed his chin.

"Things have gotten bad, Malik."

"They were already bad."

"Well, now the mayor of Atlanta, a sitting United States senator, and the governor of Georgia are awaiting a top-secret meeting with you."

32

LUCKY FLIGHT

As Malik and Ronnie walked into the dark restaurant, a young man behind the bar called out, "I'm sorry guys, we don't open until three."

Ronnie stepped forward and gave a cordial smile. "We're here to meet Governor King."

The man set down the glassware he was drying and walked around the bar. "Follow me," he said, leading them to a back corner of the restaurant. As they got closer, Malik saw Gladys King sitting at a large round table, all by herself. Her fluffy afro made her recognizable in the political world and had been prominent in her campaign materials.

"Governor King, it's always a pleasure to see you," Malik said as he pulled out a chair, unbuttoned his coat, and sat down.

"Malik, thank you for coming. And you know you don't need to be so formal. We have known each other for over a decade, after all." She tilted her face to Ronnie. "It looks like the mayor won't be joining us today."

Ronnie quickly checked his phone and winced. "I just got a message myself. He's asked me to sit in on his behalf."

.

"Ronnie, you have ambitions to run for bigger offices, correct?" Gladys asked.

"Yes, ma'am, I do." Ronnie's expression was earnest.

"Then this is where that starts. So, Malik, I heard you had to fly in?"

"That's right, this morning," Malik said, not offering more explanation.

"Today?" She sounded shocked.

Malik only nodded, figuring she would reveal the reason for her surprise.

"A lot of commercial flights were grounded today."

"Really? Across the country?"

"Worldwide."

"I flew private. I didn't realize... Is that related to the solar flares?"

"Isn't everything?" She rubbed her temples with her fingertips.

"But that's why the warning systems are in place. The version created for the FAA provides enough lead time to allow flights. And they had been rolling out the protective glass."

"That's part of why we asked you here." They hadn't heard Senator Whitman approaching. As usual, she looked impeccable, today in a pristine, all-white suit. With her tall frame, commanding presence, and blonde, straight, shoulder-length hair, she usually had no problem captivating a room of constituents. Malik wondered if she was coming from an event. He and Ronnie both stood from their seats to greet her.

"May I?" She motioned to the open chair in front of Malik.

Malik contorted his face into something he hoped resembled a smile. "Please, do." Malik inhaled deeply. *I accept this is happening for a reason.*

The senator and the governor acknowledged each other before the attention turned back to Malik.

"We know you've stepped away from the Singularity Group,

but we've asked you here for good reason. Have you seen what's been happening?" the senator asked.

Malik gave himself a moment, keeping what he knew close to the vest, and replied, "I've heard a bit."

The senator checked to make sure the bartender wasn't listening before she continued. "I'll cut to the chase. Federal funding is going to be pulled from the solar flare detection systems."

"What? That makes no sense." This was far from anything he expected to hear in this meeting.

"There was a vote to continue to pay to maintain the national solar flare detection infrastructure to keep the system live. It didn't pass. They are going to shut the system off."

"And leave people without warning?" Ronnie asked.

"I didn't know they were going to shut down the detection system," the governor said.

"It's new information," Senator Whitman whispered.

"When?" Malik asked.

"Six months. They've already allowed some gaps in system updates and maintenance."

"So, that's why flights have been canceled?" Malik asked. "If not properly maintained, the efficacy of those systems drops significantly."

"Exactly," the senator said. "Let's not even imagine what happens if solar flares knock out a plane's computer chips."

"Wait." Malik shook his head. "So, what are they going to do? Not fly planes?"

"They'll only fly planes that have the upgraded protection technology," the senator said, "which means flights will become less accessible for people. Reduced capacity, higher ticket prices, the little guy suffers."

Malik couldn't believe what he was hearing. "But I looked through the prep materials Ronnie gave me, and I was under the impression that the effects of the solar flares were becoming more evident to the powers that be."

"Well, you have those who don't believe solar sickness is real. They believe it's in people's heads. And then there are those of us who have seen how compelling the science is. I'm on a task force that has found that one result of continual direct exposure to the coronal mass ejections is the rapid decline of critical cognitive function."

"It's affecting critical thinking and even basic problem solving," said the governor, "but it's also causing the volatile behavior that's been getting more and more disturbing."

Malik looked from face to face, wondering why they were acting as though this was information he didn't know. "I—uh, I'm confused."

"Why's that?" Senator Whitman asked.

"Th—" Malik started to speak but paused. *Is this a joke? No, this must be a dream.* Malik surveyed the room. Nothing was out of the ordinary. The room didn't change. He knew exactly how he got there. And more than that, he remembered the car ride to the meeting location. He glanced at his wrist: 7.83.

"Malik?" asked the governor.

"Well…" Malik started again. "This information shouldn't be new to you. There was a prominent scientist who proposed this theory about ten years ago, suggesting the solar flares were accelerating the effects of poor consumption habits and industrial pollutants that had made their way into most people's bloodstreams. It was in the news because he became a lightning rod for the powerful people whose ventures were threatened by that idea. He was ridiculed and lost his funding. I seem to remember you, Senator, having something to say about it at the time."

"At the time, it seemed ridiculous. How was I supposed to know?" The senator was defensive, but Malik could tell she was harboring guilt for her mistake. "But now I do. Now I understand. That's why we're here."

"So, your task force, are you gaining support? If this is what you've found, why is the detection system still being defunded?"

"Well, the studies show that consumption habits make you susceptible to solar sickness. Even among those who realize solar sickness is real, there's a belief that costs are too high and the impacts are based on personal life choices. It was decided that the taxpayers shouldn't bear the costs."

"It's all about the money," Governor King said. "But we're determined to help the people of Georgia. We can't let this be."

Malik sharpened his eyes as he looked back and forth between the two political power players. "You have a plan, don't you?"

"Yes, we do," Senator Whitman said. "But we need your help."

"What's your plan?"

"Well, it's a two-phase approach. First, we launch a massive marketing campaign to convince people of the importance of changing their consumption behavior. We'll get all the native Georgian celebrities to do cameos and the whole deal. Healthy eating, whole foods, active lifestyles, et cetera, et cetera." The senator waved her hands theatrically in the air.

"How long do you think that will take to work?" Ronnie asked.

"It won't be fast enough," Malik said.

"It won't, but behind the scenes we'll be concurrently working on the other phase. This is where you come in, Malik."

"How so?"

"Our task force has been searching high and low for any viable solutions. The closest thing we have found is from that same scientist you just mentioned. We, of course, tried to find him, but have had no luck making contact. My right hand did some digging and found that he continued his research with private funding. She dug deeper and found that the private funding came from your grandparents."

"That's true until about five years ago."

"Yes, when his partner passed. And given that your grandfather passed about six years ago, I had a hunch that you may have gotten to know Anatole Patterson's research as well."

"Your hunch is right. Though I have no current contact with him. There's been no further work."

"I'm asking you." Senator Whitman's eyes pleaded with him. "We're asking you to help complete Anatole Patterson's work, however possible. With your mind, background, and resources, we know if anyone can do this, it's you."

"Between the senator, the mayor's office, and me, we can assure you the support and funding you need to make this happen for the state of Georgia," added Gladys.

Senator Whitman continued, "If you can get a viable solution, we can get the FDA to grant emergency use authorization, and with that, it'll roll out to the other states as well. You can be sure."

33

A TOKEN IS RECEIVED

MALIK REMAINED QUIET, CONSIDERING HOW HE OUGHT TO RESPOND, though, of course, this was exactly what he'd been called by Ori and the others to do.

Senator Whitman glanced over to the governor and Ronnie and asked, "Will you guys give us a few minutes?"

The two got up to leave the table. Before walking away, Ronnie placed his hand on Malik's shoulder and said, "I'll be waiting for you in the car."

Malik nodded as he regarded the senator, intrigued to hear what she needed to say without an audience.

"Listen, Malik." She sighed. "I know you're taking time away, focusing on your family. And I know this is a tall ask. I've reflected on this a great deal, and something came to me." Malik watched as the senator reached into her bag, pulled out what looked like a piece of aged paper, and slid it across the table.

Malik leaned forward but hesitated to pick up the delicate item. "What is it?"

"I found this photo among my great-grandfather's personal possessions. Lane Whitman was not only one of the greatest presidents in recent history, he was also a pillar of strength for our family. I look at his writings when I need guidance through tough situations. And that," Senator Whitman pointed at the picture on the table, "fell out of one of his journals while I was reading it and thinking about this quagmire we find ourselves in now."

"May I?" Malik asked, reaching his hand toward the photo.

"Be my guest."

Malik picked it up, and as he gained a clear view of the subjects, he got a tingly feeling down his neck. The picture quality was grainy, but Malik could make out a group of easily a dozen men. The majority had fair skin and wore some combination of sashes over their shoulders, service medals on their chests, knee-high, polished black boots, and sabers hanging down by their sides. They also each had either a thick mustache or a large beard that reached down to their chest. The only people who did not fit this mold were the two in the middle of the picture. The first, who was front and center, was a young man, maybe in his teens, with dark skin, a brimless cap, and a long, loose-fitting garment that flowed over his shoes. Standing directly behind him, dressed in a dark suit with no decorative metals or swords, was a man who looked startlingly like Malik. "Is this real? I don't understand."

"I was confused too," Senator Whitman said. "That person has an uncanny resemblance to you, doesn't he?"

"How strange," Malik said. "Who is this?" As he said those words, he realized the young man in the center was familiar, but in a different way. Malik had seen him somewhere before.

Senator Whitman shook her head. "I'm not sure. I had a few academic friends look at it. According to them, based on the way the photo was taken and how these gentlemen in their formal attire are posed, this young person was some sort of chief. The man behind him, the one with whom you share a strong resemblance, is likely his personal guard and protector."

"Okay—" Malik started.

"To make things more bizarre, look at the man on that side of the chief. You can see his coat of arms." She leaned over the table to point to the white shield with its thick, dark trim and cross-like pattern inside. "It's from the old Portuguese empire. I've had a forensics team authenticate the age of this photo, and they placed it around the early- to mid-eighteen hundreds."

"Wow," Malik said, putting it back on the table. "I would hate to damage this."

The senator stood up and came around to sit right next to Malik. She pointed to the photo. "Each of these men was the ambassador of the great European powers of the time. The mountains in the background—those are a part of the Ruwenzori mountain range between Uganda and the Democratic Republic of the Congo."

"Sounds like this belongs in a museum or archive."

"I've had historians from all over the world look at this photo, and they've said no such meeting ever took place."

"And what do you make of that?"

"I believe we are meant to work together."

Malik thought to himself, *She's not wrong. Walk through open doors.*

"You think I'm silly," she said.

"No, no!" Malik quickly assured her. "Believe me, I've recently experienced things that have opened my mind to what's possible."

"I can explain though. After everything I learned about this photo, I scoured through my great-grandfather's journals to understand how or why he had this. You'll never guess what I found."

Malik arched his eyebrows in response.

"This photo was a gift from the founder of the Singularity Group. It seems like they were friends."

Upon hearing those words, Malik remembered where he had seen the young chief from the picture. There had been a framed picture of him, though probably a few years younger, in his grandfather's office at the Singularity Group. When his grandfather stepped down, that photo was the only one he took with him. "I didn't realize your great-grandfather was friends with Leslie Ochoa."

"Not her, the man before her. My great-grandfather never mentioned him by name, though apparently that man also brought Leslie to Whitman House the night before she took over the company. But anyway, don't you see? Whether active at the moment or not, you are the head of the Singularity Group. We are meant to work with each other."

"So, it's a sign?"

"You can't tell me you don't believe in signs."

34

THE BOY IN THE PHOTOGRAPH

MALIK WALKED INTO THE HOUSE. HE SHOOK OFF THE RAIN AS BEST HE could before removing his coat. He had just sat down to take off his shoes when he heard his mom's voice.

"That was a quick trip. I thought you would have at least stayed the night."

"I wanted to get back. Where is everybody?"

"Magaly is in the shower. The boys are jumping in puddles out back. They're having a big time. I was just coming in to get some towels ready for when they're done."

"You're the best, Mom," he said, smiling and standing to give her a hug. "Is Grandma back there too?"

"Mm-hmm, she's back there watching. Is everything alright?"

"Yeah, I just want to ask her about something. See you out there?"

"Be right there."

Malik walked through the glass doors leading to the covered porch. As soon as he stepped outside, he heard his grandma say, "And just like that, he's back."

"And I do not come empty-handed." Malik pulled the

envelope out of his pocket and placed it on the table next to a cup of tea. Steam still rose into the air from the amber-colored liquid. It looked inviting on such a rainy day.

His grandma reached for the parcel. "Good thing we aren't in the splash zone."

Malik looked out to see both boys stomping around and squealing with their Opa. "He's really good with them."

"He is, isn't he?" Something about her voice sounded frailer than usual. Malik pushed the worry from his brain. His grandma was still a force. She pulled the picture out of the envelope to study it and was silent for several seconds.

"The young man in the center…" Malik spoke, breaking the silence. "There was a picture in Granddad's office at the Singularity Group, and I could swear it was of the same person, just younger."

His grandma looked closely at the picture and slowly nodded.

"That's the same person, right?"

"It is. The descendant of Queen Nzinga. She ruled over what you now know as Angola for almost forty years." She turned the photo over and examined the design along the border. "He was known as the Chief of Chiefs." Just then, Malik's mom walked out onto the porch and set towels down on an empty chair. "Nia, baby, would you do me a favor?"

"Sure, Mom, what do you need?" Nia asked.

"On the bookshelf in my room, the one next to my closet, there's a hollowed-out book with an image of the Eiffel tower on it. Can you bring it to me?"

"Will do. Malik, we've got some hot water. Want tea while I'm inside?"

"You're reading my mind. That would be amazing. Thank you!" Malik said.

Once Malik's mom went back inside, his grandma asked, "Who gave you this picture?"

"Senator Whitman. She insisted I keep it too. Turns out she was the reason Ronnie insisted we meet. Actually, it was her and Governor King."

"Senator Whitman, huh? Let me guess, she found this in President Lane Whitman's things?"

"Yeah, how did you know?"

They paused as Nia brought out the book and the cup of tea, then in unison said, "Thank you!"

Malik gratefully accepted the hot mug from her and immediately held it in front of his face without taking a sip, enjoying the feeling of the steam. His mom handed the book to his grandma before heading to the edge of the porch to watch the boys play with Jonas.

Malik watched as his grandma opened the hollow book, took out the photo he remembered from his granddad's office, and handed it to Malik. *I knew it*, he thought as he inspected the picture. Here the boy looked ten or eleven and was standing at attention, though he had a childlike grin on his face. He wore an elaborate headpiece and held a spear and shield in his hands.

"This photo." His grandma held up the one from Senator Whitman. "Did she say that what's happening in this picture isn't possible, and that this never took place?"

"Yes," Malik said.

"But you figured perhaps it did take place, just not here?"

Malik nodded. "I don't know what all this means though."

"The original owner of that picture," his grandma pointed at the picture in Malik's hand, "is the same person who recruited me to be the record keeper. He's also been aiding with your training. Ori."

"How is that possible? I thought all citizens and, uh, higher beings at the Point, you know, stayed behind the scenes."

"Well, they do. Typically. But around eighty years ago, Ori came from behind the scenes to set some things in motion. He brought to life an idea that has allowed billions of people to live a more free and prosperous life. To do that, he needed to play the role of an actual human being. Ego and the lack of awareness from some powerful people caused Ori to end that role, but not before he contained ego and preserved the legacy of what he built."

Malik was silent as he imagined this story playing out.

"Tony erased any and every trace of Ori's existence. That's why many people think of Leslie as the founder of the Singularity Group." His grandma focused again on the image in her hands. "But there's a reason this photo has surfaced. How did the meeting end?"

"They asked for my help."

"Oh, really?" Malik thought she sounded pleased.

"They asked me to find any way possible to complete the work that Anatole Patterson started."

"I think this means your training is officially over."

"What do I do?"

"Well, first I think you need to see that this photo gets returned to the appropriate reality."

"How do I do that?"

"This photo was taken in a version of reality when Queen Nzinga fought off the Portuguese well enough to unite all the tribes of Africa, which resulted in the eradication of the slave trade and foreign colonization."

"I—I…" Malik stuttered.

"Yeah, wrap your head around that."

"So, I'll need to travel?"

"Yes, but not how you might be thinking. This is kicking off your mission. How are things going with your library? Any luck reading it yet?"

"Not yet."

"I think it's time you try again. It might not be today, it might not be tomorrow, but I have a feeling you're ready."

"Where do I start?"

"Start with the journal Ori gave you. The words in that journal are the things I saw and experienced at six point one nine. This will help your brain paint a vivid enough picture of what that world looks like. When you fall asleep, you will be transported to that world. Since what you will know about that reality will be from my perspective, your ability to deviate from what I've written will be limited."

"What does that mean?"

"You'll see when you are there. Now, when you get there, you will see a face that's familiar to you. You may not consciously know who that person is, but trust them and follow them. They will help you find Gardner."

"Who's Gardner?" Malik asked.

"He's the only one who can help you find what you are looking for."

"And what am I looking for?"

"You need to know how to connect with and deliver a message to Anatole Patterson." His grandma leaned in. "This is important. You need to make sure that you find out where Anatole is most receptive."

"A frequency?"

"That's right, you need to find the frequency at which he is most receptive to a message of this importance."

"To help me finish what he started?"

"Yes, to finish what he started." His grandma closed her eyes and inhaled deeply. As she exhaled, Malik saw her smile. "Once you're able, read the book before you go to sleep. And there, you will look for Gardner and ask him where you can find the scientist. Give him this photo from Senator Whitman." She put the photo down on the table and slid it back toward him.

"How can I give him a photo in dream travel?" Malik put his hand next to the photo, but waited to pick it up.

She smiled, reached out, and gently patted Malik's hand. "I can't give you all the answers, now can I? Just trust that you'll be able to do it." She warmed her hands on her cup of tea. "When you wake up, you might notice you are pages ahead of where you were when you fell asleep. Don't worry about going back and rereading."

Just then, the boys and Jonas hurried under the porch, and Malik's mom took their raincoats. Noah grabbed a towel, adrenaline clearly still pumping from the excitement of running around and playing in the rain.

"Dad! Did you see us splashing in all the puddles?"

"I did, buddy! That looked like so much fun," Malik said, jumping up to help. He was wrapping Aries in a towel when Magaly came outside.

"Babe, you're back!"

35

ZOMBIE ANTS

"Noooo!" Noah screamed. "Aries, stop!"

Malik heard Aries shriek. Malik closed the refrigerator door and trotted to the living room, where he saw the boys playing tug of war with a bowl of popcorn.

"Dad," Noah moaned. "Aries won't share the popcorn."

"That's okay." Magaly's voice was calm as she walked past Malik toward the kitchen.

"No. It's. Not." Noah grunted as he tried his best to pry the bowl out of the firm grip of the almost two-year-old, who responded promptly with another loud shriek.

Magaly returned and bent over the two. "Aries, can I please have the bowl?"

"Mm-mm." The toddler shook his head at her.

"But you can have this one," Magaly said, as she held up the second bowl, which was larger than the one in Aries's hands. "Please."

Malik smiled in amazement as Aries released the bowl, allowing Magaly to pour almost half of the popcorn in, while showing Noah he would still get his fair share. Then she gave the smaller bowl to Noah and the larger bowl to Aries. Satisfied, the toddler hurried to the couch, pushed the large bowl up, then settled into his favorite corner seat with the popcorn between his legs.

Malik laughed. "His legs don't even fit around the bowl."

Noah positioned himself on the other end of the couch and said, "I'm ready for the movie, Dad."

"Great. Did you decide what to watch?"

"Yep, we are watching live animals that live in the," Noah pretended to have a deep voice, "Amazon rainforest."

"Excellent choice!" Malik turned to Magaly. "Are you ready?"

"I'll just grab us something to drink. You guys go ahead."

"Sit here, Dad," Noah said as he pulled a pillow next to him.

Aries looked content in his little zone, so Malik sat down next to Noah and started the documentary.

Malik tried to focus on what they were watching, knowing that Noah would have questions and want to talk about it, but his mind kept wandering anyway. After talking with his grandma, he had tried to read the journal again, but still had no luck. Then he thought about what would happen once he could read it. *Am I ready for this? If there's not supposed to be any physical interaction in dream travel, how am I supposed to hand off the photo?*

Malik's reflections were interrupted by his son's enthusiastic voice.

"Here, Dad, look!" Noah said. "That's the leaf-cutter ant."

Malik watched as the ants used their mandibles to cut parts out of leaves, which then floated to the ground to be carried back to the mound by other ants.

"Did you hear that, Dad? The ants don't eat the leaves."

"They don't?"

"Nope. They turn the leaves into a fungus and their babies eat that."

"Really?" Malik looked down at those same bright, intelligent eyes. "You're helping me learn new things."

"That's why I'm going to be a teacher."

"You'll make a fantastic teacher."

"And a scientist, and an inventor."

"I love it. That all sounds perfect."

"Oh, no!" Noah shouted and pointed at the screen. "Something is wrong with the ant."

Malik turned to the screen and saw an ant with what looked like an involuntary jerking hitch in its walk.

"What's wrong with it?" Noah asked.

"Let's listen and find out," Magaly said. "Volume up, please."

The documentary showed the ant struggling to climb up a branch. The ant appeared to slip and lose its grip, but it didn't stop.

"Closed captions on, please."

WHEN THE GUARDS *discover an ant has been infected with the spores from a parasitic fungus, they quickly carry the infected ant away to protect the colony. The guards are, in effect, committing suicide to protect the colony, because they know what happens next. The fungi, cordycep, infiltrates the system that controls the ant's body and mind. Cordycep forces the insect to go to an ideal place with the right height, temperature, and moisture, where it then forces the ant to clamp its powerful mandibles, locking the ant's body to a prime place. Then, after several weeks, the fungus develops its spores to infect more insects in the jungle.*

MALIK WATCHED the screen as the ant clamped its mandibles onto a part of a tree, then hung there, no longer moving. The documentary showed a time lapse of the process happening to the ant's body as the fungus eventually sprouted spores, which in this case looked like a whitish-purple blade of grass.

"What is that?" Noah asked.

"The program said it is a type of fungi," Magaly answered. "Not the kind the ants farm, but a different, harmful kind."

"Wait, aren't mushrooms fungi too?" he asked.

"Yes, they are," Magaly responded. "But… Pause, please."

"They can do that?" Noah's alarm was comical, but Magaly did a good job not laughing. "I'm never eating mushrooms again."

"Those aren't like the mushrooms we eat," she said.

Noah shook his head strongly from side to side. "I'm not eating them. I don't want that to happen to me."

"And it never will," Nia said as she passed by the couch.

"How long have you been there?" Malik asked.

"Oh, I was just walking through. And, Noah, you know what?"

"What?" Noah asked.

"Do you know why that bad fungi won't ever take you over?"

"Why?"

"Because Opa feeds you the good stuff." Nia winked at the child. "The good stuff helps to fend off the bad stuff."

"Really?"

"In fact, he's probably out finding some good ones right now."

Malik stood up as something clicked in his brain. *The answer's been here all along.*

"Where are you going, Dad?"

Malik turned to Magaly. "I have an idea."

"What?" she asked.

"Yeah, what's your idea, Dad?" Noah stood up too, eagerly looking up at Malik.

Malik inhaled. "Do you remember how that man was hurt at the zoo?"

Noah nodded.

"We think that the solar flares can harm people's brains and make them do things they don't want to do, kind of like what happened to that ant. I have an idea that if fungi can do this," Malik pointed at the television, "maybe there are fungi out there that can help protect against things that impact the brain too." Malik glanced at Magaly.

"That could work," Magaly said. "Assuming you find someone who has researched and cataloged the various fungi and their effect on the human body. I mean, penicillin does come from a fungus, and mushrooms have been used medicinally for thousands of years."

"I'm gonna go find Jonas."

36

THE LION'S MANE

MALIK SPEED-WALKED TO THE TREES BEYOND THE GARDEN WITH HIS head on a swivel, looking for any sign of Jonas. Before long, he saw movement in the distance. Jonas was kneeling down at the base of a tree, examining something with intense concentration.

"Jonas!" Malik called out.

Jonas, still kneeling, turned to face him. "Malik? What are you doing out here?"

"I have a question for you."

Jonas lifted his wide-brimmed hat, exposing the smudges of dirt above his eyebrows and down the sides of his face. "Of course. What's up?"

"It's about fungi."

"Excellent topic and timing." Jonas smiled as he stood up.

"We were just watching a nature documentary that sparked an idea. I was hoping to run it by you or your mycologist group."

"I'm intrigued. Tell me more."

Malik could tell how excited Jonas was to help. After Malik's father stopped visiting, Malik had made a vow to himself to become as self-reliant as possible. He did not want to feel like a burden to anyone, and he'd thought this would be the best answer. It was several years later that Jonas came into their lives. Malik's mom had wanted them to bond, and on one particular fall break, she had planned for Malik and Jonas to spend a day together replenishing firewood. Malik had approached it like so many things in his old life. While his mom and Jonas were out getting groceries, he took care of the chore by himself. He had never forgotten the look of disappointment on Jonas's face, and he'd realized his mom was not the only one who had wanted them to bond. The two men had since developed a strong relationship, and Malik appreciated the support and wisdom he had come to expect from Jonas.

"You know how the solar flares have become more harmful over the last fifteen years or so?"

"Yes, I know the protective glass was a big accomplishment for your grandfather and for you. We certainly appreciate having it on the house."

"Are you also aware of the strange, dangerous behavior that's increasingly on the news?"

"You know I don't really watch the news, but I have heard a little about that. Like what happened at the zoo before you brought your family here?"

"Yes, like that. It's been getting steadily worse, and is actually caused by exposure to the solar flares."

"Okay," Jonas replied, looking Malik intently in the eye and pushing his hat back off his head so it hung around his neck.

"There is not yet any treatment or cure. The scientist who came the furthest in understanding the cause of this solar sickness established the solar flares were causing rapid growth of the bacteria, fungi, and chemicals that lay latent in our guts. In some people, this has impacted the brain, creating a sort of fog and reduced ability to make decisions and control impulses."

"Hmmm…" Jonas looked back down at the base of the tree, and Malik could tell his wheels were already turning.

"Well, in what I was just watching with the boys, they showed the effects of a parasitic fungus on insects."

"Cordyceps?"

"That's the one. So, I was thinking, if a fungus could take over the mind and body of an insect, are there fungi that could counteract something like that?"

Jonas looked back up at Malik, his eyes wide.

"What?"

"How long has this been happening?"

"I mean, we've been seeing effects for over ten years, but the erratic behavior has been accelerating over the past three years."

"The last three years," Jonas repeated, while turning toward an area deeper in the woods. "This can't be a coincidence."

"What can't be a coincidence?" Malik asked, his stomach tightening in anticipation.

"I have to show you. Follow me."

Jonas walked ahead of Malik with a determined stride, forcing Malik to jog here and there to keep up. They ventured off the trail into a part of the forest new to Malik, where the undergrowth was high enough he was thankful he had put on boots before leaving the house. This had to be where Jonas spent a lot of his time foraging.

"This is old-growth forest, you know," Jonas said over his shoulder. "It's been left to do what it does. Only the rare mycologist friend comes into this part of the woods with me."

The trees were spectacularly large, and on the forest floor were enormous moss-covered branches and an array of vibrant green ferns.

"Come," Jonas said as he kneeled low to the ground so they were almost crawling along a log and through the bushes. "Try to walk as close to my trail as possible so we don't disturb the forest floor."

Malik did as instructed, and Jonas led them to a place where several large trees had fallen completely to the ground. "There." Jonas extended his hand, pointing to something. "Do you see it?"

There, at the base of a tree, Malik saw a large white ball with a strand-like texture.

"That's lion's mane," Jonas said. "It's a well-known supplement for healing the brain, gut, and heart. There was research that said it could even help improve neural connections in the brain."

"I've never seen it before," Malik said.

"Wait, there's more." Jonas walked them farther until he came to a stream. "Look over there."

Every single tree across the river, as far as Malik could see, had lion's mane growing at the base.

"This is the most lion's mane we have ever seen." Jonas looked at Malik. "Across the world, old-growth forests have seen a substantial increase in lion's mane."

"Not that I watch a lot of news myself, but I have heard nothing about this."

"It's probably not the type of thing that makes its way to mass media. There's more too," Jonas said as he took a few steps, kneeled, and plucked a different type of mushroom from the ground. It was flat and brown, with white stripes near the edge. "This is called turkey tail. It has been used to help boost the immune system and fight some types of cancer. Malik, this too has been growing in abundance, much more than ever before recorded, in the past two to three years. If what you are saying is true, and solar sickness has become more severe in the past few years, then I believe the earth has been giving us a cure."

37

IN SEARCH OF A DREAM

THAT NIGHT, WELL AFTER MAGALY HAD FALLEN ASLEEP, MALIK picked up the journal again to try it. He turned on the reading light and sat back against his pillows, looking at the puzzle of a book. He took several deep breaths with his eyes closed. *I can do this. I am present and connected. I am ready.* Malik opened his eyes to peer down at the book. At first, it was still all ones and zeros to him, but he didn't look away. Sure enough, the numbers on the page became blurry. Malik brought the journal closer to his face to see that the text was actually vibrating. Before his eyes, the first numbers converted to 6.19. Malik let out a quick burst of air in excitement and looked over at Magaly, peacefully sleeping, and whispered, "It's happening!"

Malik assumed he was supposed to start at the beginning, but he couldn't resist flipping through the journal. He stopped on a random selection of pages, allowing a moment on each for the numbers to transform into text. On one such page, a picture took shape instead. *What is this?* he wondered as he tried to process the image. It looked like a dome resting on the top of a pyramid. Something about it reminded him of a snow globe he had gotten in

Singapore for Noah. The souvenir had a miniature scale version of the Marina Bay Sands hotel, resembling a massive ship sitting on top of three pillars, which were actually hotel rooms. Noah still had that snow globe, and Malik laughed, thinking about how they took to calling it Noah's Ark. As he looked more closely at the drawing, he could tell there was a city inside the dome. He continued to turn the pages and found subsequent drawings with more detail of the city: the streets, buildings, green spaces, and even trees.

His eyes were getting fatigued, so he took a break and gazed out the window. There was a full moon lighting up the night. From this window, on a clear day, you could see Mount Olympus. Malik's mind wandered to the Mount Olympus of Greece and its gods and goddesses. The distant hoot of an owl interrupted Malik's reverie, reminding him that now was not the time to get lost in thought.

Malik skipped ahead to find that there were several empty pages in the back of the journal. His grandma's entries stopped about two-thirds of the way through. He was going back to the beginning when he noticed the cloth bookmark holding a place in the middle. *How did I not see this before?* Malik contemplated before he tugged on the thin blue cloth to see what it marked. The text took shape.

Today, I finally had time to visit the food and wine festival I've heard so much about. It was more expansive than I could have imagined. Countless booths lined each road inside the domed city. The booths, made mostly of bamboo, felt more like huts. Vau said it's part of the tradition. I wasn't a carefree attendee today though. I volunteered to help work the smoothie booth with Dylynn.

Malik's eyelids became heavy, so he set the journal down on his lap. He reached into the drawer of his nightstand and pulled out the photo Senator Whitman had given him. Inspecting it again, hoping that would help him know how to take it with him, he turned it over in his hands. He sighed and placed it inside the journal, turned out the light, and rested his head.

THE BLARING whir of the blender made Malik jump.

"Can we have two, please?"

Two people who were chest high to Malik and dressed in flowing robes, were standing in front of him. Malik surveyed the scene and quickly realized he was at a festival, with food stands that looked like bamboo huts as far as the eye could see. *Did it work?* Malik glanced down at his wrist, and his timepiece displayed the number 6.19. *This is real! I did it!*

"Here you go." A young lady's voice came from beside him. A woman with striking red hair extended her freckled arms to give the patrons their smoothies.

In tandem, they said, "Thank you, Dylynn."

Though they were shaded inside the smoothie booth, Malik felt beads of sweat sliding down his back. Most of the festival-goers were dressed for the warm weather. He peaked his head out, looking for any sign of some familiar landmark from his grandma's drawings. Dylynn didn't seem to notice him, so he ventured away from the booth to better assess the area. He jumped out of the way as a group of children sprinted past him, caught up in a game of chase as if no one else was around. Malik smiled and shook his head. The sight of those kids laughing and playing made him think of his sons.

That's when he heard a friendly vendor a few huts down shout, "Hello, Gardner! How are you today?"

Malik scanned the area in front of that booth, trying to discern who the vendor was addressing. He spotted a man with smooth, dark skin in a straw hat leisurely strolling along the street with his hands clasped behind his back. He had acknowledged the vendor with a warm smile before looking ahead and nodding at folks as they passed by.

The man walked right by him, but Malik froze, unsure what to say and whether this was even who he was seeking. As the man approached the smoothie stand, Malik hurried back into the hut to gain a second opportunity. He tried to wait for a break in the casual exchange between Gardner and Dylynn. Malik couldn't understand what they were saying for some reason, but he took a deep breath and jumped in. "Excuse me? Are you Gardner?"

The man turned his attention to Malik, staring at him with confusion written on his face. "Do you know me?"

"Umm, I think I know who you are. I was sent to get your help."

"Oh, you were?"

"Yes, I was told you could help me find someone, or I guess the right version of someone." Malik instinctively reached into his pockets, and in the left, found the photo from Senator Whitman. He extended it toward Gardner. "I was told to give you this."

As Gardner looked at the picture, Malik studied the man's face more closely. Strangely, he felt as though he had seen him before. In a dream, perhaps? An image of the man in nursing scrubs floated into Malik's mind. Suddenly he got a sensation of being constrained against his will, and panic seized his chest. Malik rubbed his arms, averted his eyes, and focused on his breath.

"Lucky that was just a dream, no?" Gardner said, observing Malik with understanding. "You do know me, though my role was a small one. How is your grandmother? It has been a while since I've seen the Scribe."

"She's doing well, spending more time at the Point."

"Ah, bittersweet."

Malik tilted his head, unsure of what Gardner meant by that. He waited a second, but when Gardner said nothing else, Malik refocused on the mission. "I'm looking for Anatole Patterson. I need to give him a message wherever he is ready to receive it."

Gardner glanced back at the photo. "Evelyn and Ori must really trust your bloodline for this to have found its way into your possession." Gardner returned his gaze to Malik. "There is one place where you can find him, but it's likely to be a difficult experience for you." Gardner handed the picture back to Malik.

Malik objected to taking the picture back, but as he held it, it transformed into a plain, cream-colored piece of paper. He glanced back up at Gardner. "Who are you?" Malik asked.

"I'm Gardner. I know where everything is planted and how it grows. But you've called me George." Gardner paused. "Are you sure you are ready for this?"

"I am," Malik affirmed.

Gardner smiled. "Seven point eight three zero two zero one two zero two zero."

"What?" Malik felt his pockets again frantically, wishing he had something to write with.

"That's where you will find the ideal state to reach Anatole Patterson. That's your best shot. But prepare yourself: he has trouble with sleep." With that, Gardner spun on his heel, and Malik felt himself pulled in the opposite direction, as though he were falling backward.

Malik awakened with a jump and found himself in bed with his grandma's journal open, resting on his chest. He picked it up, hoping he could remember the exact frequency Gardner had given him. Inside, he now found the photo-sized piece of paper with 7.8302012020 written on one side. On the other was a flyer for a concert at Gardens by the Bay.

38

THE MISSION BRIEF

ORI MET HIM IN THE WOODS THAT MORNING AND SUGGESTED THEY RUN together again. He set the pace at first, but then let Malik assume the lead, deciding which trails to take. Perhaps because it was up-tempo, or perhaps to let Malik focus on his surroundings and his breath, the run was a quiet one. When they finished back near Malik's grandma's house, Ori seemed pleased with the exercise and told Malik to get cleaned up and meet the team back at the command center.

When Malik got to the Point, he met the team in the octagonal room. Evelyn and Ori were in the middle of discussing something quietly, so Malik took a seat near the door. Vau came in and patted him on the back. "It seems like Gardner likes you. Well done!"

"Gabriel won't be able to argue with that," Tony said, strolling in with Vau.

"They just jump right into it, don't they?" Carlos said, trailing the duo before finding a seat across the table. "Good morning, Malik."

"Morning," said Malik, appreciating the growing feeling of being a part of this group.

Jordan flopped down in the seat to his left and seemed to address the entire room. "Isn't this a little soon to be sending him on an assignment? Let's not forget that the target barely sleeps."

Ori, who seemed to have heard everything despite his conversation with Evelyn, turned to Jordan. "Now, you know it is not our call who is and isn't ready. Malik received the token, and Gardner gave him the answer. He's got to be the one who goes in."

At the mention of the token, Malik got out the picture that had changed into a flyer with the frequency written on the back and placed it on the table in front of him.

"I know you're concerned, Jordan, but he can handle this," said Ori.

"What are you worried about?" Malik asked Jordan.

Jordan shook her head. "It's just, I've known people who have trained far longer than you have and still can't manage what you are about to do with someone who has a regular sleep pattern. We're talking about entering someone's dream, and with insomniacs, the dreams move much quicker and the mind is on edge."

"That's why Malik is needed," Ori said. "Anatole's subconscious won't feel so threatened."

"You're going to be a familiar face in the dream," explained Vau to Malik. "The face that gives the dreamer a feeling that what they are experiencing is real."

"And more than that," Ori interjected, "your presence should give the dreamer some sense of responsibility—a feeling to take action after they wake up."

"I only met Anatole in person twice, and that was about five years ago. Do you think my face will be meaningful enough to him for all that?" asked Malik.

"We do," said Ori. "You and Zach were very important in his life because of your support and passion for his research. When he sees your face, he should feel the collective influence of both you and your grandfather."

"The cause of Anatole's paranoia was how he was treated when he first shared his theories connecting consumption to the effects of intensified solar flares," Vau said. "He was treated horribly and lost his funding. Your grandparents were saviors to him when they saw past all of that, believed in him, and privately funded his work. That's a strong connection."

"The frequency Gardner gave me isn't just seven point eight three. There's a string of numbers. Will my relationship and history with Anatole be the same?" Malik asked.

"Great question," said Evelyn. "What Gardner gave you is the exact point to enter Anatole's dream. It's still in your version of reality, so all of what you know and have experienced with Anatole is valid."

"Okay, that's good," Malik said, feeling more comfortable. "So his subconscious will be less on edge. Is that also what makes him receptive?"

Carlos spoke up this time. "To you, yes. To the message, it's something else. Until now, Anatole has feared resuming his work. He has always had a tendency to work with maniacal focus, and he did not want to let that happen, look up, and have lost his daughter too. But his daughter is now getting older and is ready for more of an independent life. He's been resisting it, but down deep he knows it."

"All he needs now is a nudge from someone he trusts and a spark of inspiration to point him to the missing piece," said Evelyn. "That will give him the belief that he has everything he needs to finish his work."

"Is the missing piece what I think it is?" Malik asked.

"You tell us," said Ori.

"I don't think it can be a coincidence that lion's mane and

turkey tail mushrooms have been growing at unprecedented rates over the past few years."

"And did this discovery happen after a very clear request from someone?" Ori asked.

"Yes, it did, from a senator. And it came with an offer to secure funding."

"Manifestation," said Ori, before looking at Evelyn. "And it meets Gabriel's criteria."

Evelyn nodded at Malik. "That's the missing piece you'll point him to in the dream. Then in real life, you can facilitate the funding of the completion of Anatole's work."

Just then, a man knocked on the open glass door and said, "Am I early?"

"You're right on time, Gabriel," replied Evelyn.

Gabriel stepped into the room and quickly zoned in on Malik. "Malik, it's a pleasure," he said, extending his hand.

Malik shook Gabriel's hand and said, "Nice to meet you."

Gabriel took a seat right by Evelyn and continued talking. "I heard the good news that your training has gone swimmingly, and you're ready for the mission."

Before Malik could reply, Ori said, "That's right."

"So, what's the plan?" Gabriel asked, leaning back in his chair and propping one foot up on his other knee. "Effectively traveling into someone's dream is challenging. Are you sure you aren't rushing it?"

"It's time," said Ori.

"He was expressly asked to do this in his reality. A solution presented itself to him, and Gardner granted him the frequency," said Evelyn.

"Well, then." Gabriel eyed Malik. "Sounds like we're ready to give it a go. What's the premise?"

"Jordan," Evelyn said, "can you walk us through the background?"

"You got it," Jordan said. "Anatole has always traveled a lot, starting when he was a child. His parents took him all over the world, and he has continued that with his own family. Two places hold the most meaning for him: Singapore and New York City. Anatole's parents believed the people of Singapore knew something that the rest of the world didn't, which is why they built a giant hotel that looks like a ship on top of massive pillars. Anatole has fond childhood memories of that hotel. Then, as an adult, he got to watch the love of his life do what she loved most at Gardens by the Bay. Those are the reasons his mind often seeks solace there."

"Is that why the paper Gardner gave me is a flyer for a concert there?" Malik held the flyer up for the room to see.

"Yes, exactly. And New York City is where Anatole lives now and is where he has spent several years since his wife passed trying to create the best life possible for his daughter."

That was news to Malik. He didn't know Anatole was back in the country.

"Malik, you won't have much time. You will have two to three changes of scene max to get into position. Both locations give Anatole a feeling of joy and put his mind at ease. Just keep these locations in the back of your mind. If the dream gets chaotic, you both will have the same destination in mind, and that will be enough to reset to a much calmer scene."

"Should we walk through it?" Gabriel asked.

39

THE WALK-THROUGH

Tony took over the floor to walk through the plan. "Anatole has a recurring dream of watching one of his wife's concerts at Gardens by the Bay, so this is where it will start. Malik, since you actually attended one with Anatole several years ago, it won't seem strange for you to be in the audience. His subconscious should accept this."

"Okay, am I attending with him, like a recreation of that visit? Or do I just happen to be in the audience?" Malik asked.

"You'll sit next to him, and once he sees you, his mind should create the scene to align with the memory, especially if you activate that memory as well. Something to note, though, is that Anatole dreams in black and white and without sound. What you envision will need to match that," Tony said. "Your original visit was to express support for his research. His mind should interpret this the same way, which is perfect. During your visit, what happened after the concert?"

"We took a stroll. His daughter was there, but with friends, so we were giving them some space."

"Perfect, that should naturally happen here as well. And that's when you'll share the missing piece with him."

"If there's no sound, how do I have a conversation with him?" Malik asked.

"You won't need to talk," Tony replied. "Just keep a calm, pleasant energy. Make eye contact, and behave as though you're engaged in the conversation. Then briefly envision the lion's mane. That should translate well since it's white."

"But won't he find it odd to see large mushrooms growing out of the artificial trees?"

"Not in this dream. It's his world, all things come to him in all different ways. And since it's not an out-of-place person, it should be noticeable without being disturbing to his subconscious."

"Got it," Malik said.

"Should we expect any resistance?" Gabriel asked.

"There's a chance of that," Ori said. "Anatole's mind should associate this visit with his old research. That could trigger his fear of letting it consume him and hurting his relationship with his daughter. Just remember, Malik, don't attack, only defend. And always the extras, never the target."

"Okay," Malik said.

Tony took back over. "It's important that we bring Anatole to the present within the dream. Malik, as you pointed out, the mushrooms will be a natural thing popping up on man-made structures. We think this could actually help transition to the next scene of a natural wooded area: Central Park."

"Okay, I've spent time there too. Not with him, obviously, but I can visualize it well."

"Good. Here's where it gets interesting. The goal will then be to drive the connection home between the lion's mane and what's happening in the gut. We have an idea of how to ensure the dream stays with him vividly once he's awake."

"What's the idea?"

"Have you ever heard of Alexis St. Martin?"

"No, I don't believe so."

"He was a young Canadian fur trapper who was shot in the stomach in the eighteen hundreds. It happened in a general store when someone near him was looking at a rifle, and it accidentally went off. Alexis survived and became the subject of the first real in-depth study of the stomach. This story also plays because Anatole has read and journaled about it in relation to his own research."

"How do we incorporate something like that into the dream?"

"The first step will be to lead the stroll out of the park and into a sporting goods store. Anatole's daughter is an athlete, and her track season is starting soon. She'll need new spikes. If you envision a sporting goods store, we think he'll go along with it, especially if you don't react."

"Then I briefly think about Alexis St. Martin and a rifle?"

"Actually," Tony looked apprehensive and shifted in his chair, "you'll bring to mind the accident itself. It should play out in front of you. The shot should wake Anatole up."

Malik looked around at all the faces in the room. They were each eyeing him carefully, clearly trying to read his reaction. He hated to bring an event like that into the dream of someone already struggling to sleep.

"It won't be traumatic," Ori said. "He knows about this already. If you envision the inside of the store as a quaint place and see the young man as a fur trapper from the 1800s, it will feel like a black-and-white movie. And that's okay, because Anatole will be about to wake up anyway. It will be jarring, but not harmful."

Malik turned this over in his mind. What Ori proposed made him feel better. And if making the ending of the dream impactful was their best chance at success, he had to be all in. He nodded at Tony and said, "Got it. I can do that."

"We need a contingency plan," Jordan said. "What if fear kicks in, and the transitions don't happen as planned?"

"They can stay in Central Park," suggested Tony. "Anatole and his daughter have always liked the Alice in Wonderland statue."

"That could be good for reinforcing both lion's mane and turkey tail," Malik said. "I don't know about a jarring ending to that one though."

"Just make sure that you stay with him and make your face the last he sees," Tony said.

"Malik," Ori said, "this is where your ability to solve problems comes into play. We know his fear is being without his daughter, yet we don't know what that will look like. That could mean he gets lost in a large crowd, or it could mean he's lost his daughter at a train station. His focus will be to keep track of and follow his daughter. If things get out of hand, your task will be to do whatever you have to do to be the last face he sees before he wakes up."

"How will I know when it's time for him to wake up?"

"The third sub-dial on your watch," said Tony. "It will show the frequency of Anatole's brain waves. If the frequency is between zero point five and four hertz, then he is in a deep sleep. Since Anatole has insomnia, it's more likely that his brain waves will be between four and seven point five hertz. In that state, he is still dreaming; he's just aware within the dream. When the frequency approaches eight hertz, that means that he can wake up at any moment."

Evelyn spoke to Gabriel and Carlos. "Will you two be able to make sure no one wakes him prematurely?"

"Yeah, we can handle that," Carlos said, and Gabriel nodded.

"Malik," Evelyn's face turned serious, "although Carlos and Gabriel will provide cover, we still can't expect Anatole to be asleep for long. These transitions can happen incredibly fast, so you need to stay focused and be ready to move."

40

MISSION AT THE GARDENS

MALIK ALMOST ALWAYS WOKE UP AROUND TWO OR THREE IN THE morning and would force himself to stay in bed until five. Sometimes that resulted in another hour or two of sleep, and other times he would just listen to the owls and think about his beautiful life. Tonight, Malik wasn't taking any chances though, which is why he set a small timer to vibrate under his pillow at two thirty.

He awakened to the soft, even breathing of Magaly, thankfully undisturbed by his alarm. He lay there for half an hour, reminding himself of each part of the plan, and then, once comfortable, he cleared his mind. He could hardly believe he had finally arrived at this moment, and he had to trust he had done all the preparation he could.

Malik held his wrist up and rubbed his thumb over the face, creating a glow in the darkened room. He placed his index finger above the middle sub-dial of the skeleton watch. The face transformed into an opaque black, while the three sub-dials shone white. Malik removed his finger and watched as the middle sub-dial flashed, displaying the number 0.0. He twisted the bezel around the watch face until the number displayed 7.8302012020.

Malik extended his arms down by his sides, palms facing up. He sealed his lips, closed his eyes, and concentrated solely on his breath. *Inhale... hold... exhale... squeeze. Inhale... hold... exhale... squeeze.*

Malik felt a subtle tickle begin on his biceps and spread down his arms to his fingertips. The sensation then jumped to his toes before it crawled up to his stomach, generating a flurry of butterflies. His mind flitted to an image of black-and-orange-winged monarch butterflies, but Malik pushed it out. The flutter in his belly became a feeling of joy, and he couldn't help but smile. He breathed sharply in through his nose, to calm and focus himself once more. *Inhale... hold... exhale... squeeze.*

Malik's body became weightless, and his connection to the bedroom he was in faded away. He no longer felt the soft king-sized bed or the pillow supporting his back. He didn't feel the soft linen sheets on his skin. Malik felt the urge to open his eyes, but he resisted. *Inhale... hold... exhale... squeeze.* Higher and higher, he felt himself elevating, until he lost sense of what was up and what was down. It was as if, through no movement of his own, his body was propelled to standing. Ahead of him was a small white light coming at him fast.

The next thing he knew, he was walking along a concrete sidewalk, and with each step Malik took, a burst of light and energy radiated in every direction. He focused on his breathing. *Inhale... hold... exhale... squeeze.* As Malik continued down the path, a giant cylindrical tower dropped next to him, its landing gentle. Malik was mesmerized as pink tubes sprouted from the ground, twisting and turning, as they crawled up the sides of the tower like the English ivy that took over the pine trees behind his house in Atlanta. Next, patches of green shrubs popped out of the sides of the cylinder, starting at the bottom. Within seconds, the entire structure had vertically growing plants hanging onto and over the pink tube-like structure.

Malik craned his neck to see the top of the tower, just as a bright, violet light turned on. His attention was drawn back to the illuminated pathway as more towers sprouted. This time, almost instantly, each shined a different colored light from the top. The vibrant blue, red, green, and orange colors felt warm and welcoming. Malik strolled along until he spotted a group of people walking ahead of him. *Anatole,* Malik thought as he started after the group. He had taken only three steps when he found himself seated in the audience of the concert.

The musicians' heads and elbows moved with precision to the presto tempo of the beginning bars of Mozart's *The Marriage of Figaro.* There were bright flashes with each crescendo, and gentle pulses of light with each softer note. *The light show.* Malik realized what was going on, getting caught up in the concert. Catching movement in his periphery, he glanced at the chair next to him. To his surprise, Anatole was seated there, gazing at the orchestra. His smile was broad and genuine.

Malik focused on remaining relaxed and natural. As he faced forward again to watch the musicians, the entire scene faded to shades of black, white, and gray. And though the orchestra still swayed as each member played their instrument, Malik could no longer hear the music. He looked around the audience to see people watching with rapt attention. When Malik's eyes fell upon Anatole again, he was now regarding Malik with his brow furrowed and his smile gone. His hands were resting on his lap, his fingers keeping time with the music. Reacting quickly, Malik tapped his foot in the same rhythm, and tried to exude the enjoyment he had felt when the concert had begun. He kept his attention on the stage for a few moments before risking a glance at Anatole. It was a relief to see that he once again looked at ease.

Malik continued to tap his foot, and out of the corner of his eye, he monitored Anatole until he became still. Malik tried to assess what was wrong and followed Anatole's stare to the orchestra's cellist. It was no longer Anatole's wife. Instead, there sat a young man, maybe in his late twenties. The ground trembled as Anatole's breathing grew shallow and intense. Malik became conscious of his own breathing.

Inhale... hold... exhale... squeeze.

An idea came to him, and Malik brought to mind standing with Anatole on the path, watching his daughter run to an ice cream stand. The multicolored umbrella appeared within their view, but the shaking continued. *Now what?* Then Malik recognized his error and reimagined the scene in black and white. Slowly, the ground steadied, and Anatole's breathing normalized. As his daughter turned toward them with a smile on her face, Malik could sense the return of Anatole's joy.

Anatole stood up and walked. Malik hastily followed so he could be in stride with his companion. Anatole looked at Malik with a raised brow, as if listening to him speak. Malik wasn't saying anything and was trying to decide whether to pretend, when Anatole laughed, crossed his arms behind his back, and silently carried forward the conversation. Malik matched Anatole's body language and did as he was coached, doing his best to look pleasant and engaged. Anatole appeared to be eagerly chatting, occasionally gesturing with his hands. Malik was about to picture the lion's mane when Anatole froze mid-stride. His daughter was now standing in front of them, holding two ice cream cones that had melted into puddles by her feet.

Anatole lunged toward his daughter with open arms. As Malik looked on, a crowd took form and encircled them. Anatole's face twisted in panic, and Malik edged closer. The mob of people pressed in with a strange aggression, wedging themselves between Anatole, his daughter, and Malik.

Despite his heart pounding in his chest, Malik silently told himself, *Stay calm! Go to the contingency plan.* Malik closed his eyes. *Inhale... hold... exhale... squeeze.* Malik saw the Alice in

Wonderland statue and was careful this time to be true to how Anatole dreams.

When Malik opened his eyes, the crowd had disappeared, and the trio was now in Central Park. As Malik released the image from his own mind, Anatole's subconscious took over, and the statue came to life. Alice ran across the clearing before climbing back onto a giant toadstool and crossing her legs. Her cat jumped up and into her lap. Then the White Rabbit chased the Mad Hatter. Malik did a spin and took in the buildings of New York City, visible above the tree line, before turning back to the laughing faces of Anatole and his daughter.

Malik took a seat on the bench next to Anatole as the characters all settled back into place on the eleven-foot-tall statue. Knowing he might not have long, Malik pictured the lion's mane. As all three of them sat there observing the statue, the toadstool vibrated and transformed. The long stem widened, and the upper structure melted and dripped until it looked like Alice was seated atop a ball of white fringe. Anatole leaned forward and stroked his chin.

A buzzing sensation drew Malik's attention down to his wrist, where the third sub-dial jumped from 4.6 to 6.3. The surrounding pathways, previously clear, were now filling with people walking toward them with purpose. Anatole grabbed his daughter's hand as they were washed away in a sea of people. Malik tried to follow them, but the crowd was too thick. The harder Malik tried to force his way through, the harder he was bumped and pushed back. It felt as though he were in quicksand.

Inhale… hold… exhale… squeeze. Malik thought of his defense training. *If I can do that in reality, I can do it here.*

Malik focused on his closest threats, tucked his chin into his chest, and raised his fists, elbows up. His vision adjusted, and the air thickened. Opening his palms face down, he thrust his arms downward, the force of which pushed the crowd out, creating some space around him. He leaped onto the bench and located

Anatole and his daughter leaving the park. Malik kneeled slightly before giving a powerful jump. It was enough to clear the crowd and the trees and exit the park.

Anatole and his daughter were beginning their descent into the subway. *I've got to be there before he wakes up.* Malik moved with incredible speed to close the gap and reach the subway before losing sight of them. He jumped the turnstile to follow them onto a platform. A light flashed, alerting passengers that the train was arriving. Malik had almost reached Anatole and his daughter when the other people on the platform morphed into transit officers on alert. Malik assumed his defensive position again while his mind plotted a last-ditch effort to ensure the success of the mission. The officers ran at him right as the train rushed into the station. Malik threw his force into the wind the train created, which sent the officers sliding and tumbling backward.

Then Malik sprinted to the doors that Anatole and his daughter had walked through, his watch now displaying 8.0. He conjured an image of himself as a young fur trapper and stood before the open doors, looking Anatole in the eye. A man appeared on the platform holding a musket, examining it as if he were in a store. Anatole's eyes widened, and his mouth opened to give a warning. As the subway doors closed, a tremendous force threw Malik to the floor, and a blinding light consumed the scene.

Malik shot upright in bed, clutching his stomach. He was safely home in bed, and outside his window, a bolt of lightning ignited the dark night sky.

41

DANDELIONS AND DÉJÀ VU

JESSICA ROLLED OVER TO LIE ON HER SIDE IN A FAILED ATTEMPT TO GET comfortable. When she returned to her back, her eyes still closed, she felt her sheets stick to the exposed skin above her chest. She rubbed the base of her throat and opened her eyes to inspect the moisture that her fingertips had collected. She had been sweating. Jessica noticed that fractions of sunlight had found their way through her curtains. *I overslept?* she thought as she got out of bed.

After washing up and getting dressed, Jessica made her way toward the kitchen. From the hallway, she heard Noah roar and yell before the sound of the back door closing muffled his young, energetic voice. As she continued down the hall, she felt a shadow, shuffling his feet behind her. She glanced down to see Aries standing there, looking up at her and smiling widely enough to show his baby teeth. Jessica smiled back at his little face and said, "Hello there."

He sang something she didn't quite recognize. "Aw yoo seepeen, aw yoo seepeen." He gave her another grin and waddled along on his way again.

"Good morning, Mom," Nia's voice rang out. "How are you feeling?"

"Oh." Jessica was surprised by the question. "I'm fine." She spent a moment in her body, making sure there were no new aches or pains. "I'm just fine."

"That's good! I have some breakfast ready for you at the dining table."

"Thank you." Jessica reached up to her neck, expecting to feel the cool frames of her vision glasses.

"I put them on the table, next to your breakfast," Nia said.

"Oh, great. Thank you," Jessica responded, slightly confused because she always left them on her nightstand.

The dining room was empty, and eating at that table had an odd, formal feeling. The family only ate there on holidays or other special occasions. Although Jessica did like the view out the large bay windows. It allowed her to see the gate and driveway down below. Today, she could see Magaly, standing on the wraparound deck, applying oil paint to a sketch. Jessica looked down at her plate and picked up the blueberry muffin just before Nia brought in a bowl of grits and scrambled eggs, with the steam still rising from the dish.

Aries was right behind her, singing the same song. "Aw yoo seepeen, aw yoo seepeen."

"So pretty, baby!" Nia encouraged him in a sweet voice and then finished the song. "Brother John, Brother John. Morning bells are ringing. Morning bells are ringing. Ding, Ding, Dong. Ding, Ding, Dong."

Aries beamed and bobbed his head up and down. "Deen, deen, don. Deen, deen, don."

"I'll go get your tea," Nia said and vanished once more.

Aries came over and leaned into Jessica's leg, resting his head against her thigh and staring at something out the window. She combed her fingers through the boy's big loopy curls that were soft and loose and uniquely his. She found herself lost in the moment, staring at how the light played off his auburn locks.

"His hair reminds me of my grandfather's." Jessica looked up to see Magaly standing at the entrance of the dining room. "Is he bothering you?"

"Oh, no. He's not bothering me at all. We're just enjoying the morning and watching his momma paint." Jessica spoke to Aries: "Aren't we, little one?"

AFTER BREAKFAST, Jessica peeked into the office. Malik was entranced, reading through the journals. *He figured it out,* she thought, feeling proud and excited about the journey he had ahead. She quietly walked away and joined the rest of the family outside, having a seat on the porch where she could take everything in.

Noah and Jonas were bent over inspecting something at the far end of the yard. Nia was walking in the grass next to Aries, who picked a dandelion and tried his best to blow it. Jessica watched as a butterfly flew above his head.

"Buh figh, buh figh," Aries shrieked, and leaned back so far he almost fell backward. He stumbled, but managed to keep his balance. He clapped and laughed, waving his hands up and down to imitate wings flapping in the air.

"Oh, that looks amazing!" Malik had come outside now as well and was inspecting his wife's painting, which was out of Jessica's sight.

"Thank you!" Magaly said.

"Who is that?" Malik asked.

"Your mom told me it was your grandma's childhood friend. I found the photo in the art studio." Jessica briefly wondered what picture Magaly was referring to.

"Aw yoo seepeen, aw yoo seepeen…" Aries was by Jessica's

lap once more. His chubby hand was extended, holding a dandelion.

"Thank you," Jessica said, accepting the flower. She inhaled deeply and blew, just strong enough for some of the dandelion's pappus to float away. Aries shuffled away, intently searching along the grass.

"Mom," Malik said, holding a photo out to Nia. "What happened to her?"

"She passed away young, but…" Jessica couldn't hear what Nia said next.

Jessica's gaze drifted back to Aries, who had found another dandelion. He was squatting next to it, using all his strength to pick the flower. He triumphantly brought it over to her, putting one hand on her knee and holding out the dandelion with the other.

"You can keep it, baby," she told him.

His eyebrows were stern as he grunted and pushed it into her hand. Jessica put her hands together at heart center, smiled, and bowed slightly. "Thank you." She took the flower, and Aries flashed his dimples in return. Then, he turned to go join his big brother.

Jessica decided to go inside for a while. She took her favorite seat in the family room and placed the vision glasses on her face. As she touched the right temple of the frame, before the lenses darkened, Jessica caught sight of the young woman on Magaly's canvas. She had that unmistakable, long, dark hair, freckles, and bright smile.

Breaking news! A headline pulled Jessica's attention back to the screen. *The FDA has granted emergency approval for the new drug that will prevent solar flare sickness. Initial trials have been promising, and the FDA has deemed the drug safe for consumer use. The incredible story of the reclusive scientist, Anatole Patterson, was first covered by the*

Washington, DC-based media company, Str8 Truth Media. Jessica pulled the glasses from her face and lay back in the reclining chair, feeling a new sense of peace. She closed her eyes, inhaled, then exhaled. She heard the baby outside, as if he were standing by the glass door, singing to her.

"Aw yoo, seepeen, aw yoo seepeen?"

Suddenly, his singing became much clearer. Jessica wanted to open her eyes but resisted, until the voice changed, and the words were undeniably clear.

The voice was no longer that of a two-year-old; it had been replaced by that of a young woman. "Are you sleeping? Are you sleeping? Jess-i-ca? Jess-i-ca? Everyone is coming. Everyone is coming. La, di, duh. La, di, duh."

Jessica opened her eyes to a different scene. She was sitting on a blue reclining chair, back in Janice's manufactured home. Jessica sat up and saw a half-full glass of water on the table. She turned to the first window to see the lush green grass and the tall pine trees had been replaced by tan desert sand dotted by jagged mesquite trees.

"You must have been exhausted," Janice said from within the room. "But you woke up just in time. They should be here any minute."

"Who?" Jessica asked.

"Atu and his brother. And they're bringing a friend that we want you to meet."

"What friend?"

"This guy who's been doing his community service at the Y. He has a great story. You should write it. He went to prison for hacking, but guess how he got caught?" Janice paused, perhaps noticing a strange look on her friend's face.

Jessica had already written this story. She had lived it. She had loved it. Hadn't she?

"What?" Janice asked, still staring at her.

"Nothing," Jessica said. "I think I'm having déjà vu." She had lived it. She had loved it. She had written it, and she was enthusiastic about writing it again.

AUTHOR'S NOTE

Thank you for deciding to give your time and attention to *The Rewired Series*. Writing these stories has been a personal journey and has ultimately been a life-changing experience. Now that the third book is complete, I would like to share a few reflections.

When writing *The Recruiter*, I felt called to put positive, diverse images and messages into the world. I wanted my son to live in a world with more CEOs of color, more businesses built upon principles that improved the world, and more members of society feeling included and provided with opportunities. And so I wrote a book where that was the case.

To complete and release that novel, I had to overcome my ego. I couldn't worry about how others would receive my ideas and what they might say. It couldn't be about me. I had to trust my muse and be true to my inspiration.

I then knew I was on the right path. While writing *Deeply Rooted Dreams*, however, I still had to push through doubt and fear. Because I felt those things, I wrote them. Even once you take a leap of faith and pursue a purpose, staying the course requires belief in oneself and persistence.

It became easier to maintain that belief, inspiration, and energy when I focused on personal growth and taking great care of my family and myself. I stayed present and appreciated the journey. The stories flowed, and then came *Emergent Light*.

While writing this, we also welcomed our second child, who has been quite the night owl. Many ideas and scenes came to me in the middle of the night while trying to soothe him back to sleep. He helped me listen to the universe.

Just as I continually work to become a better version of myself, I want each book to be better than the last. This intention is my promise to you.

Thank you for your open-mindedness. Your readership means a great deal to me.

Alexander Mukte

Please consider rating or writing a review of Emergent Light wherever is most convenient for you. Or even better, tell a friend!

CHARACTER LIST

In Alphabetical Order

1. *Aja:* Council member responsible for Earth.
2. *Anatole Patterson:* Brilliant scientist known for his work studying the effects of solar flares.
3. *Aries:* Younger son of Malik and Magaly.
4. *Callie:* Malik's childhood friend.
5. *Carlos:* Council member who can identify and understand the fears of humanity.
6. *Dylynn:* Resident of 6.19 who originally appeared in *Deeply Rooted Dreams* during Match Day.
7. *Evelyn:* Council member who understands the rules and laws that govern life on Earth. Her team takes on missions to help humanity survive the reset.
8. *Gabriel:* Council member responsible for human affairs.
9. *Gardner:* An ascended being who knows "where everything is planted and how it grows."

10. *Janice:* Jessica's childhood friend who symbolizes transitions and new beginnings.
11. *Jessica (a.k.a. GG):* The Scribe and Malik's grandmother.
12. *Jonas (a.k.a. Opa):* Malik's stepfather.
13. *Jordan:* Member of Ori and Evelyn's team, responsible for field operations.
14. *Lotus:* Guide who specializes in becoming rooted.
15. *Magaly:* Malik's wife and confidante.
16. *Malik:* CEO of the Singularity Group who is taking a sabbatical to focus on his family and whatever it takes to ensure them a bright future.
17. *Nia (a.k.a. Nana):* Jessica's daughter and Malik's mom.
18. *Noah:* Elder son of Malik and Magaly.
19. *Ori:* The Recruiter himself who represents the consciousness of man.
20. *Professor Raziel:* Council member who is a teacher, mentor, and keeper of archives.
21. *Ronnie:* Malik's childhood friend who works in the Atlanta mayor's office.
22. *Senator Whitman:* United States senator and great-granddaughter of Lane Whitman.
23. *Silas:* Council member and embodiment of war.
24. *Tony:* Member of Ori and Evelyn's team and creator of the timepieces.
25. *Vau:* Anthropologist and member of Ori and Evelyn's team.
26. *Zach Carver:* Jessica's late husband and Malik's granddad.

DISCUSSION QUESTIONS

1. Have you ever meditated? If so, what was that experience like for you? What, if anything, was challenging?
2. Have you ever taken a sabbatical? If so, for how long, and what did you do during that time? Did it benefit your life?
3. Do you believe in manifestation? If so, is there anything you have manifested in your life?
4. Has a dream or nightmare ever led to actions you have taken in the waking world?
5. Have you ever felt like you were destined for a greater purpose? If so, did you pursue it?
6. If you have ever pursued something that initially seemed out of reach, were you able to achieve it? How long did it take?
7. In the book, Magaly rediscovers a childhood passion for art. Is there anything you enjoyed as a child that you've rediscovered as an adult?
8. Do you dream in color, in first person, and with sound?

9. If someone offered you the power to make anything and everything you dream up a reality, would you be excited or apprehensive?

10. Do you agree with Silas that the ego feeds on conflict, and it's very present in our world?

ABOUT THE AUTHOR

 Alexander had an active imagination his whole life, but it wasn't until the birth of his first child that he began putting the stories in his mind on paper. He wanted to be an example of someone pursuing his passion, dreaming big, and taking chances.

Alexander loves people, their stories, and their dreams. He has a passion for learning and is known by most as an intensely curious person who eagerly soaks up everything he can.

For more about him and his works, visit **alexandermukte.com**.

Made in the USA
Middletown, DE
16 January 2023

21591585R00170